TIME TO STEELE

A Daggers & Steele Mystery

ALEX P. BERG

BATDOG PRESS
KNOXVILLE, TN

Batdog Press
www.batdogpress.com

Publisher's Note: This is a work of fiction. Names, characters, places, and incidents portrayed in this novel are a product of the author's imagination.

Cover Art: Damon Za
Book Layout: ©2013 BookDesignTemplates.com

Time to Steele / Alex P. Berg — 1st ed.
ISBN 978-1-942274-09-4

1

I put my head down and shouldered my way through the unwashed masses at the biennial World's Wonders Fair. All around me, charlatans and quacks hawked everything from hair restoration tinctures to miracle balms, shouting and pointing and waving colorful flags. Legitimate scientists with exhibits founded in facts and data looked down upon them from their hardwood podiums, dour looks on their faces, and I wondered to myself what exactly about the experience was supposed to be *fun*.

Steele glanced at me out of the corner of her eyes and read my mind. "Oh, come on Daggers. Keep an open mind. You might enjoy yourself."

Shay Steele was a psychic—of sorts, anyway—but not the type who could discern my thoughts from a mere glance. That particular trick had more to do with the fact that she'd come to know me—and because the fates had cursed her with a unique blend of hormones, body parts, and personality traits that most people generally referred to as 'being a woman.'

Of course, Shay hadn't let that particular genetic handicap slow her in the least. She was sharp as a tack and quick on her mental toes, able to dodge my verbal barbs and sling them back into my own face with ease. She also possessed incredible observational skills, a trait that had quickly made her the second-most valuable homicide detective in the precinct—behind only me and my deft deductive abilities, naturally.

"You know I'm not particularly interested or well-versed in either science or technology—of which precious little of this even is," I said as we passed a greasy-haired snake oil salesman.

"Well, I'm not sure there's much I can do regarding the first part of that statement," said Shay, "but I'm actively trying to remedy the latter."

"By exposing me to guys in flat-rimmed boater hats trying to sell me on the health benefits of deer musk?"

"It's not all balderdash," said Shay. "What about the exhibit we passed concerning the improvements to the Stearns and Company water pumping system? Or look up ahead. There's a demonstration about the security of modern door locks. I'm sure we could learn something useful there."

At the exhibit in question, a man with a lengthy salt-and-pepper beard and a knee-length black wool coat gestured toward a display, a torsion wrench held in one hand and a hook pick held in the other. He spoke in a bombastic voice, one stronger than I would've expected for a man his age. "On the right, we have a conventional, everyday tumbler lock, built to standard manufacturing specifications. On the left we have a special lock of my own design, featuring not four, not five, not six, but a grand total of seven pins. Yes, ladies and gentlemen, seven. I fabricated the device using—"

Steele looked at me expectantly, her azure eyes bright in the mid-morning sunshine. A hint of a cool fall breeze flitted past, tickling the long, sleek chocolate-colored hair that hung over her pointed ears—a byproduct of her mixed human and elven ancestry. It fluttered the jacket of her tailored charcoal gray pantsuit which flared over her slim hips and hid the heel of her stylish boots.

By the gods, she was beautiful. I hadn't realized it when we'd first met several months ago in the Captain's office—which wasn't to say I hadn't noticed her narrow waist and elfin features. I'd noticed, but at the time I'd been more concerned with what her appearance suggested: youth, inexperience, and ineptitude—or so I'd assumed. Thankfully, the last part couldn't have been more false, but it had clouded my assessment of Shay. I'd always been attracted to women with a few more curves up top and below the belt, women like my ex-wife Nicole. But as Shay had grown on me, keeping step with me in our investigations, taking my jabs and delivering counterpunches in full force, so too had her arched eyebrows, sharp nose, and slim bust infected me with admiration for her beauty.

Much to my chagrin, Shay's contagious spirit had changed me, and not simply in terms of who I found my tongue lolling over. As I spent more and more time in her presence, I'd become less ornery and irritable. I'd lost some of my trademark biting humor—something I wasn't sure I could ever forgive her for. I'd even changed physically. I'd lost a few inches around my waist and was down about a dozen pounds to a svelte two ten. If only her smile and witty banter could do something to stem the premature creep of gray into my otherwise perfect crop of umber hair...

I sighed and tried to hide a smile that threatened to overtake my face. "Alright. I suppose we can check out the locksmith. Whatever he's demonstrating, it has to be more interesting than the mechanics of drawing well water."

Shay gave me a sly grin, and I pushed my way through the crowds closer to the display. I heard the announcer's voice over the buzz of the onlookers as we approached.

"—and as you can see, with a quick flick of my wrist, the traditional lock has been disarmed, its contents made available to whichever band of thieves or brigands chose to assault it. Can you imagine it, friends? Your home or apartment broken into, your belongings stolen, your sense of personal safety violated? Have any of your endured such heartbreak? Let's see a show of hands. Yes, indeed, I see. That's four hands too many. Now that's a sensation no man or woman of any breed should ever have to endure. And with my new Septasure brand of tumbler locks, you won't have to. But don't take my word for it—try them yourselves, friends. I have the tools, you have the know-how. Now who wants to take a crack at the Septasure? No one? Surely someone wishes to give it a try. I didn't mean anything by my last remark, you understand. Knowing a little lock picking doesn't necessarily make someone a bandit—"

I found a gap in the crowd where both Shay and I might be able to see the exhibit, but apparently my choice of spots was a bit too close to the action. The graybeard with the booming voice took advantage of my curiosity right away.

"You there, sir," he said. "The large gentleman with the worn jacket. You seem like a man who knows his way around a lock. Why don't you take a crack at the Septasure? Show your lady friend how secure the technology is."

Worn jacket? Was it really that bad? Shay had given me guff about my coat before, but the old piece of cowhide I kept draped around my shoulders had saved me from more scrapes, cuts, and bruises than I could remember, and it served as a perfect place for me to hide Daisy, my eighteen inch steel law enforcement companion who helped me bash civility into the brains of the unruly.

I cleared my throat, unsure how Shay might've taken the hawker's last comment. "Um...we're just friends."

It was a true statement. Despite the freshly shaken cocktail of admiration, lust, and affection which I'd developed for my partner, I was fairly sure my emotions toward her were one-sided. Not that she didn't enjoy my company—a fact I was still coming to grips with—as we often spent time with one another, even outside of work. We'd dined together a number of times, and here we found ourselves at the fair with only each other as company. But we weren't dating—the word had never been uttered in our mutual presence—and based on Steele's demeanor, she seemed perfectly happy to keep our relationship at the level of simple friendship.

"Well, that's what I said, isn't it?" said the man onstage with a flourish of his hands. "She's a lady, and your friend. A companion, perchance. Now don't blow your chance to show her your skill with a lock pick. Come on up and take a stab at the Septasure."

My smiling half-elf partner nudged me in the ribs. "Go on. Give it a try."

"What?" I hissed. "I don't have any experience picking locks. You know very well my preferred method of opening locked doors."

"I'm sure your foot will forgive you for this act of indiscretion," she said. "Now go. Consider it a learning experience. We're here during working hours, after all."

I pictured the Captain's ugly, scowling muzzle and sagging jowls as we told him we were heading out to the World's Wonders Fair. He'd only let us leave because we didn't have any active cases at the moment. If I took his kindness for granted, he might enact all sorts of punitive measures to keep me in line, and that never went well. I still remembered the murderous looks I received from the other detectives when he confiscated the department's coffee supply because of my stubbornness.

Grudgingly, I made my way up on stage. As I reached the lock salesman, I held out a hand for the tools, but the graybeard mistook my gesture. He grasped my hand in his own and shook it heartily. His coat flapped in rhythm with his arm, and scents of stale cologne and machine grease drifted my way.

"Welcome, sir, welcome," he said. "Now, before we begin, why don't you introduce yourself to the crowd."

"Really?" I said.

"*Really?* Do you hear this man, friends?" The sales-man held his hands out in appeal to the crowd. "Why, of course, sir! Don't be shy. The people want to know what sort of man holds the safety of their families in his hands—metaphorically speaking, of course."

I sighed. Might as well get it over with. "I'm Dag-gers."

"Is that an adjective or a surname?" said the lock-smith, chuckling in exaggerated fashion. "Please, sir, your full name, and profession."

"The name's Jake Daggers. I'm a detective with the New Welwic PD."

The graybeard's face lit up like a jack-o-lantern. "Did you hear that, friends? A member of the city's finest! Who better to test the impenetrability of the Septas-ure?"

"Well, actually, I'm in homicide," I said. "I don't have any—"

The announcer drowned out my protest as he jammed the tools into my hand. "Yes, indeed, a master of security is our new friend, Detective Daggers. Go on, sir, give the Septasure your best."

I had half a mind to smack the obnoxious announcer upside the head, but I couldn't very well do so with Shay and a legion of civilians watching me, so I bent down and tried to figure out what to do with the tools I'd been provided. I jammed the hook pick into the lock and stuffed the torsion wrench underneath it, hoping I was doing it right.

"There you go, sir," said the graybeard to the crowd, guiding my hands a little as he did so. "Why, you're a natural—which doesn't surprise me in the least given your occupation."

After a minute of fumbling with the tools, I stood and handed them back to the announcer.

"Well, sir...your verdict?" he said.

"I couldn't do it," I said.

The man's voice boomed forth, even louder than before. "Did you hear that, friends? The lock cannot be picked! It is impervious to all attempts!"

"Well, that's not exactly what I—"

"Give the detective a round of applause," said the graybeard, cutting me off again. "Let's thank him for his service to the city."

I returned to Shay to the sound of two dozen clapping hands. "I feel used."

"Yeah, maybe that was a bad idea," said Shay. "I can't help but feel he's going to use that in all his future marketing efforts. *The Septasure—not even police can crack it.*"

"Thanks for making me feel like everyone's going to forget my ineptitude. I appreciate that."

Shay shrugged, a malevolent smile creeping its way onto her lips.

"So, are you ready to go?" I asked.

"Are you kidding? We haven't seen the big show yet. In fact—" Shay glanced at the sun. "I bet it's about to begin. Come on. I've heard this year's display is out of this world."

2

A throng of sentience, from human to elven to dwarven and beyond, pressed itself around the World's Wonders Fair central stage on which the morning's performance would occur. Rather than push into its meaty core, I led Shay to a small hillock overlooking the stage from the right—a brilliant idea which unfortunately had already been thought of by hundreds of other fairgoers. With a little luck and perseverance, I found a free spot for two behind a small crowd of dwarves, which afforded Shay and I a good view. As we waited for the show to begin, I sent a silent thank you to the gods for the onset of fall. Without the cooler weather, the hints of body odor and ethnic cuisine funk of the various humanoids and half-breeds around me would've been a full-on nasal assault.

From my vantage point on the hill, I could easily see the stage in its entirety. On the left-hand side, a massive metal contraption consisting of an elevated box, a thick-walled steel cylinder, and a flywheel at least ten feet in diameter dominated the space. A crankshaft that by itself probably weighed twice as much as I did connected the box and cylinder combo to the giant wheel. Smoke, or perhaps steam, seeped through a valve that fed up through the top of the apparatus, and grimy workmen lounged by the side of it near a cart piled high with coal.

Sitting across from the contraption on the right-hand side of the stage was another instrument of similar size. A thick, black covering draped over the top of it, hiding its mysteries from view of the public. A trio of burly, mustachioed gentlemen that looked as if they might be brothers surrounded the hidden machine, arms crossed, their eyes trained on the crowd.

Milling behind the two pieces of equipment onstage, I noticed a few familiar faces. One was that of Perspicacious Blaze, a fire mage and owner of a number of foundries who I'd wrongly accused of murder in me and Shay's first case together. If anything, his granite-like visage had only hardened since I'd last seen him, and based on the scowl he wore alongside his vest and slacks, he wasn't particularly happy about his attendance at the event.

Behind Blaze I spotted Torg the Defiler, a goblin who, despite his name, had long since traded in his defiling business for a much more profitable one—coal production. The coal baron was one of the wealthiest humanoids in the city, as his enterprises had displaced nearly all the charcoal industries that had preceded him. A lush, ermine coat hung from his shoulders, its hem hovering an inch above the stage, and enough gold dangled from his neck to fund the operating costs of a mid-sized orphanage for a decade.

Off to the right of the stage, I noticed another wealthy business magnate by the name of Linwood Bock. Bock owned the aptly named Bock Industries, a conglomerate that dipped its fingers in everything from transport to manufacturing, including, I could only assume, the manufacture of whatever iron-clad behemoth had drawn my gaze on the stage. The man wore a tailored pinstripe suit and clutched a gleaming black cane in his right hand, which, based on the way he moved, he used more for assistance than as a full-blown crutch. A stovepipe hat sat atop his head, and a white door-knocker beard covered his upper lip and chin.

I turned my attention from the ostentatious businessmen to Shay. "So what exactly do you know about this exhibit?"

"Not much," she said. "Only that my dad insisted I attend. He says the demonstration is going to be spectacular."

Shay's father was a chemist, a point that came up in conversation more often than it should. Her upbringing had made her more adept at unraveling the mysteries of science than I'd ever be.

I opened my mouth to ask Steele when the party would start, but before I could push the words out, a hush fell over the crowd. A tall, barrel-chested announcer clad in nothing less than a tailed tuxedo, top hat, and spats walked to the front of the stage. A baton spun in his hand effortlessly, and when he spoke, his voice boomed in a large bass that put the graybearded locksmith to shame.

"Ladies and gentlemen, humans, elves, dwarves, goblins, gnomes, ogres, trolls, and faeries, citizens of New

Welwic and travelers from across the vast expanse of the lands and seas, welcome to the opening day of the biennial World's Wonders Fair, the largest, most comprehensive, most stupendous spectacular featuring the greatest feats of science, technology, and engineering derived from the minds of the world's leaders in business and industry."

As well as quackery and hogwash from scam artists, I thought.

"Today we gather here to learn, to think, and to be inspired, to open our minds to not merely the probable but the *possible*, to share in a mutual sense of wonder, and to catch a glimpse into the future, made possible through innovations that'll shape and mold our future in ways that until recently were mere fantasy. Undoubtedly you've already widened your eyes in wonder at many of the innovations throughout the fair, but it is not until now, until this very moment, that you glimpse the true future of technology and industry."

The announcer spun and pointed with his baton to the gargantuan metal contraption at his right. "Surely by now you must wonder...what is this machine that graces our fair stage? What purpose does it serve? What future does it hold in its gleaming, metal embrace? Perhaps some of you already know, but the vast majority of you undoubtedly do not. Behind me is the newly fabricated, newly redesigned, and newly christened Bock Industries crank-and-piston churned, single-cylinder, double action, high pressure, coal-fed reciprocating steam engine. And what does such a machine do, you ask? Gentlemen, stoke the fires!"

At the announcer's command, the workmen at the side of the machine jumped into action, two opening a hatch in the apparatus's side and shoveling coal in through the gap, a third working a set of bellows, and a fourth manning a set of levers poking from the top of the ensemble. The valve at the top of the machine whistled as the fourth man yanked on a chain. The crank shaft that connected the massive flywheel to the steel cylinder pushed forth, slowly at first, then back, then faster, forcing the mighty flywheel into motion.

As the machine roared to life, the announcer continued to speak, becoming more animated the faster the flywheel spun. "Ladies and gentlemen, it's not mere hyperbole for me to state that this machine will transform the world around us in ways we cannot yet fathom. The Bock Industries reciprocating steam engine harnesses the power of the earth and transforms it into real, usable work. This spinning wheel represents far more than a mere technological proof of concept. It represents the milling of grain, the pumping of water, the turning of presses. No more will mankind be subjected to the vagaries of wind and water for his needs. No more will—"

As the baton-wielding announcer droned on about the implications of the machine, I found my eyes drifting to Perspicacious Blaze, the fire mage, standing in the back. He stared at the proceedings, unblinking, and I recalled a thought I'd had during our case with him: a passing bit of mirth in which I'd pictured Blaze and other similar working mages put out of work by technological advances, forced out onto the street, angry and with grudges against society. The vision was coming to pass—except for the fact that Perspicacious Blaze owned two-thirds of the foundries in the city. I doubted he'd lack for funds anytime soon.

"This is amazing," I said to Steele. "I hate to agree with Baton McTwirlsalot, but this could impact a lot of businesses."

"Well, it *is* amazing," said Shay, her eyes on the stage, "but it's not really the draw of the presentation."

I scrunched my brow. "Huh?"

"This technology's been around for a while," she said. "Don't get me wrong, the improvements made to the reciprocating steam engine by Bock Industries are impressive. That thing's purring like a kitten. But the scientific basis for steam power isn't new. People have been working in earnest on it ever since Torg the De-filer established his coal empire."

"You're kidding," I said. "How come I'd never heard about this?"

Shay looked at me, tilting her head and giving me a smirk. "I thought we already established you're not par-ticularly well-versed *or* interested in science. Your words, not mine."

I frowned, unconvinced.

Shay decoded my expression. "If I'm wrong, then why was the engine uncovered? Whatever's beneath that black shroud is the real draw here."

As if on cue, the announcer flicked his baton at the workmen. As they closed the coal hatch and played with the levers, the flywheel began to slow, and the announcer switched his attention to the other side of the stage.

"But, ladies and gentlemen, as magnificent, as astonishing, as portentous, and as awe-inspiring as the manufacture and functions of the Bock Industries reciprocating steam engine are, the implications of this next feat of science and engineering are even larger, even greater, and even *more* momentous.

"Picture for a moment, as I stand here in front of this thick span of canvas, the state of the world in which we all live and work. Long has mankind achieved mastery of three of the four elements: fire, which we use to heat our homes and light our dark streets, water which we use to power our mills and churn our grindstones, and wind, which we use to fill the sails of our vessels. Earth we've used to grow our crops and build our homes, but with the advent of the Bock Industries reciprocating steam engine, synergy—" The announcer intertwined his fingers. "—has been achieved between the elements. Earth and fire combined to produce the energy previously harnessed from water and wind. But is there more? Are there other secrets, other natural phenomena, other elements which we've yet to harness? Well, friends...yes. There are. Lads, harness the machine!"

Shay groaned as the mustachioed brothers removed the black canvas. "I'm glad my dad's not here. He'd probably have a heart-attack hearing this guy talk about 'fire' and 'water' as elements."

Even I knew better than that. I shrugged. "He's feigning ignorance to pander to the crowd. I hope..."

The black covering fell under the combined pull of the burly-armed trio, revealing another curious contraption. This one also featured a large flywheel, but instead

of steel it appeared to be made of copper, and it sat between arms wrapped with thick coils of wire. In front of
the machine, up out of arm's reach, were two broad
metal plates that faced each other about an arm's length
apart.

As the flywheel from the engine finally slowed to a
stop, the workmen brought out long, heavy belts which
they used to connect the two machines. A young man
with medium-length brown hair and a thin mustache,
dressed in a white overcoat, separated himself from the
crowd onstage and stood next to the newly revealed
machine. Once done with the belts, the workmen ran
back to the Bock Industries engine and stoked the fires
with more coal. The flywheel began to turn again,
spinning the copper wheel along with it.

"Ladies and gentlemen," said the announcer, "although it goes against my nature, I'll try to be brief. As
this Bock Industries reciprocating engine spins—need I
remind you, fueled by the power of the earth underneath our feet—it brings to life a new Bock Industries
creation, one that'll let civilization harness a power
heretofore only dreamed of, the power of nature, the
power of the heavens, the power of the gods above."

The announcer cast a glance at the young man with
the lab coat. With both flywheels spinning rapidly, the
young man placed a hand on a lever at the side of the
newly revealed instrument and gave the announcer a
nod.

"Ladies and gentlemen...may I present the Bock Industries Gen-er-ator!"

The young man flipped the lever. The air before us
crackled, sparkled, and hissed, and with a resounding

pop, a bolt of lightning materialized out of thin air, convulsing and pulsating but contained between the two metal plates in the air. A gasp erupted from the crowd, interspersed with countless 'oohs' and 'aahs' and followed by a thunderous crash of applause.

For once, Shay looked as slack-jawed as everyone else in attendance.

I, however, had maintained full control over my facial muscles. "Well, it's cool, I'll give them that. But unlike the engine, I'm not sure what use it'll be to anyone—unless someone plans on starting a tree-splitting service using it."

Steele picked her jaw up off the ground before answering. "Your problem is that you don't have any vision. And before you crack any jokes about my psychic ability, yes, I can envision numerous applications for such a device."

"Such as?"

"Well, for starters—" My partner raised a finger, but before she could respond, the crowd parted behind us, spitting out a familiar blond-haired, blue-eyed, smooth-cheeked face. For once, it didn't carry with it a perfect, white-toothed smile.

"Rodgers," I said. "What are you doing here?"

Gordon Rodgers adjusted his coat and snorted. "Taking in the sights, what do you think, Daggers? I've been searching for the two of you for the past hour. If you weren't up on this hill, I'd never have found you."

Rodgers wasn't as ardently opposed to aerobic exercise as I was, but I couldn't imagine he'd tramped all over the fairgrounds for his health. I deduced the obvious. "There's been a murder?"

"Your deductive abilities are unparalleled, old chum," he said. "Come on. Quinto's already on the scene."

3

Rodgers led us to an apartment building on Height Street—a fairly new, tan brick structure in a city where 'fairly new' generally meant anything octogenarians couldn't remember existing in their spoon-fed years. Based on the first floor windows and the richly furnished lobby, I guessed the dead person's abode would be on the nicer side of the housing spectrum, and as I slid past a bluecoat standing guard at the door of the second-story apartment, I found I wasn't mistaken.

A pair of matching beige upholstered sofas shared the middle of a living room with a wide, rectangular ottoman while a mahogany coffee table sat over to the side, lonely and forgotten. The room's shutters had been thrown open, allowing light to flood into the room and glide over a broad writing desk, a round eat-in table, and a quartet of chairs. A couple of technicians from the precinct hovered over the desk and table, dusting the hard surfaces for prints.

"Seems pretty idyllic." I walked in and ran my hand across the top of the padded couch. "You sure this is the right place?"

"The body's in the bedroom," said Rodgers. "It's not quite as *idyllic* in there."

A shadow filled a portion of my vision, and I heard a familiar rumbling, gravely voice. "Not so much. Although it is more colorful. You know, because of the blood."

Detective Quinto, Rodgers' partner, filled a doorframe at my right. At six foot three and over two century-notes, not many people dwarfed me, but Quinto did by a good four inches and at least a hundred pounds. As if his size wasn't distinctive enough, his mismatched buckteeth, buzz cut, and grayish skin—a byproduct of his alleged half-troll heritage—really rounded out the package. Despite his intimidating appearance, the guy had a good head on his shoulders, and he was a bit of a teddy bear at heart—unless you insulted his mother.

"Hey Quinto," I said. "I didn't see you over there."

The big guy smiled. "I find that hard to believe."

"So, Quinto," said Steele, "based on your comment, I'm guessing this one's messy."

"It's not the worst I've seen," said Quinto. "But it's far from the best. Come on. I'll show you. Cairny's checking out the body as we speak."

I was an awful whistler, so I settled for nudging Rodgers in the ribs. "Nothing stokes the fires of passion like a murder investigation, wouldn't you say, pal?"

Quinto glared at me. He and Cairny Moonshadow, the precinct's coroner, were dating, but it wasn't common knowledge. Certainly the Captain didn't know, and Quinto and Cairny intended to keep it that way.

Even though Rodgers had been working on his quip game lately, he kept his mouth shut following my jab. He was stuck with Quinto nearly twenty-four-seven, and he knew better than to piss him off. Instead he shrugged, and we all followed Quinto into the bedroom.

Due to the angle of my entrance into the room, the first thing I noticed was the massive canopy bed, complete with ornamental drapes, padded headboard, plush comforter, and silk sheets. The second thing I noticed was the dead body strapped to a chair at the foot of the bed.

The victim was a man, in his mid to late thirties if I had to guess based on his hairline and complexion. His arms had been strapped to those of his chair, and the tips of several of his fingers ended in twisted, mangled stumps. Bruises marred much of his face, and dried blood covered the majority of his chin and neck. It also matted his light brown hair, and I didn't have to look hard to spot the source. The entire top right of his skull had imploded, revealing lots of icky bits that nature dictated shouldn't be visible to the eye.

Cairny poked the body in the midsection with an extended finger, but she popped up as soon as she saw us enter, sending a ripple through her otherwise motionless waterfall of midnight-black hair. "Detective Daggers. And Steele! What a surprise to see you here, bestie."

Rodgers furrowed his eyebrows. "Um...Cairny, I told you and Quinto I'd find Daggers and Steele and meet you guys here. Right after the runner dropped by the precinct. Remember?"

Cairny blinked her big moon eyes. "Oh. Right. Well...welcome."

In addition to being a half-faerie, Cairny was a bit of a space cadet, but she was good at her job. Unlike most people, being presented with a dead body had a way of sharpening her focus. Sometimes I thought she'd be an excellent artist, what with all the time she spent day-dreaming, but she'd probably only get any real work done in a studio surrounded by cadavers, and that wasn't something those of us in police employ particularly condoned.

A grin crept onto Quinto's face as he gazed at the coroner, probably without his knowledge. I think he still couldn't quite believe he and Cairny were dating, and with good reason. With her ivory skin and soft features, she was far too pretty for him. Not that she was a ten by any means—she was too gangly and mooncalfish for my tastes—more that Quinto was that ugly. I'd mentioned his luck to him before, and he'd been quick to remind me of my own limitations in the physical appearances department. I'm not sure if he'd meant it as an insult or as a way of giving me hope.

"Alright, gang," I said. "Give us the rundown. What do we know so far?"

"Well," said Quinto, getting serious, "as far as we can tell, this man was murdered."

"Oh, wait. Hold on." I held up a finger, then reached into my coat pocket and extracted Daisy, which I held out to Quinto. "Here you go."

Quinto lifted an eyebrow. "Um...why would I want your truncheon, Daggers?"

"First, refer to Daisy by name," I said. "And second, this isn't a truncheon. For the purposes of this exercise, this is the Captain of the Obvious baton. Go on. You've earned it." I waggled the steel headknocker at Quinto again.

He reluctantly took it, scowling at me as he did so.

"Why don't I begin?" Cairny smiled. I couldn't tell if she was trying to defuse the situation or wasn't even aware of her boyfriend's lack of mirth. She pointed out various body parts as she provided her diagnosis. "As you can see, our victim was tied to this chair and tortured. Given the facial bruising and missing teeth, I assume the victim was punched repeatedly before having his fingers smashed with a hammer, as you can see here." Cairny drew her hand down to the armrest. "Eventually, said hammer was used to provide the killing blow to the victim, as you can see by the fractured cranium. The head of the hammer appears to have impacted right at the front of the parietal bone."

"Did you find the murder weapon?" I asked.

Cairny shook her head.

"And when did he die?" asked Steele.

"Based on lividity?" said Cairny. "Early this morning. Maybe between five and eight. I'll need to get him back to the lab to give you a better answer."

"Alright," I said. "What else do we know about the victim?"

Quinto maintained his vexed expression, but he responded. "His name's Darryl Gill. He owns a repossessions business smartly titled Gill's Repossessions. We found some files of his with business info. Tax records, bank notices, that sort of thing."

"Repossessions?" I said. "As in take stuff from people and give it back to the bank sort of repossessions?"

Quinto held out Daisy. "Here you go. You've earned this back."

"Thank the gods," I said, retrieving my nightstick. "I'm the king of *something* again."

That earned a smile from Quinto. Good. I hadn't meant to actually anger the big guy.

"What about his personal life?" asked Shay.

"I talked to some neighbors," said Quinto. "They said Gill wasn't married, nor do they think he was seeing anyone on a regular basis. No kids. And nobody recalled seeing anyone out of the ordinary late last night or early this morning."

"*Really?*" I said with a raised eyebrow. "This guy got tortured and beaten to death with a hammer and nobody heard anything?"

"I should note the victim was gagged when we found him," said Cairny. "You can see some of the bruising at the sides of his lips from where the muffle was placed."

"To be fair, one neighbor did hear some thumping," said Quinto. "She thought Gill was rearranging furniture."

"At five in the morning?" I rolled my eyes. "Sheesh. Apparently we won't be able to count on the neighbors for much assistance. You guys get anything else useful so far?"

Quinto shrugged. "We found some assorted cash and valuables around the apartment, so it doesn't appear to have been a robbery. Lab techs are working on getting prints from surfaces."

I drummed my fingers on my chin, scraping them against my stubble. "Ok, so we have a torture and murder—possibly a crime of passion. I'm guessing it might've had something to do with his profession." I gave Shay a look. "You want to make a trip out to Gill's place of business?"

"Seems as good a place as any to start," she said.

"Quinto, you said you found bank statements," I said. "You mind swinging by his branch office and seeing if you can spot any red flags on Gill's finances?"

The big guy groaned. "Why me? I always do the bank runs."

"Because you're so good at it," I said. "I'm honestly not sure how you get in and out so fast. You must sweet talk the tellers."

I flashed Quinto my best smile, but I think it was Cairny's giggle that convinced him to abandon his resistance.

"You ready?" I said to Steele.

"Wait," said Rodgers. "What about me?"

I shrugged. "Pick your poison. Gill's Repossessions, the bank, or stay here and help out the lab boys."

Rodgers and Quinto went way back. They'd been partners for the better part of a decade, but no amount of brotherly camaraderie could convince Rodgers to voluntarily take part in a bank run. He came with us.

4

Shay and I caught a rickshaw outside Gill's apartment, but since there was only room for two, Rodgers was forced to commandeer his own unit. Apparently, Rodgers' driver had eaten a few too many pancakes for breakfast, because we quickly outpaced him and his slow-footed chauffeur. By the time we reached Gill's Repossessions, my old detective pal and his human-powered transport were nowhere to be seen.

As we waited for him to arrive, I studied the façade of Gill's business venture. The place was little more than a shack attached to the exterior of a warehouse, with a sign hanging over the front of the hut that read, simply, 'Gill's.' An indeterminate half-breed equipped with a mop and bucket worked at the side of the warehouse, scrubbing graffiti painted upon the wall in bright green ink, graffiti that currently read 'VAGES.' I dearly hoped some of the word had already been washed away.

I turned my eyes back to the street as I heard the distant pattering of footsteps and clattering of rickshaw wheels upon cobblestones.

"Something on your mind?" said Steele.

I glanced at her and blinked. "Huh?"

"You've got that blank look on your face again," she said. "You wore it most of the ride over."

Rodgers' rickshaw appeared from behind a bend. "You wonder what's going to happen to all these rickshaw drivers?"

Shay tilted her head. "What do you mean?"

"The expo this morning," I said. "That machine was second to none at spinning wheels. It's only a matter of time before it replaces rickshaws."

Shay gave me a dubious look. "Daggers, that Bock Industries steam engine was roughly the size of a skiff and certainly weighed far more than one. I don't think it's going to replace rickshaws any time soon."

I snorted. "Now who's the one without any vision. I bet the horses didn't think they'd get displaced either."

"Probably because horses don't spend much time thinking about their job security."

I neglected to follow that comment with a response. I knew from personal experience horses were deceitful, malevolent creatures that knew far more than us sentient races gave them credit for, but I didn't think it was worth arguing that point with Shay.

Once Rodgers arrived and paid his driver, the three of us walked over to Gill's and tried to make ourselves obvious. After a few moments of warming our pockets with our hands, a guy emerged from the shack, clipboard in hand and a pencil tucked behind his ear—his pointed, furry, wart-infested, greenish-blackish atrocity of an ear.

I tried to convert my slack-jawed expression into some facsimile of a yawn to avoid appearing rude. The guy must've fallen off the ugly tree and hit every branch on the way down. A squatty, smashed nose dominated the center of his face, sitting underneath sunken eyes and brows in desperate need of trimming. A thick, golden hoop hung from his jutting lower lip, and his pock-marked skin was the color of gangrene—perhaps an indication of mixed goblin and ogre heritage?

"You guys need something?" he asked in a voice reminiscent of rocks being ground into sand.

I cleared my throat. "Um...yes. Is this Gill's Repossessions?"

Green, Black, and Terrifying pointed up. "I feel like the sign's pretty descriptive."

"You work for Gill?" I asked.

"No, I'm robbing the place," he said. "This clipboard and pencil is the best loot I could find."

"A sense of humor, eh?" I said. "Good. That'll come in handy once I break the news to you."

"News?" he said. "What news?"

I reached into my jacket to extract my badge. "I'm Detective Daggers. These are Detectives Steele and Rodgers. We're with homicide."

The goblin ogre—gogre?—scrunched his face up, more so than normal. I feared it might soon collapse under its own weight. "Um...ok."

Steele took over. Her feminine charm made her better at delivering sour news than me. "I hate to tell you this, but your boss, Gill? He's dead. Murdered this morning in his apartment."

The gogre's face fell. "What...?"

I'd expected any number of reactions from the tough guy—confusion, stoic indifference, possibly even tight-lipped denial—but I certainly didn't expect to break the dam holding back the dude's emotional reservoir.

Tears welled in the gogre's eyes, and he stumbled backwards, his legs wobbly. Rodgers had to step in and help him before he fell. As he sagged into Rodgers' shoulder, he started babbling. "Darryl... No, no, not Darryl. This can't be happening. He was such a good guy. He didn't deserve this. Oh, gods..."

Steele again came to the rescue. "Look, it'll be al-right. Here, let's find you a seat." She turned to me. "Daggers, go see if you can find this man a hot bever-age."

"A what now?" I said.

"A hot beverage," said Steele. "They're very sooth-ing to people in distress. Now go!"

"But..."

Steele glared at me. I gulped and made myself scarce.

I returned a few minutes later with a cup of steaming hot chai tea I'd purchased at a bodega down the street. Steele and Rodgers had settled the unpleasantly-skinned repo employee in a chair up against the side of the shack in front. Tears dripped down his cheeks, but his breathing had returned to normal.

"I, uh...got you some tea," I said.

The gogre accepted it with his warty hands. "Thank you. Thanks. This means a lot."

As he sipped the beverage, taking deep breaths to try and calm himself, I pulled Rodgers to the side. "So, did you two learn anything useful while I went on my spiced tea run?"

"His name's Gronk Turbot," said Rodgers. "He's the manager here. Apparently he was pretty close to Gill."

"Apparently," I said, glancing at the emotional wreck. "That it?"

"Steele didn't want to press him too much until he'd calmed down," said Rodgers. "Probably a good idea. Most of what I told you was deciphered through a wall of blubbering and sobs."

Suddenly I didn't feel so bad about being relegated to the role of beverage jockey. I joined Steele at the gogre's side. She knelt by the chair, her hand resting gently on the guy's knee. I suppressed a shudder, telling myself it was simply a show of concern. At least the dude was wearing pants.

"So tell me, Mr. Turbot," said Shay, "did Gill have any enemies? Anyone who might want to make him suffer?"

The green and black guy shook his head. "No. Not at all. He was a lover, not a fighter. People liked him."

"But surely not *everyone* liked him," said Steele. "He ran a repossessions business. I have to imagine some people got upset with him, and with you, when you came to collect on their debts."

Gronk nodded. "Yeah, sure. Most of them do. It comes with the territory. They get heated and yell, sometimes they even make threats, but it's all unfounded. Nobody ever takes action. That's part of the reason Darryl hired me—to scare people into submission while we repoed their stuff."

"Do you recall anyone you dealt with who got particularly animated?" asked Steele. "Preferably recently."

Gronk nodded again. "Yeah. Just yesterday, as a matter of fact. Darryl and I called on a guy, something Patterson. Rudolph, I think. He owned a small rickshaw business where he'd rent the carts out to freelance drivers, except he was way behind on his payments, so we came and rounded up all the rickshaws to return them to the bank. He got mad. *Real* mad. Had some choice words about our sisters and where we could stuff things. Screamed at us as we left, saying stuff like 'I'll get you' and 'I'll show you.' I thought he was full of hot air. I had no idea..."

The waterworks started again. Great...

"Hey, Gronk," I said. "I don't mean to be rude, but do you have an address for this guy? And a physical description, perhaps?"

He did, for both his home and his business. We collected the information and headed out, leaving Gronk to drown his sorrows in warm chai.

5

The business address we culled from the gogre's paws was close enough to Gill's Repossessions that we decided to walk, saving the department a few coppers on the monthly transportation budget. Besides, it was a beautiful day. Cool and crisp, with the city's summer scents of sweat and warm garbage having been whisked away on the arms of the wind.

All around us, people took advantage of the weather while they could, chatting on terraces, sipping coffee at cafes, and snacking on meat pies purchased from unlicensed mobile food carts. Soon enough, the bitter winds of winter would arrive, driving people back into their homes and making my complaints about the summer heat seem unfounded in comparison.

Hints of butter and rosemary tickled my nose as we passed a trio of dissimilar ethnic pasty carts, awakening my salivary glands and stomach in quick succession.

"You know, we should probably stop and grab something to eat," I said. "It's about that time."

Shay gave me a halfhearted roll of her eyes. "You always think it's time to eat."

Rodgers chimed in. "As true as that may be..."

"You're hungry, too?" asked Shay.

Rodgers shrugged. "We didn't have much in the house this morning. Breakfast consisted of a slice of wheat bread and a glass of milk."

"Just bread?" I said. "Not even toast? You should file a civil complaint against Allison." She was Rodgers' wife.

"I'm trying to get back into her good graces, not end up like you, Daggers."

"Ouch." I held a hand over my heart. "Fair enough. I admit it was mostly my own incompetence that led my marriage past the point of no return."

"*Mostly?*" said Steele.

I gave her the evil eye before turning my gaze back to Rodgers. "Anyway, what are you trying to atone for?"

"The usual," said Rodgers. "Staying at work too late. Snapping at the kids when it's been a rough day. That sort of thing."

Rodgers' problems sounded like a carbon copy of mine while I'd been married to Nicole, except I knew when Rodgers left the office, and he wasn't anywhere near as much of a workaholic as I'd been during the period that preceded my divorce.

"Don't take that first one for granted," I said. "Spending time with your family is more important than any job. I think even the Captain would agree with that."

Shay looked at me with a smile on her lips, the kind that said she was about to hit me with a verbal jab but that, secretly, she admired what I'd said. "You know

Daggers, for as often as you head home early, I have a hard time believing you ever burned the midnight oil to the point where it interfered with your marriage."

"That just shows I've learned my lesson," I said. "And before you say it, the fact that I have no family at home to return to anymore is immaterial. It's a lifestyle choice. Reduces stress."

Shay snickered. She appeared to be in a good mood, so I pressed my luck and suggested grabbing as a to-go option for our lunch some of the freshly baked beef-and cheese-filled pockets of goodness we'd passed our noses across. Normally, Shay would've declined. She was a stickler for finer dining—plated meals that weren't complete without garnishes and sprinkles of spices and herbs and drizzled sauces. I, on the other hand, much preferred the simply glory of the sandwich and its many close relatives, namely wraps, calzones, and pasties, in whatever language or form they came.

In an act of magnanimousness, Shay allowed us to stop and fill up on street food, but probably only because she knew Rodgers shared my culinary sensibilities. She also insisted we pitch in and buy a bag of pasties for Quinto. Given he'd grudgingly taken on the loathsome bank run, that seemed like a fair trade. I snagged a few beef and raisin filled pockets for myself, then filled a bag with an assortment for Quinto, everything from ham and cheese to potato and salted cod—a combination I personally couldn't stand, but the big guy had a stomach that could withstand offerings even vultures would turn their noses up at.

We shot the breeze as we ate and walked, discussing the more pressing issues of the day such as why pastries were sold by the dozen when ten was such a more logical number. We'd long finished our lunch by the time we arrived at our destination, a warehouse about an order of magnitude smaller and more decrepit than Gill's establishment. The metal roller shutters over the warehouse doors were locked tight, but as luck would have it, a horse-faced gentleman wearing a ratty jacket and khaki pants was exiting through the main door as we appeared. Based on Gronk's description, I ID'd him as Rudolph Patterson, the rickshaw business owner.

"Excuse me, Mr. Patterson?" I said as we approached, stretching a hand into my coat for my badge.

The guy at the door took one look at us and bolted.

"Hey, wait!" I yelled, my arm still plugged inside my coat.

Rodgers and Steele took after the guy with me a bare two steps behind. At first opportunity, Patterson weaved into an alley. We barreled around the corner behind him, Rodgers and Steele making the turn cleanly while my momentum carried me into a stack of ill-placed metal trashcans. Ignoring their clatter, I kept going down the alley, skirting puddles of urine, feral cats, and a wine soaked hobo as the baggie full of Quinto's lunch swung wildly in my off hand.

Unfortunately for us, Mr. Patterson had inherited more than just a face from his horse-like ancestors. The guy zipped along the deserted thoroughfare at a quick canter, not even pausing to glance back at us. Thankfully, Rodgers, with his light frame, was a match for him—something I'd have to thank Allison for later. He pulled away from Shay and I, closing to within a few arm lengths of Patterson before the alley spilled into the street.

Patterson darted into the traffic, narrowly avoiding a guy pushing a cart full of radishes. Rodgers wasn't so lucky. He met the cart stomach first, sending a bushel of the small red and white tubers flying as both he and the cart crashed to the pavement.

"Go," he croaked, waving his hand as we passed him. "Get that SOB."

I tossed him the baggie with the pasties and nodded. I wouldn't have stopped—it was just a radish cart, after all—but Rodgers' command lessened my guilt over leaving him behind. Not that I had much time to think. Patterson had already ducked into another alley, and he'd gained ground on us. Steele had a better bead on him than I did, but as we entered the mouth of the second alley, I could tell we weren't going to catch the guy. So, I did what anyone in my position would do and took a flyer on an action that had a chance of success somewhere in the teens.

"Steele! Duck!" I yelled.

Despite her usual argumentative nature, she did.

In one smooth motion, I ripped Daisy from the interior of my jacket, planted my foot, and threw her at the back of Patterson's head with all the precision of a weekend barroom darts player. Through some act of magic or divine intervention, my truncheon flew true, impacting Patterson's skull with a ringing thwack.

"Grawha!" he yelled, or something to that effect, as he crumpled to the ground, holding his injured decision maker.

I was on him in a New Welwic second, pulling his arms behind his back and securing him in my iron grip.

Quickly forgetting his pain, Patterson started thrashing underneath me. "Let go of me, you cur! Who do you think you are? I'm an honest man, you savages!"

I cuffed him in the back of the head again to get him to shut up as Steele approached.

"Nice shot," she said.

"Thanks," I replied. "It's all in the feet, or so a professional knife thrower once told me. Can you snag Daisy for me?"

She did, wiping Daisy off on the hem of Patterson's now somewhat rattier coat before leaning in close and sliding her back home into the interior of my jacket. As she did so, I could feel her breath on my neck and smell a hint of her perfume—lilac scented, if I wasn't mistaken. Shay pulled back, taking with her a sliver of my own heart, one that wished I could tell her how nice it would be to have her that close to me more often.

"You ok, Daggers?" she said.

"Um...yeah," I said, dragging Patterson to his feet. "Let's go see how Rodgers is doing."

6

Rodgers was fine, though chagrined that he'd been bested by a gaggle of root vegetables. With Patterson in tow, we hightailed it back to the precinct, though Rodgers limped a little as we walked. I asked him if he wanted to spring for a rickshaw, but he seemed determined to walk his injuries off, so much so that he offered to go rustle up some background info on Patterson for use in our case against him.

Who was I to turn down an offer like that? With a tip of my hat, I bid him adieu, then stuffed Patterson into an interrogation room at the precinct and cooled my heels at my desk for a half hour or so while I indulged myself in the finest coffee-flavored sludge the 5th Street Precinct had to offer.

Shay sipped a mug of tea in the seat at the desk across from me, as cool as a cucumber. She'd come a long way since our first case. I could remember her, pacing back and forth, wearing a rut into the floor of the pit as we waited to interrogate our first suspect, a drug addled dwarf. At the time, she hadn't understood one of the fundamental principles of interrogation: that time is one of your best friends. The longer the suspects sat in the interrogation room, working up a sweat while staring into the bright lights and shiny mirrors, the easier the truth would flow.

I glanced to my side at the Captain's office, a glass-walled cubby that made the communal workspace the rest of us detectives shared and affectionately referred to as 'the pit' seem like the very thing we'd nicknamed it. The Captain, who sat at his desk staring into a stack of papers, looked as if he'd been chiseled out of stone. His high and tight sat motionless on the top of his head as he flipped a page. Only a flicker of his jowls revealed any hint of humanity in the old bulldog.

As if sensing the weight of my eyes, the Captain turned his gaze up and glared at me. I didn't think I'd done anything to anger him—I'd cleared my morning trip to the fair with him before leaving, after all—but years of my pig-headedness had made that his go-to look whenever he regarded me.

Shay finished her tea and set it down upon her desk. "You ready?"

Eager to remove myself from the Captain's line of sight, I nodded. "Let's go."

We set off down the hall, working our way through the center of the pit over to our destination. Upon arriving, I twisted the knob and entered the interrogation room, where I found Patterson seated behind a metal table, his wrists shackled to its surface for good measure. A trickle of sweat dripped down the side of his strangely equine face. The lights had done their trick.

"Hey, there you are," he said. "I've been calling for someone to get me a glass of water, but no one would answer the door. I was afraid you guys forgot about me and went home."

That was the point, but I didn't bother explaining it to him. I sat down across from the guy, and Shay took the seat to my right.

"Rudolph Patterson?" I asked.

"Yeah, that's me," he said. "Look, I know I ran and everything, but are these shackles really necessary? They're kind of cutting into my wrists."

"You tell me," I said. *"Are* they necessary?"

Patterson didn't take the bait. Instead he looked at me with furrowed brows and a half-open mouth. "Huh?"

I tried a different approach. "You own a rickshaw business, don't you?"

Rudolph's face darkened. "Well, I did...until all my cabs got repossessed. I'm not sure I have anything left now other than a few office supplies and a lease I'm three months delinquent on."

"Losing those cabs must've hit you pretty hard," I said.

"Yeah, no shit, Detective," he said. "Those rickshaws were my livelihood. What the hell am I supposed to do now? How am I going to feed my family? Huh?"

Shay poked her nose into the conversation. "We talked to an employee at the repossessions company that reclaimed your rickshaws yesterday. He said you had some pretty *vicious* words for him and the business's owner, Mr. Gill."

"Yeah, yeah I did," said Patterson, his cheeks flushing. "And you know why? Because that guy's a vulture.

A goddamned vulture, that's what he is. Preying on innocents like me. I'm just trying to make a living. I was *trying* to pay off the bank. I thought we'd come to an agreement on a delayed installment plan, and then those damned savages show up and take all my rickshaws, claiming they had no idea what I was talking about and to take it up with the bank. So yeah, I got pretty damn *vicious*. That bastard Gill deserved it. I told him to—"

Patterson stopped abruptly. He closed his eyes and took a deep breath, then opened his hands and held them before him as best be could. "Look. I know why I'm here, ok? I know what I did was wrong, and though I don't regret it, I *am* sorry. Is that what you want to hear? I'm sorry. I've learned my lesson, and I won't do it again. Now can you just slap me with a fine or whatever it is you need to do and let me get on with my life?"

I shared a look with my partner before looking at Patterson. "Yeah, buddy. I hate to break it to you, but the punishment for murder is a little more severe than that."

Rudolph suffered an eye tic. "Wait...what?"

"We found Darryl Gill murdered in his apartment this morning," said Shay. "Care to tell us where to find the hammer you used to kill him?"

"WHAT?" Patterson tried to stand, but his shackles kept him tied to the table. "Whoa-whoa-whoa-whoa. Whoa. WHOA. I did not murder anyone. I have no idea what you're talking about."

"Then why did you just confess to us?" I asked.

"I wasn't confessing to *murder!*" said Patterson. "I vandalized Gill's repo business. I swung by there last night and wrote 'Savages' on his warehouse exterior in green paint. That's it, I swear!"

I recalled the half-breed cleaning the warehouse, and the letters reading 'VAGES' on the wall. 'SAVAGES' made much more sense.

Patterson kept talking. "Seriously, you have to believe me. I had no idea the guy'd been killed. Look, I was angry with him, but I'd never *murder* anyone!"

"Where were you last night?" asked Shay. "And early this morning?"

"Like I said, I went and vandalized Gill's storefront," said Rudolph. "I came home probably around midnight, then slept in with my wife before heading out to my office in the late morning. I've been there ever since, trying to pick up the pieces of my life. Seriously, ask around. I'm sure people saw me."

I shared another silent look with Shay before standing up. "Alright, Patterson. Hang tight here for a bit. We'll be back."

7

Shay and I waltzed back to the pit, but before we made it to our desks, a combination of moans, grunts, and satisfied sighs distracted me. Figuring nobody would be stupid enough to engage in any hanky-panky in the middle of the common area, I was only mildly surprised when I realized the guttural noises were coming from the direction of Quinto's desk.

"Hey big guy," I said as I walked over. "I take it you found the bag of assorted street goodies we left for you."

Quinto turned in his chair at the sound of my voice. "Daggers. Hey. Thanks for the vittles," he said around a mouthful of bread and filling. "The bank run took longer than I expected. I was about ready to eat a horse by the time I got back here."

"Well, for all you know, you are," I said. "You never know what kind of mystery meat makes it into those pockets."

Quinto chuckled. "Wouldn't be the strangest animal I've eaten. But regardless, this one's definitely horse free." He held up a half-eaten pasty. "Salted cod and potato. These are delicious! You should've filled the bag with these. Want a bite?"

I made a face. "No thanks. I already ate. And I wouldn't be caught dead filling my belly with those things."

Quinto raised an eyebrow at my partner. "Whatever happened to the sense of culinary adventure you were instilling in him?"

"It's a work in progress," said Steele.

"Hold on now," I said, holding up my hands and turning to Shay. "You wouldn't have touched those salted cod concoctions with a ten foot pole either, so don't give me that."

"Maybe not," said Shay, "but I'd be perfectly happy to sample a nice salted cod brandade if I knew where it had been prepared and where the fish had been caught. Really, this is more about your unwillingness to try anything new than anything else. Isn't that right, Quinto?"

The big guy nodded.

I gave Shay a squinty-eyed sort of glance.

She responded with a slightly tilted head. "You have no idea what a brandade is, do you?"

"Not a clue," I said.

"It's a dish made from pureed salted fish, oil, cream, potatoes, and garlic."

"That sounds hideous," I said.

"You realize you're making my point for me, right?" said Steele, crossing her arms.

Quinto popped the last of his cod pasty into his mouth and licked his fingers. "So, anyway...scuttlebutt has it you found a guy."

"Yeah, we found *a* guy," I said. "But not *the* guy."

"What makes you so sure?" said Quinto, searching through the bag of goodies for his next victim.

"Well, this guy would have to be the world's biggest idiot if he were the killer," I said. "He confessed to the crime, except when we told him Gill had been murdered, he about soiled himself. Said he was admitting to vandalism, not murder. His story seems to hold water, though. His description of his adventures in building defacement matched the tags we saw on the side of Gill's repo warehouse this morning."

"Nonetheless," said Steele. "We'll need to check into his alibi. Make sure he was at home during the murder window."

"Not necessary," said Rodgers as he popped up behind me. "I already did."

I blinked and shook my head. The sunny-faced one had crept up on me from out of the blue. "Hey, you're back. That was fast."

Rodgers' chest rose and fell rhythmically, and he'd pulled his lips back, displaying his teeth. "Eh...I jogged a little on the return trip. Helped work out some of the kinks."

Quinto frowned and lifted an eyebrow. "Kinks?"

I opened my mouth to make a snappy remark about the radishes, but Rodgers caught my gaze and gave me a subtle, pleading shake of his head. Apparently, he was more embarrassed about the cart incident than he'd let on.

I settled for an off-the-cuff quip. "I think Rodgers is trying to fit his exercise regimen into company time. Can't blame him though. It's tough working out with kids, and they say the last five to ten pounds of post-baby weight are the hardest to get rid of."

Shay rolled her eyes. "Get anything useful, Rodgers?"

"Yeah," he said, his breath still a bit uneven. "I hit up Patterson's apartment and talked to his wife. She said her husband came home late last night and stayed home until about ten or eleven."

Shay emitted a hum that stopped short of being a grunt—it was too cute and high pitched for that. "Well, that matches Patterson's story. Though she's his wife. I'd imagine she'd cover for him if he was our guy."

"Which is exactly why I corroborated the story with some neighbors," said Rodgers. "Two of them confirmed Patterson was at home this morning from around eight thirty to nine thirty. One of them also remembers seeing Patterson leave the apartment building sometime after ten."

"*Two* neighbors can confirm his presence at home this morning?" I asked. "We're never that lucky. And before he even left?"

Rodgers smiled. "Yeah, well, neither neighbor actually *saw* Patterson during those hours, but they did hear him—and his wife. By all accounts, they engaged in some epically loud sex this morning. Apparently, Patterson's wife was trying to console him after his business went down the drain."

"Seriously?" I said. "He loses his job and his wife rewards him with ear-splitting sex? Someone should give this woman the Wife of the Year award."

Rodgers shrugged.

"Ok, so Patterson's not the killer," said Steele. "Good to know our character judgment abilities aren't way off. But where does that leave us?"

Quinto held a finger in the air as he finished chewing and swallowing the remains of another pasty. "You know, no one's asked me about my trip to the bank yet."

We all stared at Quinto. He stared back.

"Well?" I said.

Quinto shook his head. "Really? That's the best you can do? No, 'why did it take you so long, Quinto?' or 'why don't you tell us about your experience, Quinto?'—the place was swamped, by the way, and I met a nice young gnome teller by the name of Sheila who was more than happy to help once the opportunity arose. But, nope, you just want the facts."

I nodded. "Pretty much."

"Figures," said Quinto. "Well, I found that Darryl Gill was making fairly regular withdrawals of money from his account."

"That's not too out of the ordinary," said Steele. "Everyone needs cash for day to day expenses."

"True," said Quinto, "but Gill was withdrawing more than he'd need for regular purchases. And while the amount of some of the withdrawals varied, others, which occurred about every two weeks, were always for the *exact* same amount of money."

"Hmm." I scratched my chin. "That does sound a mite suspicious. Maybe it was hush money? Or bribe money?"

"Could be Gill's murder *is* related to his business," said Rodgers, "but not necessarily in the way we expected. Maybe we should take at look at his business's financials in addition to his own."

"Not it," said Quinto, throwing up his hands. "It's somebody else's turn to go to the bank this time."

"Whatever happened to the budding relationship you described between you and Bank Teller Sheila?" I asked.

Quinto shrugged. "I may have exaggerated a little. It's called poetic license."

"Why don't we head back to Gill's Repossessions, instead?" asked Steele. "They should have copies of the business's financials on hand, and that guy Gronk was pretty accommodating last time. He should be able to help us sort through any inconsistencies."

That seemed like as good a suggestion as any. While Quinto finished his lunch, I packed a thermos of hot coffee for Gronk—on Shay's insistence, of course—before the four of us hit the road.

8

ill's Repossessions looked exactly as we'd left it, except the sun's rays landed on the other side of the sign and the half-breed janitor had finished cleaning up the last of the green paint from the side of the warehouse.

I popped my head into the shack at the front of the place in search of the soft-hearted manager with the face of nightmares, but the only trace of him left was his lingering smell—a cross between dirty gym socks and halitosis. Even the guy's clipboard and pencil were missing.

Hoping he hadn't gone to a bar to drown his sorrows or crept back under whatever rock he lived, I dove into the warehouse with the rest of my fellow detectives in search of him.

Given that Gill was in the repo business, I'd expected his warehouse to be full of used equipment and supplies, but I didn't anticipate the sheer quantity of stuff that would be in there. Piles upon piles of goods, from all different sorts of trades: sewing machines, display racks, and spans of treated leather for shoemaking, gleaming copper brew kettles for fermenting beer, pots and pans and utensils for cooking or confectionery, and, of course, rickshaws, whether repoed from Patterson or some other poor sap, I couldn't tell.

Some of the stuff had cobwebs on it, which I found surprising. Didn't the banks come calling for the goods, or did they simply have Gill hold on to the stuff while they tried to reach an agreement with the debtors? Or did Gill pay the banks a fraction of the original cost of the goods in exchange for the rights to the property, which he could then auction off at his leisure? Despite being an officer of the peace, I had no idea how repossession law worked. I was sure I could ask Gronk about it, but the response might bore me to tears, so I decided against it.

Eventually, we found the sullen-looking gogre moping around in a pile of lumber and pig iron, clipboard in hand.

"Gronk! There you are," I said.

The poor guy nearly jumped out of his shoes. "Good gods!" he said in his grating, raspy voice. "You scared me. I didn't hear you coming."

I turned to Quinto, who followed a couple paces behind me. "I think he's saying you're light on your feet, big guy."

The green and black-skinned manager rubbed a hand against his forehead. "No, no, that's not what I meant. I meant..." He sighed and sat down on one of the cords of wood. "Oh, I don't know what I meant. I'm drifting, that's all. Drifting in a sea of my own thoughts."

I hoped the guy wasn't going to start waxing poetic on me. Impromptu, depression-induced spoken word events rarely went well for anyone.

Shay squeezed by from behind Quinto and poked me in the ribs. "The coffee," she said.

"Oh. Right." I handed the thermos to Gronk. "We brought this over from the precinct. The quality's nothing to get excited about, but, well...you know."

He accepted it, unscrewed the cap, and took a sip—right from the thermos. I shuddered. At least the thing wasn't mine. I'd leave a note with it when I returned it to the precinct with instructions for it to be sterilized.

"Thanks," said Gronk. "I appreciate it. Really. But why are you back? Did you find that Patterson guy?"

"We did," said Shay. "But he's not the killer. Though he was responsible for that nice piece of street art that graced the side of your warehouse this morning."

"Oh. Well, that's a shame," said Gronk. "Well...not a shame, really. I don't have anything against the guy, I just meant that..." The manager rested his face on an upraised palm. "Argh. I'm a mess. Don't mind me."

"We'll try not to," I said. "We're actually here for a different reason, though. We found some discrepancies in Gill's personal finances, and we were hoping to take a look at the business's records to see if the problems spilled over here as well."

"Discrepancies?" said Gronk, looking up. "What sort of discrepancies?"

"Mr. Gill was withdrawing abnormally large sums of cash from his bank account on a somewhat regular basis," said Quinto. "More than he'd need to get by.

We're thinking perhaps he was being extorted—or something worse."

"Oh. Wow. Ok," said Gronk. "Well, sure. You can come up with me to the front. We've got all our records there. But I don't think you'll find anything strange. I do the business finances myself—"

I snorted, not entirely of my own volition.

Gronk noticed. "Don't worry. I don't take it as an insult. I get that a lot. But as I was saying, I do the finances, and I don't remember stumbling across anything that raised any red flags." The guy picked himself up off the lumber and took a step toward the front before pausing. "Wait. How much cash, exactly, was Darryl withdrawing?"

Quinto told him.

"Oh..." Gronk lifted a hand and played with the weighty, golden hoop that hung from his lower lip. "I, uh...think I might know what that money was for."

I gave the gogre a moment to respond, but he didn't, so I filled the void of silence. "We're all ears."

"Well, Darryl needed the money for something discreet," said Gronk. "Something he wanted to keep to himself, if at all possible."

I rolled my hand in the universal gesture of encouragement. "Such as...?"

"I guess he's dead, so it doesn't matter," said Gronk, flicking his lip ring with his finger. "Darryl had a bit of a taste—for prostitutes. One in particular. A dark elf by the name of Passion Faust. She works over at the 9's."

"Passion Faust?" I said. "I'm guessing that's a stage name."

"Your guess is as good as mine," he said. "I've never met her. But from the few conversations Darryl and I had about her, I think he was pretty crazy about her. And they might've had more than a passing relationship. If Darryl was involved in anything shady, she might know about it."

"Good to know," I said. "Can you tell me about the place she works at? You said it's called the 9's?"

"It's a club over on Flatley," said Rodgers. "Real name is Undressed to the 9's, but that's too long, so everyone refers to it as the 9's. I know where it is."

Rodgers had been standing in the back, making himself invisible. We all turned to face at him.

"What?" he said. "Don't look at me like that. I'm a married man. I only know about it because of a case we had back in the day. You remember which one I'm talking about, right Quinto?"

The big guy blinked. "I'm drawing a blank."

"No, no, come on. You remember," said Rodgers, chuckling nervously. "We even joked they should call it the 10's instead, because all the girls were so pretty, but that wouldn't have worked because of the idiom they based the place's name on... Seriously, don't leave me hanging."

"Nope. Doesn't ring a bell." Quinto shook his head and stuck out his lower lip, but he did it a little *too* convincingly.

"Oh, stop it," said Rodgers. "You remember."

I turned my attention to Steele, but she preempted the conversation before I could snag it. "Don't act like you're not going to enjoy this."

"Me?" I said innocently. "I take no pleasure in ogling pretty ladies in the name of justice."

Shay rose her eyebrows. "Sure you don't..."

I wanted to make a witty remark, but the only one that came to mind was, 'You know I only have eyes for you, babe.' Unfortunately, that hit a little too close to home for comfort, so I shut my quip-maker and told Rodgers to lead the way.

9

Roughly one-half to two-thirds of all the brothels in New Welwic could be found along a mile-and-a-half long stretch of Flatley Street. You could argue for multiple reasons as to why that might be the case. Having all of them in close proximity made it easier for patrons to pick and choose the sorts of service providers and acts they were interested in, or mix and match between the services of multiple bordellos. Having the enterprises close together also made it much easier to collude on price—something the cynic in me always assumed occurred whenever there were at least three similar businesses on the same street corner—but I'm not sure that was the main draw in the case of the brothels. For this particular trade, the reason for their close proximity was, I think, a little more practical: ease of self-regulation.

Prostitution wasn't illegal in the city of New Welwic, but it wasn't precisely *legal* either. It sat in a sort of purgatorial gray area as far as the lawmakers were concerned. Nobody who ran for public office wanted to support it outright for fear of angering the religious nuts and conservatives, but most logical politicians—of which there were precious few, to be fair—realized it was completely impossible to rid the city of it. Prostitution was known as the oldest profession for a reason. And so it was tolerated, but not really regulated.

The end result, in practice, was that the businesses were taxed—which the bean counters loved—and sex workers weren't prosecuted for performing whatever acts they decided to accept money for, but cops steered clear of the places like vegetarians at a barbeque joint. The brothels were expected to police themselves—and they did, with plenty of hired muscle, strict codes of conduct, rules posted on every window and door, and even dress codes in some locales.

Given that it was the middle of the afternoon, foot traffic on Flatley was light, but the hired peacekeepers were out in full force. Thugs patrolled the sidewalks and alleys in pairs, all of them smartly dressed in olive green jackets and black trousers. Most of them carried truncheons like me, but they did so in plain view as a deterrent to idiots who might not understand the way things worked in the district.

I nudged Quinto in the ribs as we walked. "You know, if we ever get tired of our detecting gig, I think I know where we can find work."

Quinto raised an eyebrow at me. "Huh? I thought you knew."

"Knew what?" I asked.

"I worked here, once upon a time," said Quinto. "Had about a six month stint as a private head knocker with the green jackets before I joined the force."

I knew Quinto had done private security in the past, but I hadn't realized it had been for the bordellos. "How is it you didn't know where the 9's club was, then?"

The big guy smiled. "I knew. I was just screwing with Rodgers."

"Knew it," said his partner, glancing back at us.

Shay walked at Rodgers side. She glanced back, too. "You wouldn't last a week, Daggers. You'd get too bored."

"You're right," I said. "Though not for the reason you voiced."

"No?" she said.

"Too much walking," I said. "Those green jackets' feet are probably one big callus."

Quinto nodded. "Two, technically. But yeah. I found it was hardest on my back."

After a little more walking, we arrived at the 9's, a three story rectangular brick of a building that more than made up for its lack of architectural panache with aftermarket additions. Metallic overhangs protecting the windows had been bent and tucked to resemble dress ruffles. Red velvet drapes that hung in the windows had been bunched at the top and bottom but spread wide in the middle, as if in representation of a lady's privates— an effect only furthered by being positioned directly underneath the skirt-like overhangs. In the middle of the building, above a set of golden double doors flanked by musclebound toughs, an eight foot sign lounged at a rakish angle, one depicting a cherry-red number nine slipping out of a babydoll, a discarded pair of panties draped over the top right-hand corner of the number. It was cute—if such a description could be used to describe the sign to a pleasure house.

The brute squad at the door stopped us before we could enter.

"Spread your arms," said the bouncer as he prepared to pat us down.

"We're cops," I said. I showed him my badge.

He took a good look at it, to make sure it was real. "Alright. You know the rules. Don't make any trouble." He glanced at Quinto as he said that last part, probably in the hopes we'd follow his orders.

The bouncer opened the doors, and we stepped into a sea of ruby. Practically every surface was covered in the stuff. Chairs and sofas were upholstered with it, tables were painted with it, rugs were infused with it. The only deviations in color came in the form of ivory white columns—carved to display the most curvaceous elements of the female torso—and a spotless, sparkling white marble countertop that stretched across the lobby from left to right. Scantily-clad harlots drifted around the room, mostly human and elven but I spotted a few members of other species as well. Some tickled the chins of patrons, draped across their laps as they lounged in the overstuffed sofa chairs, but most milled around aimlessly, waiting for the mid-afternoon doldrums to be replaced with the evening rush.

A trio of girls, two humans and an elf, approached us. The lead cheerleader twirled her golden curls with a lazy finger. "Hi boys. Looking for a good time? And don't worry, sweetie—" She placed a hand lightly on Shay's forearm. "We'll take care of you, too. Our man candy is second to none."

I cleared my throat. "Um, thanks for the interest, but we're with the police. We're investigating a crime."

The finger-twirling came to an abrupt halt. "Oh. Talk to Fanny at the bar. She runs the place."

The two human girls flitted away, but the elf girl, who wore a sleek little number that paired nicely with her long, jet-black hair, lingered for a moment and wiggled her hips as she turned.

"If any of you change your mind..." She lifted an eyebrow and ran a tongue across her lips as she pointed to a far corner of the room.

"Alrighty then." Shay clapped her hands as the elf girl undulated off. "Daggers, let's talk to this Fanny lady, see if we can find Passion. Rodgers and Quinto, why don't you two split up and canvass the rest of the girls and staff. See if you can learn anything about Gill we don't already know."

Rodgers looked at Quinto. "Want to flip a coin to see who gets the girls and who gets the staff?"

I tried to keep my eyes from drifting off toward the elf girl's rear. "Um...I could talk to the girls, too."

Shay gave a tight-lipped smile. "I'm well aware of that. Come with me."

Shay took my arm and led me to the bar, where a middle-aged woman wearing a low cut dress with copious amounts of ruching over the bust worked the marble. "Can I get you two anything?" she said as we approached.

"You Fanny?" I asked.

She nodded.

I showed my badge.

"So?" she said.

"We're with homicide."

"Crap." Fanny knew as well as we did that even though brothels policed themselves, murders were our business no matter where they occurred. "So what happened? Someone get a little too frisky with one of the girls on the street, or did the hired muscle use too much vigor in teaching someone a lesson?"

"Neither, most likely," said Shay. "We found someone tortured and murdered in their home, a Mr. Darryl Gill. We understand he came here frequently. Was sweet on one of your, uh...*service providers*, should we say. Passion Faust?"

Fanny sighed. "Damn. Yeah, I know Darryl. Knew him, I guess. Good guy. Good customer." She sighed. "Hang out for a minute. I'll get Passion."

Fanny scurried off, leaving Shay and I to wallow in the splendor of the 9's. I passed my eyes over the interior of the club, trying not to let my eyes linger on any one bulging bosom too long. Through my peripheral vision, I could tell Shay was watching me.

"I should've asked for a drink before Fanny left," I said, hoping to distract my partner from my wandering eyes.

"We're working, remember?" said Shay.

Someone tapped me on the shoulder. I turned around to find myself face to face with a really, really, really, ridiculously good-looking dark elf dude wearing nothing but a sequined G-string. He stood with one hand on his hips and his head tilted to the side, his golden blond hair—dyed, surely—draped across the side of his face. "Hello, there."

"Um, thanks, but I'm not interested," I said.

"I'm confused," said the dark elf. "You asked to see me?"

"Excuse me?" I said.

"I'm Passion Faust."

10

"Wait, *what?*" I passed my eyes between Shay and Passion. "He's a dude. You're a dude."

"In the flesh." Passion held out his hands and gyrated in a manner I'm sure most women would find extremely seductive.

I looked at Shay—partly just to get my eyes off Passion and his nearly naked body. "Am I crazy? Gronk said Passion was a 'she,' right?"

"You must be mistaken," said Passion. "There is only *one* Passion Faust." He performed a double snap and point, bringing his fingers to point toward his crotch.

"I'm thinking Gill didn't tell his manager the whole truth about his sexcapades," said Shay. "Mr. Faust, you want to sit down so we can talk?"

"Preferably in a dark corner," I said. "Somewhere you might get lost in the gloom."

"Or not," said Shay with a bit of a grin and a moony look in her eyes. "You know, whatever."

"Follow me," he said, bringing his hand out gracefully.

We settled for a mood-lit ring of sofa chairs in the back. Passion's glistening caramel skin shone in the low light, but at least I couldn't make out the bulge of his man parts against his sparkling thong anymore.

"So," said Shay. "I don't know what Fanny told you, but we're investigating the murder of one of your clients. Darryl Gill?"

"Yes. Extremely sad," said Passion, drawing an index finger and thumb across his smooth cheeks. "I liked Darryl very much. He was one of my favorite clients. Very gentle hands. Coarse, but tender."

"I'm sure," I said. "When was the last time you saw him?"

"Last night," said Passion.

I raised an eyebrow. "Really?"

"Yes," said Passion. "He came in at his usual time, around eight. We spent a passionate few hours together, and he left around eleven."

"Did Darryl seem nervous or agitated at all?" asked Shay.

"Not especially," said Passion, shifting in his seat. "He'd had a bit of a rough day—endured some verbal abuse from one of his work encounters—but nothing out of the ordinary. If he'd carried any tension in his shoulders, it was *long* gone by the time I was done with him."

I suppressed a shudder. "Did Gill confide in you much?"

"Of course," said Passion. "We were lovers, in every sense of the word."

Except in the sense that didn't involve payment, I thought to myself. "So did Gill mention to you any trouble he might've been in? Did he ever talk to you about anyone who he thought might be out to get him? Or hurt him?"

Passion shook his head. "We took part in some rather *imaginative* role-playing on occasion, some involving compromising situations, including, dare I say it, one involving naughty police officers—" He lifted a high-arching eyebrow. "—but no, he never mentioned anything like that to me."

"Can you think of anything about Mr. Gill that might've seemed odd or unusual?" asked Shay. "Even small details may be helpful to us in solving his murder."

Passion tapped his chin as he stared at the paneled ceiling. "Hmm. I'm not sure, detectives. Gill was a sweet man. Lonely, and a little misunderstood—he mentioned on several occasions how his heart wasn't in his profession. It caused too much strife in his life. But apparently the money was good. He never lacked funds to pay me, that's for certain." Passion flicked his hand in the air. "And that's about it, I suppose. I'm not sure what else to say."

I sat there, rubbing my hands together and wondering if there was a reason Passion wasn't making eye contact when Rodgers and Quinto returned.

"Hey guys," said Rodgers. "Looks like we might've caught a break."

"Yeah?" I said.

"One of the bouncers at the door was working last night," said Quinto. "Said he noticed a creeper hanging outside the front. Bouncer said he knows the type. Dirt poor, loveless, sullen. Says some of them walk up and down the street, hoping to catch glimpses of naughty stuff through the windows. But this guy wasn't walking. Just hung around the club."

"The bouncer didn't think anything of it," said Rodgers, "until we mentioned Gill's name. Then the bouncer remembered—the guy who was hanging out disappeared around the same time Gill left."

I smiled. "Well...that's an unlikely coincidence."

"Did the bouncer get a good look at the guy's face?" asked Steele.

Rodgers nodded. "Yup. We should be able to get a sketch."

I clapped my hands and stood. "Excellent. Mr. Faust? Thanks for your time. I'd say it was a pleasure, but I don't want to get charged."

"Nonsense," said Shay. "We appreciated your help, and all of your *assistance*—in its various forms."

I glared at Shay. I couldn't tell if she was being nice to the guy in order to make me uncomfortable or it she actually liked him. I don't know why she would. What did he have that I didn't, other than glistening, caramel skin, washboard abs, and a face that could be used to grate cheese?

"Come back any time to see me, detectives," said Faust. "I do special group rates. I could service the two of you simultaneously, if you like. Whatever floats your boat."

I shared a look with Shay, both of our cheeks warming in the wake of Faust's comments. We skedaddled before the awkwardness reached a critical pressure.

11

The sun glinted off the massive seal of justice that hovered over the entrance to the 5th Street Precinct—a bas-relief carving that displayed a soaring eagle clutching a pair of scales between its blade-like talons. I kept my eyes trained on the seal as we walked along the street toward the precinct's front doors, but not because I had any particular interest in it. To be fair, the massive seal still gave me chills—despite my cavalier approach, I took my pursuit of justice seriously—but I'd walked under the seal so many times, I could describe every pock mark, scratch, and imperfection on its surface while drunk and blindfolded. I just needed somewhere to rest my eyes.

The walk back from the whorehouse hadn't done much to alleviate the weirdness that lingered between us. I blamed Shay. If it had been me and the guys, I'm sure we would've traded off-color jokes about the ladies at the 9's, remarking upon their various overflowing assets—which, specifically, depended on our own personal preferences—but we couldn't very well do it in

Steele's company. It'd be uncouth. Besides, Shay's presence reminded everyone of the real women in their lives: Allison for Rodgers, Cairny for Quinto, and, well...nobody for me, though I doubt I'd impress the young lady beside me by reminiscing about the rump on the elf floozy at the club.

As we reached our desks in the pit, I forced my mind back to the case at hand. "Does anyone want to go find Boatreng? We need to get a sketch of that creep hanging around the 9's ASAP."

Boatreng was our resident sketch artist. A short, squatty man with a shaved head and a crop of chin fuzz, he wasn't exactly the friendliest chap in the department. I sometimes wondered if his surliness stemmed from the fact that his years of toil in art school had only netted him a low-paying job as a public servant.

"You've been delegating work all day," said Quinto as he slumped into his chair. "Why don't you do it?"

"Because Boatreng hates me," I said.

"He doesn't hate you." Steele draped her coat across the back of her chair before settling down into it. "He just harbors a high level of dislike for you because you treat him like something that's stuck to the bottom of your shoe."

"What?" I said. "That doesn't sound like me."

"Really?" said Rodgers, joining me at my desk. "How long has he worked here?"

"I don't know," I said. "A few months?"

"Try two years," said Rodgers.

"Really?" I said. "No."

"I bet you don't even know his last name," said Quinto.

"What are you talking about?" I said. "Of course I do. It's Boatreng."

"Boatreng is his *first* name," said Rodgers.

I blinked and shook my head. "You're kidding. What's his last name, then?"

"Davis," said Rodgers.

"Boatreng Davis?" I said. "Are we sure his parents didn't mistakenly swap his first and last names on his birth certificate?"

"This is exactly what we're talking about, Daggers," said Steele. "You minimize everyone else. Turn everything into a joke. That's why he dislikes you. Give him a chance. Talk to him. You'll find he's a pretty nice guy once you get to know him."

Shay smiled as she said that last part. Were we still talking about Boatreng, or had she snuck in a jab about me there at the end?

"Hold on a moment," I said. "You know Boatreng?"

"Sure," said Steele. "I introduced myself within a few days of starting here."

I looked around at my compatriots, and they all gave me same sort of look. I sighed. I wasn't about to get any sympathy. "Alright. I'll tell him about the sketch we need. And I'll be civil. I just have one problem."

"Being?" said my partner.

"I don't know where his desk is," I said.

"Second floor, near the back stairs," said Rodgers.

I picked myself up, trudged up the stairs, and fumbled around on the second floor until I found Boatreng and his gleaming head near where Rodgers said I would.

I cleared my throat. "Um...Boatreng?"

"Yes?" he said, looking up from his work.

"We've got another case that needs your expertise," I said. "A bouncer at a club on Flatley, called the 9's, saw someone who may have been involved in a murder. If you could head down there, that would be great. You know, when you get a chance."

The sketch artist looked at me quizzically. "Um...sure. I'll get right on it."

"Thanks." I turned before he could ask me what was wrong and headed back down the stairs. I found the gang huddled together where I'd left them, chuckling.

"What did I miss?" I asked as I sat down.

"Oh, nothing," said Quinto as the mirth died down. "We were just mercilessly mocking you like a bunch of bratty schoolgirls."

"Sure you were," I said with a roll of my eyes. "Everyone here knows *I'm* the leader of this pack."

"A pack leader who likes to mix and match teenage girl and dog metaphors, apparently," said Shay.

I wanted to argue that witty, off-the-cuff comedy had an inherent fail rate and that I'd be happy if even forty percent of my barbs made others chortle, but I'd spotted a runner enter the precinct and head for the Captain's office. The fleet-footed youngsters delivered messages around the city, and they knew if they brought useful news regarding cases back to our headquarters, they'd get paid for their efforts. I thought of them as similar to crows in terms of their portentous ability. They always brought bad news.

"Uh-oh." I pointed.

The runner sped into the Captain's quarters. Through the glass walls of the office, I saw the urchin whisper into the bulldog's ear. The Captain's eyes widened, and he stepped to the door. We all held our collective breath.

"Detectives," barked the Captain. "Looks like we caught a break. A neighbor reported a break-in at Darryl Gill's apartment. If you hurry, you might be able to get there while the scent is still fresh."

I released my breath in a puff. "Good news from a runner? The stars must've aligned while we weren't looking."

"Well, they're going to unalign themselves if you don't get moving." Steele had already sprung out of her chair and snagged her coat.

I followed her lead and called out to the Captain. "Boss, can you let Boatreng know to stop by Gill's apartment after he's finished at the 9's?"

My gruff-voiced commander-in-chief delivered a curt nod in response. Shay gave me a curious look out of the corner of her eyes, as if admonishing me for not doing it myself, but she couldn't actually come out and say it. We needed to get back to Gill's place, stat, and nobody could claim that trying to catch a thief and potential murderer in the act wasn't a good reason for avoiding the shiny-headed sketch artist.

12

We had our pick of the litter of all the rickshaw drivers outside the precinct, so Shay and I enlisted the one that looked the healthiest and best fed and promised him an extra silver crown if he got us to Gill's place in record time.

We hadn't even pressed our bottoms into the hardwood bench before our driver took off like a horse at a steeplechase. Foot traffic scattered before the guy as he booked it down the street pell-mell. Unfortunately, despite his superhuman effort fueled by the promise of enough silver for a gourmet dinner and a new pair of shoes, we couldn't quite make it. The intruder had fled the scene by the time we arrived.

I stood in the middle of Gill's living room with my hands on my hips. When the morning crew had left, they'd transferred Gill's body to the morgue so Cairny could continue her analysis, but otherwise, they'd left the place as it was, which meant the intruder had largely done the same. The furniture was where I remembered it, including the upholstered sofas and the coffee table and the eat-in with the chairs, but someone had gone through Gill's desk.

Files had been withdrawn and tossed on its surface, the pages within scattered—in search of what, who knew. I hadn't searched through the documents myself for fear of contaminating the crime scene. I figured the lab techs would be on their way soon, and even though paper wasn't an ideal surface for pulling prints, they'd gotten lucky in the past. From what I could see right off the bat, the documents on the desk weren't financial in nature, nor were they related to Gill's repo business in any way. Instead, they appeared to be letters. I spotted numerous names and signatures at the bottom, right-hand corners of the pages.

The intruder had also rifled though Gill's closet, turning coat and pants pockets inside out, and we'd found a few boxes of curios and collectibles—also from the closet—upended in the bedroom and sifted through. We'd never bothered going through the boxes and cataloging the belongings during our morning session in the apartment, so I had no idea if anything had been taken or not, but there didn't appear to be anything of value among the remaining mementos.

Given the evidence, two things stuck out to me. Based on the disorderly state of the letters and knick-knacks in the bedroom, the intruder had been rushed. They knew we'd be back, which meant they knew about Gill's murder. That meant there was a high probability the trespasser *was* our murderer. Second, the intruder was after information—personal information based on what we'd found upended in the apartment. That, in turn, meant Gill's torture in the morning likely wasn't passion or rage driven but rather *information* driven. Did the murderer come back because they didn't get what they needed the first time around? Or were two parties after the same piece of knowledge?

Shay walked into the living room from the bedroom, rubbing her chin between her index finger and thumb.

"Find anything?" I asked. I'd done my own sweep of the premises, of course, but I'd learned to defer to Steele's superior observational skills when analyzing crime scenes.

"For once, I think I'm going to disappoint you," she said. "No."

"You didn't find any mysterious crumpled notes?" I said. "No used handkerchiefs or scuff marks from shoes or anything else that might help us identify who was here?"

Shay shook her head. "Zilch. Just the curios and letters on the desk. Although I did notice something about the knickknacks in the bedroom." She smiled and tilted her head almost imperceptibly.

I waited a moment before responding in kind. "Are you going to make me pull it out of you?"

"You always do this to me," she said. "You claim it increases the pleasure of the reveal."

"Well," I said. "Is it working?"

"I'm not sure," said Steele. "I haven't revealed anything yet."

"So hit me," I said.

"There are three piles of stuff from Gill's boxes in the bedroom," said Shay. "The contents of one seem to have been sifted through more than the other two. Another difference is the contents of the pile that received the most attention have more wear than the contents of the others. They're older mementos."

"You think the intruder is after a clue from Gill's past?" I asked.

Shay snapped and pointed her finger at me.

"Hmm." I tapped a fist against my chin as I let that sink in. "Interesting. But more importantly...how did the reveal feel?"

Shay shrugged. "About the same. I'm not sure why you love keeping things from the rest of us."

"Who knows? Maybe I was ignored as I child."

Shay raised an eyebrow. I shook my head. I hadn't been ignored, but that didn't mean my pint-sized years had been filled with puppies and rainbows. Between my mother being murdered when I was a spry thirteen, my father falling into a spiraling depression that forced me to care for my younger brother, and the resulting cycle of misery that steadily pushed the three of us apart, it was a miracle I'd blossomed into a somewhat functional, productive member of society.

Thinking about my dad and brother made me realize how long it had been since I'd seen either of them. I told myself I should make a greater effort to mend the fences between us all, but I had enough trouble making time for the fruit of my own loins. I figured if anything, helping sculpt a well-rounded, mostly undamaged child was a better use of my time and energies than trying to glue the pieces of two broken relationships back together.

I heard footsteps and turned to face them. Rodgers walked in through the front door with a charge in tow—a square-faced guy wearing a flat cap and vest and with his shirt sleeves pushed up to his elbows. Rodgers and Quinto had lagged behind Shay and I in our silver coin-powered rickshaw, but when they did arrive they'd gone to work on the neighbors to see what they could tell us about the second crime in one day at Gill's. If looks were any indication, Rodgers had found a long-shoreman with information worth sharing.

"Hey, Daggers," said Rodgers, stopping in front of me. "This is Yancey O'Brien. He's the neighbor who called in the break-in."

"Ah." So his attire was cultural, not work-related. "Thanks for the notice, pal. We appreciate it."

"No worries, mate," the guy said in a rolling accent. "Gillsie was a decent bloke. It's the least I could do."

I thought about Passion Faust and the fact that Gill had been murdered, most likely, over some piece of clandestine information and thought maybe the man hadn't been as decent as everyone thought. "So, Yancey, you witnessed the break-in. Did you by any chance get a look at who did it?"

"Blimey, but I did," he said. "Won't soon forget the lad, neither."

I wondered what he meant by that. "Great. We're going to send a sketch artist by in a bit to work with you. He's a, uh..." I considered making a disparaging remark about Boatreng, but I felt the heat of Shay's eyes on the back of my neck and thought better of it. Besides, the guy wasn't really that bad. "He's a short guy, bald, with a goatee. But while we wait for him, why don't you tell us about this unforgettable character you saw."

Yancey nodded. "Well, he was youthful chap, no older than his thirtieth, with wavy, shoulder length black hair like me nuncle's. Seemed like he was in a hurry, which makes since 'cause he was knockin' into Gill's place. But the real kicker that caught my eye was the bloke's nutty dressing gown."

I glanced at Yancey's wharf rat outfit and held my tongue. "Wait...so you're saying the guy was wearing a dress?"

"No, mate," said Yancey. "A *dressing gown*. As if he'd just taken a bath."

I wracked my brain. "You mean a robe?"

"That's what I said, ain't it?" said Yancey. "Look, his gown was a deep violet, so dark it was almost black—but that's not the half of it. The bloke's gown was covered in astronomical symbols, moons and stars and whatnot, like he was some sort of storybook magician's apprentice."

"Really?" I glanced at Rodgers. He shrugged. "That sounds like something out of a P. D. Wentwick swords and sorcery pulp."

Yancey shrugged. "Never heard of him."

"Her," I corrected. "The 'P' stands for Patricia, I think."

"You're proving my point," said Yancey.

Shay sighed and joined me at my side. "Don't worry, Mr. O'Brien. Detective Daggers' fictional interests are pretty esoteric."

I smirked. Shay could joke all she wanted, but my passionate love of old mystery novels had helped solve one of our more recent, high-profile cases—at least, that's how I remembered it.

"Alright, I think that's all we need, Yancey," I said. "Are you on this floor?"

The wannabe wharfie nodded. "Flat 204."

"Great. Thanks," I said. "The sketch artist'll be by soon."

As Yancey left, Quinto entered, leading a team of lab techs that spread out and got to work dusting and cataloging.

"Did I miss anything?" asked Quinto.

"Depends," I said. "How good are you with dialects?"

Quinto frowned and cast a glance at Rodgers.

"It's a joke," said his partner. "But not a very good one."

"Hey, that's unwarranted," I said. "I'm doing the best I can with a limited arsenal. I don't see you slinging around any one-liners, today."

Rodgers smiled. "I'm saving my ammunition for a worthwhile occasion. Like when we catch the killer."

"Let me know if you come up with anything good," said Shay. "We could always collaborate to clobber Daggers with a one-two punch of zingers and withheld information."

I glanced at Steele. "I thought you didn't enjoy that."

"I'm trying a new strategy. One with more snark." She smiled. "So far it's working better."

I grumped and expended my negative energies on the lab techs, expounding upon the virtues of hard work and explaining how the prints wouldn't document themselves. They didn't care for my hovering, so I rounded up my fellow detectives and headed back to the precinct.

13

I sat at my desk in the pit with the two reports from the lab techs clutched in my mitts, the ones from both morning and afternoon sessions at Gill's place. Apparently, berating the technicians regarding their timeliness was an effective strategy. They'd delivered their second report to me less than an hour after returning to the office. Of course, judging by the glare the tech had shot me as he handed me the file and the crude frowny face blowing a raspberry that had been inked onto the bottom of the folder, I guessed I might've made another enemy in the precinct besides Boatreng.

I scanned the results once again, to make sure I'd read them correctly. The prints collected from Gill's place in the afternoon *weren't* the same as those found in the morning. I'd anticipated the possibility, but I'd hoped the murderer would be the same person as the intruder. The case made more sense that way.

Shay's left hand held the top of my chair back as she leaned over me and read the reports I held in my

hands. Her fingers pressed lightly into the space between my shoulder blades, and her gentle, warm breath
wafted past me as she scanned her eyes across the
pages. I filled my lungs with the scents of the office,
scents of staleness and ink and warm coffee, but also
Shay's subtle perfume. It was definitely lilac. I was sure
of it now.

As she stood there reading, I wondered if she had
any idea the effect she had on me—the way she sometimes made my heart flutter with a heartfelt smile, the
way my stomach sank when I made a quip that went a
little too far or hit in a spot I hadn't intended, the way
she could simultaneously make me feel strained and at
ease, something no doctor equipped with a stethoscope
and one of those arm wrap thingies would ever believe
possible.

The way Shay stood behind me, relaxed and focused
on the reports, made me think she had no clue how I
felt—something that seemed at odds with her otherwise impeccable observational sense—but how *could*
she know? I'd never explicitly told her how I felt about
her. Instead, I'd gone to great lengths to bury the well
of emotions she'd helped me uncover. I'd only recently
come to grips with the feelings myself, and, moreover,
admit I wanted those feelings of love and affection in
my life again—along with everything that went with
them. The painful feelings. The feelings of uncertainty
and rejection and doubt.

A miasma of those latter feelings swirled around me
as my eyes burned holes in the technicians' reports.
Maybe I shouldn't share my emotions with her. After
all, what would Shay want with someone like me? A

good ten years her senior, jaded, divorced, with a kid. Someone her age should be having fun and getting into trouble. Not that Shay was the type for that—she was far too focused on her career for that sort of nonsense, just as I'd been a decade ago when I was in her exact position...

Her position? That thought gave me hope. In many respects, we were so similar. At Shay's age, I'd also been looking for companionship, hoping to fit it into my busy schedule. Maybe she wouldn't reject my feelings out of hand if I shared them.

Of course, there *was* also the job angle. If Quinto and Cairny's romance was a taboo subject, what chance did a detective partner pairing have of succeeding? None, I suspected. But then again...

Shay clapped me on the shoulder. "Well, I can't say any of that helps us much, but it's good to confirm it."

I blinked away the fog. "Uh...you mean the fingerprint stuff?"

"That, and Cairny's report."

"Cairny gave us her report?" I asked.

"She wrote her notes at the bottom of that second page." She flicked the reports with a fingertip. "Where it confirms Gill died between six and seven this morning? Honestly, Daggers, were you even reading these?"

"I...uh..."

Boatreng saved me from having to answer. He walked up to my desk, a couple of pages held in his small, stubby hands. How the man managed to wield a pencil with as much skill as he did with his sausage-like appendages, I'd never know.

"Got your sketches," he said. "Took longer than expected, mostly because I couldn't understand half of what the witness from the break-in at Gill's apartment was saying. Anyway, here's the sketch of the lurker outside the 9's club, and here's the intruder at Gill's place."

Boatreng handed me the two sketches. The first was of the guy the bouncer spotted. It showed the face of a guy maybe in his early forties, grizzled, with a four day beard and a faded scar trailing from underneath his left eye. A hood hid his hair, but it appeared to be close-cropped. The other sketch put some detail into the description we'd already received from Yancey the Deckhand. It featured a youthful face, clean-shaven, with a slim nose, thick eyebrows, and the aforementioned shoulder-length, wavy black hair.

"Thanks, Boatreng," I said. "These are perfect."

Our sketch artist nodded. "No problem." He turned to walk away.

A thought hit me. "Hey, just a sec."

Boatreng paused. "Yes?"

"You know," I said, "it occurs to me I've never asked if you prefer to go by Boatreng or Davis."

Boatreng shrugged. "Either's fine. I don't have the same aversion to given names you detectives do."

"Ok," I said. "Just checking."

Boatreng retreated to the stairs, and I handed the sketches to Shay. As I did so she gave me a slight nod and smile, as if in approval of my civil interactions.

"Well, we've got two sets of prints, and two different sketches," said Shay as she regarded the drawings. "The question is, what do these people have in common, and what's their connection to Gill?"

"I've been wondering that as well," I said, "but a more pressing concern is, now that we have these sketches, which one of us is going to grab the cork board?"

"Well," said Shay, "seeing as Rodgers and Quinto aren't within shouting distance at the moment, you could go get it."

"Or, we could play a quick game of fire, water, magic wand." I made my eyebrows dance.

"*Really?*" Shay regarded me with disdain.

"Why not?" I asked.

"I haven't played that since grade school," she said.

"I guess that'll make it all the easier for me to beat you then. Come on, stick out your hands."

Shay sighed, but she complied.

"On three," I said. "One...two..."

Fire, water, magic wand was mostly luck based, but it involved an element of psychology as well, and for that reason, I knew Shay would play along. Because of my personality, Shay would assume I'd choose fire, meaning she'd choose water. But she'd also know I'd suspect her of knowing that, which means I'd choose the magic wand to freeze her water, and she'd in turn choose fire to burn my wand. That meant if I wanted to win, I needed to choose water to douse her fire.

"Three."

I held out a single finger for a magic wand. Shay steepled her fingers in imitation of a fire.

Shay snorted. "You're too easy, Daggers. Cork board's in the closet. Remember to grab the new spool of yarn."

I suppressed a smile. "I'll beat you next time."

I trudged over to the closet, retrieved our trusty cork-faced crime fighting companion, and wheeled her over to the side of our desks. Using pins I'd liberated from the face of the board, I tacked the sketches up and made their acquaintance to a couple strips of paper on which I wrote 'Murder Suspect' and 'Trespasser.' With that done, I plopped down in my chair. The bolts that held the thing together squeaked in response.

Shay hadn't retreated to the confines of her desk. Rather, she sat on the edge of mine. It gave her better access to the face of the board, and she liked being close to the action.

"Alright, let's go over what we know," she said. "The victim, Darryl Gill, was tortured and murdered in his apartment early this morning—between six and seven, by Cairny's estimations—most likely by our scar-faced suspect. As far as we can tell, he didn't take anything of value from the apartment. Then at around three thirty, a separate individual—do you want to give him a nickname, Daggers?"

I pursed my lips. "How about Bathed and Confused?"

Shay furrowed her brows. "Huh?"

"You know, because he was wearing a bath robe," I said. "Oh, come on. That's funny."

"It's a bit involved," said Shay with a frown. "Do you have anything else?"

"Um...we could call him Sweet Cheeks, on account of his boyish face. Or just Cheeks for short."

Shay rolled her eyes. "I shouldn't have asked. Ok, so at three thirty, Cheeks—"

"Wait," I said.

"What now?"

"The other guy," I said. "The suspect. He needs a nickname, too."

Shay rubbed a couple fingers against her brow. "Now I'm really regretting this. How about Scar Face?"

"That's a little tired, don't you think?"

"And you have better suggestions, I assume?" said Shay.

"How about The Bearded Wonder? Or The Eleven O'Clock Shadow? Or we could get fancy and pick something like Grizzles McFacescruff."

"Scar Face it is," said Shay.

I snorted, and my partner continued. "So at three thirty, Cheeks breaks into Gill's place. He sifts through his things, paying special attention to his personal effects and his past correspondence, which we've gathered here." Shay pointed to our work spaces, upon which a few bags of evidence sat. The letters had been split between Rodgers and Quinto's desks.

"Now," said Shay. "We know Gill owned a repossessions business, and he didn't make many friends in that line of work. He also had expensive tastes in prostitutes—of the male persuasion, to be specific. However, Gill's torture and the break-in at his place points to a search for *information* from our two perpetrators. Gill probably wasn't murdered in a fit of passion, so I think we can rule out jilted ex-lovers and angry repossessed business owners as potential killers."

"But who does that leave?" I asked. "What information does someone like Gill, a reasonably successful small business owner but someone in no real position of authority, have that could be worth killing over?"

Shay sucked on her lower lip. "Maybe it was an extortion case gone wrong. Maybe someone was blackmailing him over his sexual exploits, and he refused to pay. Or perhaps he owed someone a lot of money and *couldn't* pay."

"But that doesn't jive with his personal finances," I said. "Unless his business was in serious debt, and... Wait. Come to think of it, we never *did* take a look at those records. We got sidetracked while talking to that gogre Gronk."

"*Gogre?*" Shay shot me a narrowed eye, raised brow sort of look.

"Oh. Right." I'd kept that part in my head. "Part goblin, part ogre. I assumed, based on his appearance..."

"We could always go back to the repo warehouse," said Shay.

"We could." My stomach grumbled. "On the other hand..."

"Are you hungry *again?*"

I glanced at the windows outside the Captain's office. The sun painted the sky a fierce yellowy-orange, its fiery halo already hidden behind the city's rooftops. "Well, it's about that time. And besides, I'm a growing boy. Though most of the growing nowadays occurs in directions I'd rather it didn't."

Shay took another glance at the sketches on the cork board, cracked her knuckles, and snapped her fingers a few times. "Fair enough. I need time to mull over these clues, anyway. You want to grab some dinner?"

The phrasing of the question was always similar. Do you want to *grab* some dinner, do you want to *get* some dinner, should we *snag* some dinner, or the occasional deviation: you hungry? We could try fill-in-the-blank's. Never was the question posed in the most logical manner: do you want to *go out* to dinner? Because that might imply, in some infinitesimal way, that we were actually *going out*, or dating.

I'd blame Shay for the awkward phrasing, but I did the exact same thing. Neither one of us wanted to step on the other's emotional toes, I guess. But as I thought about it, I realized that *of course* Shay must know about my feelings for her, otherwise why would she avoid using those words? Right? But there was an alternate possibility. Did she avoid the *go out* terminology because she didn't share the feelings I harbored for her, or because she feared I might not share the feelings she had for *me*?

"Daggers?" she said.

I blinked. "Food. Right. Where do you want to go?"

14

Shay surprised me. Instead of a fancy joint fit for pretentious epicureans, she picked a bar—and not just any bar, but a popular one, a place by the name of The Bleating Goat. The sign over the door pictured a portly goat trapped between two oversized buns, screaming its lungs out.

When we ventured inside, a cacophony of conversation slapped me in the eardrums, dozens of voices from high-pitched pixies, booming ogres, and bass-voiced dwarves weaving together to form a wave of sound. As it broke over me, a more pleasant sensation arrived, too. Meaty, savory aromas filled my nostrils, those of seared beef and stewed pork and buttered bread, but they were just the tip of the iceberg. I detected rosemary and thyme and pepper and spice and the greatest aroma of all, the sudsy, rich, bitter smell of the most delectable of all beverages—beer.

A hostess took our names and told us it would be a few minutes, so Shay and I found seats on a bench in front and got busy waiting. I must've looked like a total fool, because when I finally finished scanning the joint and sucking in its varied scents through the wide proboscis on the middle of my face, I noticed Shay peering at me, a cute smile stretched across her lips.

"I thought you'd like this place," she said.

"So far, it's in line to get tops marks on my report card," I said. "The question is, what do *you* like about this place?"

"It's a gastropub," Shay said matter-of-factly.

"That sounds like a medical procedure I'd rather not get."

"A gastropub is a bar that serves high end food and beer," said Shay.

"Oh."

"You don't have to sound so crestfallen," she said. "They still serve bar food, it's just much higher quality than your typical fare, which is all I'm after. As much as I enjoy the occasional fine dining experience, what I crave is food that's cooked and served properly. Ingredients pieced together such that they fulfill their potential."

"And what exactly does this place specialize in?" I asked.

"Burgers and fries, mostly. And beer."

I smiled. "I take back everything negative I've ever said about you. You're the best partner ever."

"I'll remember you said that." Shay lifted her eyebrows. "You know, for future blackmailing purposes."

The hostess called our names and led us to a booth in the back situated next to a raucous party of dwarves who might've been over served—though it would be hard to tell with their ilk. Dwarves were notorious for both their rowdiness and their prodigious alcohol tolerance.

The hostess handed me a one page menu with a bare ten items printed on the front, which was a nice change of pace from most of the places I visited with Shay. A full half of the menu items were different iterations of flame-grilled ground beef patties slapped between the two halves of a bun. All of them sounded delicious. Bacon and blue cheese, pickles and mustard, shaved red onions with a homemade sweet and savory glaze.

Within a minute a waitress came by to take our drink orders—a mug of house lager for me and a cup of hot tea for Shay—but with the menu being so compact, we had our food choices picked out as well. We both ordered variations on the beefy house special, but I went with the traditional fried potato side while Shay opted for something called manioc. When pressed, she assured me it was another sort of fried tuber, so I let it slide.

The waitress returned with our drinks. We clinked glasses and sipped them in mutually shared quiet contemplation, or as close as we could get to that with the boisterous, laughing dwarves at the table behind us. Their shouting made conversation nearly impossible, which actually worked in my favor. It gave me a chance to overanalyze everything that had happened between Shay and I over the past few hours.

My partner had willingly brought me to a bar, one that served beer and everything. I know she'd given it a fancy name and made the excuse that the food was top notch, but that didn't fundamentally change the sort of establishment it was. Was she buttering me up? Did she have a favor she needed to ask of me? Or was she genuinely taking my thoughts, wishes, and concerns into consideration when making her meal choices?

As I sat in the booth, my mind, heart, and gut waged an internal war, and not over how much beer I should drink or how quickly I should consume it. Should I be honest with Shay? Tell her how I felt about her? If so, how much should I say, and how should I say it? No plan of attack I could come up with played out anything less than disastrously in my mind. No matter how I considered it, I saw heartbreak, awkwardness, and in the worst case, unemployment in my future.

But what if I was subtle? Perhaps I could initiate the dinner invitation the next time and ask if she wanted to *go out* for a bite, breaking our unspoken code. If she accepted, surely that would indicate her interest, and if she declined...well, that must mean she knew what I was asking and not want any part of it. Right?

Our food arrived as the dwarf party behind us shuffled away, giving our ears a bit of a breather. I wrapped my meaty hands around the burger and took a hearty bite. Rendered fat and mustard oozed over the sides of the patty and pickles crunched under the weight of my teeth. Steele took a more conservative approach, slicing her burger in half with a knife before taking a modest bite. I liked my no-holds-barred method better, but my methodology did have something to do with why I inevitably left restaurants with more stains on my clothes than when I'd entered.

"So," said Steele around a mouthful of meat and bun, "how's your son doing?"

The question caught me a little out of left field. "Tommy?"

"No, your other son," said Steele. "Of course, Tommy. Unless you have other children you've been keeping secret from me."

I swallowed my food. I wasn't entirely sure how to answer, but the question gave me an opportunity to stop obsessing over me and Steele's nonexistent romantic relationship and focus on reality. "He's good. We've been spending more time together, especially at the park. Man that kids loves the monkey bars. You should see him. He's like a...like a..."

"Monkey?" offered Steele.

"I was looking for a less obvious comparison, but yes." I snorted and smiled. "He's going to be bummed when the snows arrive."

"You can play on the monkey bars in the snow, you know," said Steele.

"Oh, I know," I said, taking another bite. "And he'd love to. Tommy's completely immune to the cold. But I'm not, and someone needs to watch over him."

Shay stuffed a few pieces of the fried manioc into her mouth after dipping them in a viscous, amber-colored sauce. The suckers really did look almost exactly like potatoes, though perhaps fluffier. I might have to try them at some point.

"And how are things with Nicole?"

Try as I might, I couldn't help but wonder why Shay was asking me about my ex. I tried to answer truthfully. "Not bad, to be honest. I think we're both finally past the awkward stage where we think there might be a chance for us to work it out in the end."

"From everything you've told me, it sounds like Nicole was past that stage before she'd even signed the divorce papers."

"Possibly," I said. "But I wasn't. And...now I am. It's nice, to be honest. Everything feels less strained. Less forced. We can finally spend time together with Tommy without it feeling like someone's going to start yelling or crying at any moment."

"Sounds idyllic," said Shay as she dipped another fry in her sauce.

I snorted and took another large bite from my burger.

"So what changed?"

I raised an eyebrow as I chewed.

Shay gestured toward me with a fry. "Something must've changed to initiate this new state in your relationship."

Steele was serving them up to me on a platter today. Could she *really* not know how I felt?

I lied. "I'm not sure. Perhaps I'm maturing."

Shay laughed out loud, then stopped when she saw the look on my face. "Oh. Sorry. I didn't realize you were serious."

"Yes, well, perhaps that was an exaggeration," I said. "Maybe it's just time, then. They do say it heals all wounds."

"Hmm." Shay's eyes twinkled as she looked at me. "Perhaps."

Perhaps? What was that supposed to mean?

Before I could suss out an explanation of that peculiar one word response, the waitress brought over our check. Shay insisted we split it.

15

The sun's rays had barely cleared the top of the building across the street from the precinct when I set foot into the pit the following morning.

My presence did not go unnoticed. Shay looked up from her desk as I approached.

"Daggers?" She glanced out the windows. "Isn't it a little early for you to be in? And by a little, I mean a lot."

I shrugged. "I couldn't sleep."

"Was that herd of cats that lives outside your window back? I'm sure you could leave a bowl of milk or a fish out in the alley and they'd leave you alone."

"And encourage them to come back?" I snorted as I sat in my chair, tossing my jacket across the seat back. "Not on your life. Besides, they didn't show up last night. I couldn't sleep for other reasons."

"Thinking about the case?" asked Steele.

"Among other things, yes."

Like you, I thought. After much tossing and turning in bed, I'd come to the decision that I'd *absolutely* go through with my plan of asking Shay out to dinner, using those exact words. I'd do it tonight...or possibly tomorrow. Maybe. Perhaps. Or not.

Shay held a knuckle up to her chin. "Hmm. Perhaps you were right last night, after all."

"How so?" I asked.

"Maybe you *are* maturing," she said. "Thinking about the case after hours? I can't remember that ever happening before."

"What are you talking about?" I said. "I was obsessive during that case with the icy stilettos."

"Obsessive over that Rex Winters novel you were convinced had something to do with the murders," said Steele. "Not obsessive over the case itself."

"Hmm. I remember it differently."

Shay turned her eyes back to a stack of files she had on her desk, including one page she held between her hands. I also noticed the sketches Boatreng had produced for us of our two suspects taking up space on the far corner. Who'd put the cork board away?

"What've you got there?" I asked.

"Gill's letters," she said, without raising her eyes. "I liberated the pile from Quinto's desk when I arrived this morning."

I glanced over at Quinto's barren slab of pine. "Where is the big fellow, anyway?"

Shay shrugged. "Not sure. I saw Rodgers a few minutes ago though. I think he grabbed some coffee and started making his rounds."

"Oooh. Coffee." I got up and headed to the break room to pour myself a steaming mug. While I manned the pot, I spotted the thermos I'd leant to Gronk the previous day sitting upside down on a drying rack. Someone braver than me had cleaned it—or maybe they didn't know who had borrowed it.

Mug in hand, I returned to my desk. Shay continued to read.

"So, find anything interesting?" I asked as I sat.

She looked up, face stricken. "You didn't get me any?"

My heart sunk. "What? I thought you weren't a drinker."

"I'm not. I'm just razzing you." She smiled. "Anyway, yes, I did find something interesting. You know the report we got from the lab techs yesterday? They listed the prints they found on the items from Gill's place, including those they lifted from these letters, but they also catalogued how many prints they detected on each individual page. I figured that might be a good way to narrow down what particular piece of information yesterday's intruder was after."

"Cheeks," I reminded her.

"Yes, Cheeks," she said with a roll of her eyes. "Now, admittedly, if Cheeks found something important on a letter, he probably took it with him, and the technicians' techniques aren't foolproof. They always miss some prints. But if nothing else, it gives us some indication of what letters Cheeks spent more of his time on."

I tapped my fingers on my coffee mug as I sipped the warm joe. "Ok. And?"

"I'm getting to that." Steele pointed to a stack of correspondence on her desk. "These letters are from a variety of people—men and women. Most appear to be from ex-lovers, based on the contents. Yes, including the ones from women. I think Gill went both ways, and, well...let's just say he was involved in some rather *lurid* relationships. But these letters—" Shay shook the one she held in her hand. "—are from a woman named Anya. They're the ones with more prints on them, according to the techs' report. And something I discovered while you were grabbing your coffee..." She handed the letter over and pointed at a spot on the page.

I looked at the phrase in question. "*Our dad?*"

Shay nodded. "That's right. This woman is Gill's sister."

"So that's the piece of information Cheeks and Scar Face were after?" I asked. "They were searching for Gill's sister? I wonder who she is, and how she fits into all this."

"And why her identity was worth murdering Gill to obtain," said Steele.

As I mulled the new information, I noticed the front doors to the precinct open, followed by a shadow and a walking mountain of a man with crooked teeth. Quinto spotted us and waved before walking over.

"Hey big guy," I said as he approached. "You're just in time. My partner had a bit of a breakthrough."

"Daggers. You're in early." Quinto glanced at the letters on Shay's desk and the one I clutched in my hand. "You figured out the bit about Anya, I take it?"

"You knew?" asked Steele.

The big fella nodded. "I stayed late last night reading that stack, figuring it might provide some clues. Of course, by the time I got done with it all, Taxation and

Revenue was long closed. I had to wait until this morning to drop by."

Taxation and Revenue was exactly what it sounded like: the city's headquarters for all things tax and revenue related. We had a close relationship with them, mostly because if we needed to find someone elusive, they were generally the best place to ask. It's true what they say about death and taxes. The T&R guys were nearly impossible to avoid. In the past, they'd given us addresses for hobos living in random alleys in the Erming. They were that good.

I tsked. "Don't tell me...you already went there."

Quinto raised an eyebrow. "You wanted to go instead?"

"No," I said. "But I'd held onto a faint ray of hope that I'd legitimately beat you into work for once."

Quinto grinned, showing off his big, square chompers. "No such luck."

"So, did you get an address?" asked Shay.

"I'm afraid not," said Quinto. "They didn't have an Anya Gill on file."

I snapped my fingers. "Well, that settles it. She's off grid. In hiding somewhere. That must be why Gill was tortured—to give up her location."

"Possibly," said Steele. "But even if that's true, we don't know why anyone would be after her. We don't know anything about her, unfortunately. Unless there's something hidden in these letters, but the few ones from Anya seem pretty mundane. They're full of exactly the sorts of stuff you'd expect cordial but not particularly close siblings to tell each other."

"That's the same conclusion I came to," said Quinto. "But regardless, we need to hunt her down. If someone killed Darryl Gill to get to her, there's a chance the killer wants to hurt her, too."

"Anyone have any smart ideas on how to find her?" asked Steele.

I rubbed my chin. "If she was even remotely close to Darryl, he may have mentioned her to people he confided in. At least, I hope he did. Steele, why don't we head back to the 9's? See if we can find Passion. If he loved the guy as much as it seems he did, he might've mentioned Anya. And Quinto, why don't you grab Rodgers and head back to Gill's Repossessions? Gill and Gronk were close. Maybe he knows where to find Gill's sister. And look at the business's financials while you're there. We never checked them yesterday. I want to rule out Gronk as a potential suspect."

Quinto nodded and left to find his partner. Meanwhile, Shay and I grabbed our coats. The clock was ticking, and we had leads to follow.

16

Flatley Street had seemed sluggish the previous afternoon, but that's only because I hadn't yet visited in the early morning. Not a single patron entered the red light district, though I saw a handful stumbling away. Most of them held their heads and looked disoriented, probably wondering what exactly their money had bought them. Even the hired thugs in the green jackets were largely absent, thought I spotted a few pairs lounging against building façades or sitting under porticos cooling their heels.

When we arrived at the 9's, I found the same two bouncers as before guarding the castle gates. The head hooligan remembered us and nodded for us to go through.

"You guys ever sleep?" I asked as we reached the doors.

The head honcho shook his head. "Not when there's money to be made."

I thought up a droll remark about how now, with the sun barely scraping past the roof tiles, might not exactly be the bonanza hour, but I saved my zinger for later. My wit would be wasted on the flathead.

A couple girls cast glances our way as we entered, but none of them bothered soliciting us. I spotted goldilocks from yesterday with her feet propped up on a divan. She must've spread the word. Much to my dismay, I didn't see her two friends, including the elf girl with the long dark hair and the vibrant rump. It was probably for the best. Shay had a long memory and a way of turning casual glances into biting conversation fodder.

We had to search a little to find the madam in charge—she wasn't at the bar, but neither were any patrons—but when we finally located her, going over expense accounts at a small writing desk crammed into a nook in the back, she informed us Passion was upstairs in one of the bedchambers. Alone, she thought, though she couldn't remember. I made a mental note to knock and provide ample time for the guy to throw on a robe.

We whisked back around to the front and up a broad set of hardwood stairs covered in the middle by a once plush, ruby red carpet. The railing at the side of the staircase ran glossy and smooth, and I wondered how many lace glove-clad hands had slid seductively across its surface over the years.

I stomped my feet as we walked to the room that supposedly held our quarry, and I put the full weight of my beef- and cheese-fed physique into a hearty knock on the door. Shay gave me an out of the corner of her eyes sort of look. I shrugged in response. There was a method behind my madness.

A rustling sounded from inside, followed by the squeak of the door's hinges. When the hardwood pulled back from my face, I found Passion Faust and his chiseled physique staring back at me, nude except for a delicate pair of silk boxers he wore over his man parts. I thanked the gods for that minor boon.

Passion ran a hand through his flaxen locks and stifled a yawn. "Aaaahhh. Excuse me, detectives. Pardon me for my weariness. It was a late night." He winked seductively. "So, how may I be of assistance to you two today? What *services* may I provide?"

Passion performed the same little gyration he'd shown off the previous afternoon. I suspected it was his *thing*.

"No services, Passion," I said. "We're here to ask you a few more questions."

"Well, I'm not working at the moment, so I suppose I can indulge you." The gigolo swept his hand into the bedroom. "Please, come in."

Besides a bed, which was wide, overstuffed, and draped in velvet, the room held a pair of stud-edged padded chairs, a delicate three-legged cherry wood table, and a couple of coat racks, but the racks held everything *but* coats. There were a few normal items of clothing hanging on the racks' knobby arms—hats, a shawl, and a pair of ladies' stockings—but most of the attire was for costume rather than function. A pink feather boa, a fishnet chemise, and a pair of tan leather chaps caught my eye, among other things.

Passion waved us toward the chairs while he lounged on the bed, resting his head on a pyramid of down. "So what brings you into my warm embrace today?"

"Same thing as before." I tested the chairs with a finger to make sure they weren't sticky before sitting down. Who knew what sorts of unmentionable activities they'd seen in their years. "Darryl Gill's murder."

"Ah, Darryl," said Passion. "I liked him quite a lot, you understand. He had such soft, gentle hands."

"Yes, you said the same thing yesterday," I said.

"Did I?" Passion raised an eyebrow. "Perhaps I did. The mind tends to wander when the body wants." He drew a hand across his smooth, exposed chest and took an exaggerated breath.

I tried not to gag, then turned to my partner. "You mind?"

She knew what I meant. I have a long history of distaste for naked and nearly naked dudes.

"Look, Mr. Faust," said Shay. "Your warm and compassionate nature is something I'm sure we all appreciate—"

I snorted.

"—but at the moment, we need to employ a bit of haste. The man who murdered Gill? We think he may be after one of his relatives, too. His sister, specifically. Did Darryl ever mention her to you?"

The man whore tilted his head and put a finger to his chin, which was such a stereotypical display of remembrance that for a moment I wondered if he might be faking it, but I didn't think he possessed the brain power for that. Rather, I think Passion fancied himself a performer, except his acting abilities only extended to bedroom theater.

"Well now," he said, "as a matter of fact, I think he did. Darryl had a tendency to get chatty after sex. He'd drone on about all sorts of things. Business, past relationships...though inevitably the conversation always turned back around to *me*." Passion twirled his finger.

"That's great, Faust," I said. "But what can you tell us about his sister?"

"Well..." Passion tapped his chin. "They were twins, though not particularly close despite it. Their family life wasn't particularly pleasant, I do remember that. Darryl once mentioned his father was never around, and his mother died young, I believe. Not sure from what."

I could commiserate. Gill's story sounded extremely similar to my own—except for the twin sister and premature death parts.

"Please try to think, Passion," said Shay. "Did Gill say anything else? Did he mention where she lived or any places she frequented? Bars, restaurants, social clubs, anything like that? We need to find her."

"No, no, I don't think so. Not that I recall anyway." Passion sucked on his thin lips and shook his head slowly, all the while continuing to tap his chin. "Goodness, *what was* her name? For the life of me, I can't remember."

"Anya," I said.

Passion snapped his fingers. "Yes. That's right. Anya. Thank you. Anya Crestwick."

Shay and I glanced at each other.

"Crestwick?" I said.

"Yes." Passion gave me a blank stare. "She's married."

17

Steele and I flagged down the first rickshaw driver we could find and instructed him to double-time it over to Taxation and Revenue, but I didn't offer an extra silver crown as a carrot this time. The department's transportation budget could only be stretched so thin. Nonetheless, the driver gave it the old college try, and we arrived at the hallowed halls of the old T&R building in a bare twenty minutes.

Hallowed might've been a bit of an exaggeration. Old was spot on though. The headquarters for the city's tax collectors recently hit its bicentennial anniversary, and it showed—not necessarily in terms of grime or general decrepitude but in style. Thick, ionic columns ran across the building's façade, and inside, virtually everything from walls to floors to desks to partitions was fashioned out of thick slabs of granite.

Badges out, Shay and I hustled inside, forcing our way to the interior of the tax collectors' den where the gremlins and boggarts lived—figuratively speaking, of course. Most of the T&R employees were humans or dwarves. There, we recruited a young man in a bowtie named Teller to help us locate the last known coordinates of Anya Crestwick, which the young lad did at government speed.

With the address in hand, we brushed the cobwebs off our jackets and burst out of the building in search of another rickshaw. Once our bottoms were firmly pressed into a fresh bench seat and the wheels had started clattering against the cobblestones below, my mind began to wander, and not to its normal destination full of busty women serving free beer. I was worried about Anya, and rightfully so.

To our knowledge, she had both a murderer and a thief after her, and there was good reason to suspect either or both of those individuals knew where she lived. But it went beyond that. I had a gut feeling our efforts would be too little and come too late. I couldn't vocalize the concerns to Shay, of course. She'd brush them off as hokum—which was amusing given her own particular talents, or lack thereof—but my gut had been correct often enough that I knew better than to dismiss my own unfounded worries.

By the time our rickshaw driver pulled onto Anya's street, I'd worked myself into a frenzy of despondent certainty, but as I saw the neighborhood unfold before me, I felt like perhaps reality might prove my gut wrong.

A dozen brown brick row houses, split level homes that had surged in popularity around the turn of the century, stretched along the side of the street, partially hidden behind evenly spaced oak trees that dotted the sidewalk. The trees sighed and hushed one another in the gentle fall breeze, rubbing leaves that had only just started to turn the color of fire. Further down the street, a cry sounded out, not of distress but of a small child. I noticed a young mother walking under the boughs of the trees, the handles of a stroller grasped lightly in her hands.

We hopped off the rickshaw in front of Anya's house, the third home along the line if the T&R folks could be believed. Crocheted curtains hung in the front window, knitted from interwoven threads of violet, blue, and gold. They looked like the love child of a rainbow and a snowflake.

I paid our driver and approached the front door.

"Let's hope Anya's home," said Shay.

Part of me hoped she wasn't, and that she hadn't been since yesterday morning, but perhaps I was over-reacting, seeing connections and possibilities where none existed. Perhaps my years as a homicide detective had jaded me and predisposed me to expect the worst.

I lifted my hand to knock. I paused. The door was ajar.

Despite my surly, hard-boiled persona, I wasn't prone much to cursing, and even less so since I'd taken up working with Steele. She had this miserable effect on me where she made me want to be a better person. Still, even her sunny personality couldn't keep my mouth under control when the appropriate situation presented itself.

"Shit." I reached into my coat and wrapped my fingers around Daisy's cold, hard body. "Stay behind me and keep your eyes peeled. And stay quiet."

I pushed the door open with my free hand, slowly, hoping the hinges wouldn't squeal. To my right, an artificially distressed entrance table leaned against the base of a set of stairs. To my left, sunlight filtered in through the doily-clad window, painting a sitting room with bright, flowery shades. Nothing seemed out of place.

I stepped in further, past the staircase and toward the back. I gripped Daisy hard, my muscles tense. I scanned my eyes from side to side, taking in the home, preparing myself for action but expecting the worst.

The kitchen came into my field of view. Natural wood cabinets and marbled backsplashes. Pots and pans hanging from a rack over an island, gleaming in the mid-morning sun. A cup of tea, devoid of steam, sitting on an otherwise empty butcher's block.

I turned to my right, pushed through a door, and found, presumably, Anya. The similarities between her and Darryl were immediately apparent—the curvature of her nose, the color and wave of her hair, the shape of her jaw, all similar to her brother's—but unfortunately, the similarities didn't end there.

Her body sagged, lifeless, in a chair, secured to it with a length of rope just as Gill's had been. Bruises and welts marred her otherwise lovely face, toothless gaps loomed in her mouth, and blood darkened her light brown hair. I glanced at her fingers, then at her temple. Same method of torture and murder as her brother, based on the mangled stumps and fractured skull, but the blood near the wounds glimmered, wet and fresh. Anya had died recently.

Still tense, I cast my eyes around the room—a guest bedroom, if the furniture was any indication, though I doubted anyone would stay there in the near future. Blood spatters on the floor, walls, and across the bed's dainty, crocheted coverlet gave the space an air of the macabre.

I thought I heard a rustling to my right. Shay must've heard it, too.

"Daggers," she hissed almost inaudibly. She tilted her head toward the sound.

I nodded and followed both of our instincts to another door, this one heading back toward the front of the home. I paused and held my breath, my ears straining. Another rustle. Definite, this time.

I kicked open the door and lunged into the room, Daisy held out before me and ready for action. A young man jumped at the sound of the splintering doorframe, papers flying out of his hands and fluttering across a desk over which he'd been leaning. His thick eyebrows shot up in surprise, and he brought his hands up, placing them palm forward at the sides of his oval-shaped face and wavy black hair.

"Don't move a muscle," I said.

We'd found our intruder, the guy from the second sketch, Cheeks. The wharfie at Gill's place had depicted him perfectly, though he'd sold him short on the *dressing gown* bit. It was more of a monk's robe than a bath robe—it didn't open in the front, for one thing, and the weave of the cloth was heavier—but its deep violet color was interspersed with yellowish-white star and moon emblems, just as described.

Cheeks glanced at me, then Steele, then Daisy. He tried to keep his voice steady when he spoke, but he

couldn't quite keep a bit of a nervous warble from creeping in. "This...isn't what it looks like."

"Really?" I said. "Because it looks like you're rifling
through the belongings of a dead woman. A woman
who was alive very, very recently. A woman whose
brother was found dead yesterday morning and who *you*
robbed posthumously, according to eye-witness accounts. You think I'm going to find a bloody claw hammer underneath those stylish robes of yours?"

The young man shook his head. "No. No, you've got
this all wrong. I didn't kill Anya, or her brother."

"Then what the hell are you doing here?" I asked.

"The same thing you are," he said. "I'm looking for
their killer."

I scowled and raised a suspicious eyebrow. I didn't
know what the young punk's game was, but given that I
could implicate him in the gruesome murder of multiple citizens of my jurisdiction, I planned on pulling out
all the stops to find out.

18

I sat in my hard-backed desk chair at the precinct, another cup of hot coffee grasped between my hands. Steam rose from the surface of the mug in lazy curls, and ripples pulsed out from the center of the dark liquid rhythmically as my leg bounced up and down.

Shay rapped her fingers on her desk and stared at me. "Surely we've waited long enough by now."

I shook my head. "Not yet. Give it another ten minutes. Trust me, I don't want to sit here any more than you do this time, but we do it for a reason. He's young. Inexperienced. We need to wait. The lights'll break him."

After arresting Cheeks at Anya's house, we'd summoned beat cops to take care of the mess and hustled back to the precinct where I promptly put the smooth-faced trespasser in the interrogation room—the same one we'd placed Patterson in yesterday, the one packed with mirrors and lights. We had another interrogation room in the basement, a dark, dingy, depressing space capable of putting even the sunny-dispositioned Rodgers into a funk. We used it on occasion, but its gloom was more useful when paired with a 'wait and see' approach, where we'd leave suspects in there for hours on end without seeing another sentient being. Neither Shay nor I had the patience for that strategy at the moment.

I took another sip of my coffee and noticed a lithe, angelic form clad in all black approaching from the stairs to my right. Cairny. I nodded to Shay so she'd know.

She turned as the coroner approached. "Hey Cairny."

"Hey Shay," said Cairny.

I passed my eyes between the pair. "You guys are on a first name basis, now?"

"Um...yes. We *are* friends." Cairny tilted her head toward me and raised her eyes at my partner. "And he thinks *I'm* batty."

"What?" I sat up a little straighter. "I never said—"

"Don't worry," said Cairny. "I don't take it personally. I know my mind tends to wander. I'm not sure why, really. I suspect genetics, but perhaps its due to an environmental factor, maybe something from my childhood I don't remember..."

Cairny's eyes fogged as she focused on something indistinct, essentially proving her own statement.

"So, Cairns," said Shay. "What's up?"

Cairny blinked. "Oh. Right. The body you discovered. The woman? She arrived. I haven't performed my full analysis, but I figured I'd tell you my initial impressions seeing as I heard you have a suspect in custody."

"A suspect, yes, though who knows how he's involved," I said. "So lay it on us. What can you tell us about Anya?"

Cairny tucked an errant strand of her long, shimmery black hair behind her ear. "Well, I can't say this with a hundred percent certainty, you understand, but I'm almost sure the killer is the same as that of the man we found yesterday. Not only was the placement of the blow to the skull nearly identical, but based on the amount of damage to the woman's skull and the fracture pattern, I'd wager the force applied in the blow was similar."

"Anything else?" asked Shay.

Cairny nodded. "She died about an hour before you arrived on the scene. Maybe a little less, but certainly not more than an hour and a half."

"Thanks. You're the best," said Shay.

"If you need me, you know where to find me." Cairny winked, and she and Shay shared a look. They both smiled.

I glanced at Cairny as she walked away, then turned my gaze onto my partner.

"What?" she said.

"I consider myself a facial expression guru, but sometimes I have a hard time figuring out what the two of you are sharing."

Shay regarded me with pressed lips and a single raised eyebrow. "A *guru*? Seriously?"

"What?" I said. "I'm great at reading emotions."

Shay rolled her eyes. "Yeah… I'd say your skills are very much gender dependent." She tilted her head toward the interrogation chamber. "You ready?"

As I chewed on that piece of fat, I nodded. "Let's go."

I let Shay lead the way, and not because I wanted to get in a few surreptitious glances at her backside for once. Rather, I didn't want her to see me flustered, and her comments had done just that. What did she mean my emotional sixth sense wasn't tailored to the fairer sex? Was that a subtle dig at our whole *hanging out* but not *going out* situation? Did she know how I felt about her, and was this her method of conveying her own complete and utter lack of interest? She had rolled her eyes, after all.

The walk to our interrogation room took all of a minute, and for perhaps the first time in my life, I gladly would've exchanged the short jaunt for a much longer one. It would've served to help clear my mind, but seeing as I was unwilling to let Shay know her comments had jostled me, I settled for shaking my head vigorously as Shay turned the knob to the room, hoping my own personal doubts might get displaced like a bout of drowsiness.

Cheeks sat in the interrogation chamber, squinting in the bright lights while sweat beaded at his temples. Like Patterson, his wrists had been chained to the table keeping him immobile and, more importantly, uncomfortable. His moon and star-encrusted robe looked even more out of place against the sterile white backdrop of the questioning chamber than it had at the scene of Anya's murder.

Shay sat across from the young man, and I did the same. Instead of speaking, I stared at the kid, hard-faced and iron-jawed. I'd learned the trick from my ex-partner Griggs, a dour, grumpy, dust-ball of a man who'd rather chew his own lip to pieces than utter a single word. The hard stare I'd stolen from him might loosen additional bits of evidence from Cheeks, and, as an additional plus, keeping my eyes trained on him meant I didn't have to make eye contact with Steele, who I didn't trust myself with at the moment. Seriously, what had she meant by that eye roll?

I reached into my coat pocket and produced a sketch. I slid it across the metal table. "Does this person look familiar to you?"

Cheeks glanced at the drawing. "Of course it does. It's me." He spread his fingers and held his palms toward us, at least as well as he could given the circumstances. "Look. Before you start, hear me out. Yes, I was at Darryl Gill's apartment. I did break in, and I know that's against the law. But I needed information, or at least some direction. And I did break in to Anya Crestwick's apartment, too. But I didn't murder either of them! I was trying to stop their murders from happening. If we don't start working together, more people are going to die, and if that happens? Heh, well...let's just say the consequences might get *really* dire."

I raised an eyebrow. After we'd arrested the kid, he'd clammed up, choosing not to divulge anything as we rushed him back to the precinct. Apparently the application of the lights and mirrors had done the trick.

"Ok," I said. "Why don't we start with something simple? What's your name?"

"Harland," he said. "Harland Wyle."

"And what were you doing in Darryl and Anya's apartments?"

Wyle sighed. "Look, I already told you. I was searching for their killer."

"This guy?" I produced Boatreng's sketch of the murder suspect from my coat pocket and slid it across the table.

"Yeah," said Wyle. "I think."

Shay leaned in. "What do you mean, *you think?* You're not sure?"

Wyle shrugged. "He matches the description I was given."

"So you don't know the killer?" asked Shay.

"No," said Wyle. "I've never met the guy. But I know he's a bad apple. From everything I've heard this guy is a total whack job."

"Hold on. Back up," I said. "You said this drawing—" I tapped it for emphasis. "—matches the description you were given of the killer. Who gave you the description? Why did they send you after this guy? Who are you? And more importantly, why did this guy go after Darryl and Anya?"

Wyle glanced at the floor, then at the wall, before briefly making eye contact with me. "I, uh...can't tell you."

"What?" I said. "Why not?"

"Because...it would affect things," he said.

"You're damn right it would affect things," I said. "It would help us understand what in the world is going on. It would help us find the killer. And it might even absolve you of murder, something which your current testimony is doing a terrible job of."

Wyle clenched his fists and released them. "Look, how many times do I have to tell you people, I didn't murder anyone!"

"To be honest, I don't particularly think you did," I said. "At least not Gill. Not based on the evidence we found. But unless you explain what the hell is going on, I plan on implicating you in everything I possibly can. You ever heard of aiding and abetting?"

Wyle took a deep breath and clenched his teeth. I could envision the gears in his mind churning.

Steele tapped a finger on the table and cupped her chin with her off hand. "Look, Harland? You said you were trying to prevent Darryl and Anya's murders. You said we needed to work together. So, let's work together. Tell us what you know. We'll do what we can to help."

Wyle shook his head. "You're not going to believe me."

"Try us," said Steele.

Wyle sat in his chair, shifting his gaze from Steele to me and back. Eventually, he spoke. "Ok. But what I tell you can't leave this room. I mean it. I don't know what the effects of this will be, but we have to keep as tight a lid on this as possible."

I glanced at Steele. She shrugged.

"Very well," I said, not really understanding Wyle's concern. "Tell us what you know."

Wyle leaned forward and glanced at the door, perhaps to make sure we were truly alone. "Alright. Here goes. That man, the murderer in the sketch? He's a member of a radical anti-technology group bent on preventing the rise of the industrial age. And if we don't stop him, he might just succeed."

"An anti-technology group?" I said.

"Yes," said Wyle. "Citizens for Simplicity. We've been keeping an eye on them."

"And who is we?" I asked.

"My organization. SPTM."

"SP what?" I said.

"SPTM. The Society for Practitioners of Time Magic." Wyle spread his hands as best he could. "I'm from the future."

19

I wiggled a finger in my ear. "Sorry, I think I misheard that. You're from where?"

Shay apparently trusted her sense of hearing. "That's impossible. There's no such thing as time magic."

"Oh, I'm sorry," said Wyle, with a raised eyebrow. "Are you an expert on magic?"

"Sort of, yeah," said Steele, crossing her arms.

"Well, then, tell me," said Wyle. "How do you use fire magic to form ice? And how do you transfer a psychic conduit from a medium to a normal?"

"The former is impossible," said Steele. "And I'm not entirely sure I understand what you mean by the latter."

"The former *isn't* impossible," said Wyle. "You merely haven't uncovered the art of inversion in this age yet. Nor do you understand the fundamental mechanics behind psychic conduits. And, thankfully, you haven't discovered time magic at all."

"*Thankfully?*" said Steele.

Wyle snorted. "Oh yeah. From what I've seen so far, I'm surprised the sentient races even made it to my time. I don't know how civilization didn't collapse on itself from the weight of its incompetence."

I stuck a finger in the air as I found my voice. "Hold on. I need to get this down." I pulled a spiral bound notepad and a pencil from my jacket interior, then flipped the pad open to a free page. "So let me make sure I heard this straight. You claim you're from the *future?*"

Wyle sighed. "I knew you wouldn't believe me. I don't know why I bothered."

I waggled a finger. "Now, now, hold on. I haven't passed any judgment yet. But I need to hear this story. And I mean the whole thing."

I felt the weight of Steele's blink on the side of my neck. "You've *got* to be kidding me, Daggers."

I glanced at my partner. "He's our only suspect. Let's hear him out."

I got another eye roll in response, but at least I knew what this one meant. I turned my gaze back to Wyle. "So, as you were saying...you're from the future?"

"That's right," said Wyle.

"And you were sent back to stop this man from going on a killing spree?" I tapped the sketch of Scar Face.

"Yes."

"What's so important about him?" I asked as I scribbled notes in my pad. "Who does he kill? Just Gill and Anya, or someone else, too?"

"I don't know," said Wyle.

"What do you mean, you don't know?" I said. "If this guy is as important as you say he is, shouldn't he be infamous? I imagine he's all over your history books."

"No," said Wyle. "I don't know because he hasn't done it yet. At least I don't think so. He's from the future, too."

I blinked and shook my head. "Wait, what? Scar Face is *also* a time mage?"

Wyle frowned and furrowed his brows. "Scar Face?"

"This guy. The murderer." I tapped the sketch again. "I like to give people nicknames. You were Cheeks until I learned your name."

Wyle gave me an odd sort of look. "I'm not going to ask. But no, Scar Face, as you call him, isn't a time mage. He's just a psychotic nut."

I leaned back and squinted. "I don't understand."

"I didn't think you would." Wyle tapped his fingers on the table and leaned a little closer over the table. "There are multiple branches of time magic, and people who excel at one discipline usually don't exhibit any ability in the other branches. The most common discipline is temporal dilation. That involves manipulation of the rate at which time passes for either the mage or the party being manipulated, either in terms of a rate increase or decrease. Much less common are the temporal distortion skills. Some people excel in psychic or kinetic temporal distortion, people who can influence thoughts or object motion in the near past or future.

"Then, there's temporal reconstruction. This involves the manipulation of the time streams to send objects, or even people, backwards or forwards in time. It's how Scar Face made it here. A reconstructionist sent him. Temporal reconstruction is a very rare skill, but even it's common compared to tempomorphy. Tempomorphs can move backwards or forwards in time themselves, and, as far as I know, there's only one of those who's ever existed, at least though my time."

"And what's this tempomorph famous for?" I asked. "Anything we'd remember?"

"Well, nothing yet," said Wyle. "The tempomorph isn't responsible for any changes to the history streams. Unless...Darryl and Anya's deaths changed things."

"Wait..." I said. *"You're* the guy?"

Wyle shrugged. "I'm the guy."

Steele leaned back in her chair, arms still crossed. "How convenient."

"Hey, you think I *wanted* to go back in time to stop a murdering psychopath?" said Wyle. "I'm useless in a fight, and I don't know the first thing about tracking, except what I'm able to accomplish through observation of the time ripples. But I was the only one who'd be able to travel back to the present. Or future, for you two."

I madly jotted down notes in my pad. "Ok, so let me get this straight. Your story—" I looked at Steele and reemphasized the word. *"story,* of course—is that you used an as yet undiscovered form of magic to travel back in time and stop a psychotic, anti-technology nutbag from changing the course of humanoid events for the worse. Correct?"

Wyle nodded. "Yes."

"Ok," I said. "Let's assume this is all true. Answer me this: why did this madman murder Darryl Gill and his sister Anya? What do they have to do with the advancement of science? And if they're dead, why hasn't anything changed?"

"I have no idea how Gill and his sister are important," said Wyle. "Honestly, there's no mention of any Gills in our history books referencing this time period. They're nobodies. I don't know why Scar Face would want to kill them. But regarding your last question—I'm not sure, but I have a few theories..."

"Go on," I said, letting my pencil hover over the notepad.

"Well," said Wyle. "Our society is split in thought between two theories regarding time travel. One is that events in time are set in stone. They can't be changed. If Gill and his sister are murdered, then they've *always* been murdered, and it's part of the set time stream. But we don't know if that's the case. It's possible events in time *can* be changed. We don't know which theory is true, but the latter theory is frightening enough that we had to try to stop this temporal reconstruction attempt from Citizens for Simplicity.

"Now, there's two additional possibilities. It could be that Scar Face's actions have already irreparably damaged the time streams, and the world as I knew it no longer exists. I'm not much of a fatalist, but I admit that's a possibility. Not a strong one—the ripples in the time streams have been small so far. But if so, that means Darryl and Anya's lives didn't matter, which means they weren't Scar Face's ultimate target. Which is why we need to work together to find him, and we may not have a lot of time, so..." He nodded toward his handcuffed wrists.

I set my pencil down on my pad, leaned back in my chair, and used my now free hand to stroke the stubble on the sides of my mouth and on my chin. I glanced at Shay, and she returned my gaze with an eyebrows raised, lips puckered, stone eyed, I'm not amused sort of glance. I knew the look from my married days.

I looked back at our prisoner. "So, tell me Wyle, does everyone in your time period have as unique a flair when it comes to fashion as you do?"

Harland looked at his robe. "What? This? No way. This was a mistake. We thought this was what mages in your age wore. Apparently our history texts aren't quite as *complete* as we thought they were."

"I see." I slipped my notepad back into a coat pocket. That last remark had clinched what I'd already suspected. The guy was a total kook. "Look, Wyle, Steele and I are going to see what we can do. In the meantime, hang out, ok?"

"No, please, come on," he said. "Don't leave me in here..."

I stood, and Steele followed my lead, but another thought hit me as I approached the door. "By the way, Wyle...what did you take from Gill's place that eventually led you to Anya?"

"Nothing," he said, exasperated.

"You didn't take anything?" I asked.

"No," said Wyle. "I didn't know who Scar Face was after."

"So how did you find Anya?" I asked.

"I followed the time streams," said Wyle. "I told you, changes in the time streams leave ripples. If they're large enough, I can follow them. Let's just hope they don't turn into a tidal wave."

I wasn't sure I understood, but I excused myself from the interrogation room before I let any more of Wyle's crazy get all over me.

20

"You know he's bonkers, right?" said Steele.

"Oh, without a doubt," I replied as we headed back to our desks. "The guy's wackier than one of those carnival games with the fake moles. But his complete and total craziness doesn't explain his involvement in the murders, nor does it give us any clue as to the identity of the murderer."

"Not yet, anyway," said Steele. "But maybe things'll start to make sense once we dig into the guy's past."

I nodded. "Hopefully."

I spotted Quinto and Rodgers and we entered the pit, Quinto lounging in his poor, abused chair and Rodgers sitting on the edge of Quinto's desk. I made a bee-line for them. They'd want to be briefed on our findings.

"Daggers," said Rodgers as Steele and I approached. "We heard about Anya." His grim face said the rest.

I shrugged. "Can't save them all. We'll get the bastard before his third one though." *Or at least we'd try,* I told myself.

Rodgers and Quinto nodded, which was about the extent of anyone's ability to mourn in the precinct. Thick skin was a necessary condition for admittance into the brotherhood of homicide detectives, and anyone who didn't have one coming in grew one real fast, even Steele.

"So, tell us about this guy you brought in," said Quinto. "Suspect number two, right?"

I glanced at my partner. "You want to field this one?"

"Sure," she said. "The guy's completely crazy. Certifiable, even. He thinks he's a time traveler sent back to our age to save humanity from certain destruction."

"Well, that's a bit of an exaggeration," I said. "He never said anything about the destruction of all the sentient races. More of a...readjustment of his known reality."

"Close enough," said Steele.

Quinto and Rodgers shared looks, then the big guy spoke to my partner. "Did you lose a bet to Daggers or something?"

"Oh, no, I'm serious," said Shay. "You can go talk to the guy yourself if you don't believe me."

As if on cue, shouts erupted from the far side of the pit. A pair of bluecoats were escorting Wyle to a holding area for further evaluation, and he took the opportunity to try to get our attention.

"Detectives! Detectives! Hey, there's been a misunderstanding. Come on, you have to let me out of here! We don't have time for this. You have to believe me!"

The bluecoats pushed Wyle around a corner.

Rodgers whistled. "Alrighty then."

"Yeah," I said. "What about you guys? I'm guessing Gronk didn't have anything else useful to pen into our tale of misery and woe?"

"Not a single stanza," said Quinto. "Gill's Repossessions was honestly run. We didn't find a single misplaced zero or decimal point in the financial files we sifted through. And Gronk didn't know anything about Gill's sister: her last name, her whereabouts, nothing."

"However," said Rodgers, "while you guys were interrogating the lunatic in the wizard's robe, Anya's husband dropped by. What was his name?"

"Mel," said Quinto.

"Right. Mel. Apparently a runner tracked him down and told him what happened. He's over in the sitting room." Rodgers gestured across the pit to the right of the break room. "He's pretty shaken. Maybe you should let Steele handle him."

I crossed my arms. "What are you trying to say? That I'm insensitive? Boorish? Rude?"

"Yes," said Rodgers.

"Oh. Ok then," I said, uncrossing my arms. "Just so we're clear."

Shay gave me one of her smiles, the kind that made me think she thought I was a huge dork, but that perhaps, just perhaps, she liked huge dorks.

"You can come with me," she said. "But let me do most of the talking. I don't want you badgering this poor man over his lost wife with ill-conceived references to time travelers."

"Fair enough," I said, and then to Rodgers and Quinto, "We'll be back. Hold down the fort."

"We always do," said Quinto.

Thinking Quinto could probably hold down anything shy of a seven-foot tall werewolf, I followed
Steele to the waiting room, a simple space adorned with
framed quotes from retired captains and a map of the
city from circa fifty years ago. An old worn couch made
of tanned lambskin populated the room along with a
pair of matching deep-seated club chairs, all of which
remained in miraculously acceptable condition only
through the unrelenting will of the Captain. Any detectives caught lounging in the chairs outside of official
interviews were given a stern reprimand. Apparently,
only civilian posteriors were good enough for padding
and leather.

In the middle of the couch sat a man with short
brown hair, lighter in color than mine, wearing a pair
of maroon slacks and a white collared shirt with the
sleeves unbuttoned and rolled to mid forearm. His head
hung so low I wondered if he might be inspecting the
floor for cracks, and he clutched a mug of steaming pre-
cinct-issue coffee between his shaking hands.

Shay paused inside the open door and knocked on
the side of the frame. "Excuse me...Mr. Crestwick?"

The man's head shot up in surprise. Tears streaked
his face, and I realized he'd been hanging his head to
hide his pain.

He wiped the trails of despair from his face with his
palm hastily before responding. "Um...yes. Yes. I'm Mel.
Mel Crestwick. Anya's... Anya's husband."

"I'm Detective Steele. This is my partner, Detective
Daggers." Shay shot a thumb at me, and I gave a halfhearted wave. "Mind if we sit?"

"Oh, yeah. Sure." Mel gestured toward the club chairs. "It's your office."

Steele and I sat. As we did so, Steele reached a hand out and lightly touched Mel's knee.

"I know it doesn't mean much, but I'm sorry for you loss," she said.

Mel nodded without speaking, but I could tell the gesture put him slightly more at ease. Shay had that effect on people. Not on me, of course. I think she intentionally inflamed me. Perhaps it was in retaliation for all the guff I gave her day in and day out, but she certainly saved her aura of caring and calm for others. Victims and witnesses, mostly. So what did that say about me? Did it mean she cared even *less* for me than she did a stranger?

Don't do this to yourself, Daggers, I told myself. *Not now. Focus.*

"I know how difficult this is for you, Mr. Crestwick," said Steele. "But do you mind if we ask you some questions? Your answers could help us solve this tragedy involving your wife."

Mel brought the coffee to his lips, his hands shaking so much I feared I'd be placed on spot janitorial duty. "Sure," he said between sips. "Sure."

"Mr. Crestwick, did your wife have any enemies?" asked Steele. "Anyone who might've wanted to hurt her?"

Mel shook his head, and his eyes glistened. "No. No. Absolutely not. She was a kind, sweet woman. The best. I can't imagine why anyone would..." His voice cracked, and the rest came out in a whisper. "Why...why would anyone do this to her?"

"We're trying to find out, Mr. Crestwick," said Steele. "Daggers. The sketch."

"Oh. Right." I fished the drawing back out of my coat pocket and handed it to Shay.

She smoothed it and showed it to Mel. "Does this man look familiar, Mr. Crestwick? We think he may be responsible for your wife's murder."

Mel shook his head again wordlessly, perhaps not trusting himself to retain his forced stoicism if he opened his mouth.

"Were you aware Anya's brother, Darryl, was also murdered yesterday?" said Steele.

Mel looked up and blinked. "*What?* No."

"This man in the sketch is our primary suspect in his murder," said Shay. "We have good reason to believe he's behind your wife's murder as well. Are you sure you've never seen him? There may be a connection between him, your wife, and her brother."

Mel looked at the sketch, more carefully this time, but again he shook his head. "No, I'm sorry, Detective. I've never seen this man before. I'm sure I'd remember if I had."

I spoke up, but I tried to keep my voice warm and fuzzy. "Do you mind telling us where you and your wife were yesterday morning, Mr. Crestwick?"

"We were at the World's Wonders Fair," said Mel. "To see the exhibits. We spent the majority of the day there. Didn't get home until late."

"What time?" I asked.

"I'm not sure," said Mel. "Maybe eight or nine in the evening."

I tried to envision Scar Face's movements, stalking Anya and Mel's home after having tortured the address out of Darryl, but eventually giving up after not finding them at home all day. We'd have to canvas Anya's neighborhood to see if anyone could corroborate my theory. Surely someone would've noticed a creep like Scar Face hanging around.

"And this morning," I asked. "What happened? Could you run us through your schedule?"

"Sure." Mel dropped his eyes back down to the floor. "We...went through our normal routine. I got up just after sunrise. Had breakfast and was out the door by seven thirty, at the latest. Anya stayed home, like she always does."

"Was she unemployed?" asked Steele.

Mel shook his head. "No. She had been, for a while, but she got proactive. Started up her own events planning business. She worked small functions. Parties for businesses, birthdays, even weddings, though she hadn't scheduled any of those yet. She'd just begun a few months ago."

"And what do you do?" I asked.

"I'm a guidance counselor," said Mel. "I help young people get their lives on track. Help them figure out what sorts of careers and paths to consider."

A thought struck me. "So...you work with trouble-makers, then?"

"Not really," said Mel. "They're misguided, but they're good kids. They just need, well...guidance for lack of a better term."

"So none of them ever threatened you or your family?" I asked.

"No. No, they..." Mel looked up, and I could tell someone had connected the hoses in his mind. "Wait. Actually, there was one kid. A young gang member. You know the type: cocky, self-assured, brash. He didn't want to be in my office, but he had to be as part of his parole agreement. I was trying to be sympathetic—only the gods know what sorts of things these kids go through—but then Anya dropped by to deliver some lunch. Left the bag on my desk, leaned over to give me a kiss, and out of the corner of my eye, I saw the kid ogling her. And then he made a—" Mel clenched his teeth. "—a *rude* remark, one that's not fit to be repeated in public. And so I told him to get lost. To get the hell out. I wasn't going to help him. And he gave me this look. Like a real, malicious, *evil* sort of look." Mel shook his head. "I don't know. Maybe I'm imagining things. But it gave me a bad feeling about the kid."

"When did this happen?" I asked.

Mel shrugged. "I don't remember. A few weeks, maybe a month ago?"

"And do you remember this kid's name?"

"Yeah," he said. "It was Zander, though I can't remember if it was his first or his last name. He was sent to us from the Our Lady of Hope and Salvation halfway house. The one on Crown Street, south of the Erming. We have a relationship with them." Mel leaned forward a little. "Look, you don't think that incident had anything to do with Anya's...murder, do you? I mean, how would that kid be connected to the guy in the sketch?"

"I don't know, Mr. Crestwick," said Steele. "Chances are there *is* no connection." She glanced at me pointedly as she said that. "But we need to look at this case from all possible angles. Who knows where a lead will surface?"

Mel nodded again, glumly, as if he wanted to drown himself in his coffee.

"I know this is hard, Mr. Crestwick," said Steele, "but do you mind staying here a while? We don't understand the motivations behind your wife's murder yet, but between her and her brother, it would appear someone's targeting her family, or yours. Did Anya have any other relatives?"

"No," said Mel with a sigh. "It was just her and her brother. Her mother's long dead, and her father's been out of the picture almost as long."

"Alright. Thanks," said Steele. "We'll try to send some officers out to check on the rest of your family members."

My partner stood and gave me a nod. I considered leaving Mel with my condolences, but I knew better than to think they'd make any difference. The only thing that could fill the hole in his heart now was his own misery, and chances were the hole was deep enough it wouldn't fill for years.

21

Shay and I returned to the pit where we found Rodgers and Quinto exactly where we'd left them. Well, not exactly—Rodgers had shifted from the top of Quinto's desk to his own seat, but neither detective looked to be involved in anything particularly useful, unless a discussion on how a guy like Gronk Turbot could come to be conceived could be considered useful. From what I caught of the conversation, Rodgers and Quinto were split between copious amounts of alcohol, a curse, and divine fury as the most likely causes.

Rodgers broke off his jibber jabber as we approached. "That was quick. Get anything useful from Mel?"

"Not much," I said. "The name of a possible suspect, a punk kid parolee. The only other thing I carried away from that interview was a lingering stink of sorrow."

"And what does that smell like?" said Quinto.

"Coffee and old leather, mostly," I said.

Shay snorted. "You know that kid's not involved, right, Daggers?"

"He could be," I said.

"He's not," said Shay.

"Oh, so suddenly your psychic sensibilities are acting up again?" I said.

Rodgers chuckled, but my partner didn't seem to think it was funny.

"We *have* a suspect," said Shay. "The guy from the sketch. I think it's pretty clear he murdered Darryl Gill, and the MO for Anya's murder is exactly the same."

"Exactly," I said. "We *suspect* Scar Face is the murderer, but we don't know for sure. To our knowledge, no eye witness noticed him at either Gill or Anya's places, and the only person who's been able to implicate him in the murders is that nutball Wyle. Maybe this punk who insulted Mel has something to do with the murders."

"Alright," said Shay. "Let's say this Zander kid is somehow involved. Let's say he wanted revenge on Mel for a proposed slight. Why would he go after Darryl Gill first? By all accounts, he and his sister weren't exactly close."

I shrugged. "I don't know. But I'll ask."

Shay threw her hands up in the air. "Whatever. If you want to go after this kid, be my guest. I'm going to spend my time pursing more fruitful avenues."

"Like?" I asked.

Shay smiled and raised her eyebrows. "Oh, wouldn't you like to know?"

"Well, yeah. I would," I said.

Shay shook her hands and frowned in overexaggerated fashion. "No, no. You go and track down the gang member. I'll pursue my own gut for once."

"That's not really how this works," I said, crossing my arms. "We're partners. What if you get into a jam?"

"I'll be fine," said Steele. "My investigative path has a lot more pencil pushers than vicious murderers populating it. But if it makes you feel better, I'll take Rodgers with me and you can take Quinto to protect you from that dangerous juvenile parolee Mel told us about."

Rodgers groaned, but he hid his displeasure on receiving a glare from Shay.

I turned to Quinto. "Well, bud. Looks like you got conscripted into my army. You up for taking a trip to the Erming?"

"Does *anyone* ever want to take a trip there?" said Quinto with a grimace.

The Erming was by far the worst slum in all of New Welwic, a place so miserable and destitute even rats avoided the place for fear of being turned into a rat casserole that was light on the cheese and potatoes and heavy on the rat.

"To be fair, the place we're heading to is south of the Erming," I said. "And we can grab lunch on the way back."

Quinto flashed his buckteeth. "Sold."

I straightened my jacket and gave my partner and Rodgers a two finger salute. "Well, then. Enjoy the stacks of records or files or whatever it is you plan to delve into in my absence."

Shay smirked. "We'll cherish the silence."

I held my hand out for Quinto. He led the way, but Rodgers stopped us with a call before we'd taken more than a few steps toward the door.

"Daggers?"

"Yes?" I said.

"Pick me up a sandwich on the way back, will you?" he said.

"How'd you know we were going to get sandwiches?" I asked.

"Do you have to ask?" said Rodgers.

"Fair enough," I said. "Steele, you want anything?"

She dropped her indignant act and regarded me with a more serious gaze. "Um, no. It's ok. I'll be fine. Thanks."

I sighed and headed for the exterior, my mind trying to process Shay's comment. *It's ok. I'll be fine. Thanks.* I didn't want to overanalyze everything she said, but by the grace of the gods, what in the world did *that* mean? Was she unwilling to accept an offer of free food from me? Did she think that by breaking that social convention she'd be accepting my advances? She could've paid me back for the sandwich if she'd wanted, but the conversation had never advanced to that point.

Quinto flagged down a rickshaw driver, the one with the widest cab he could find to accommodate our combined bulk. I glanced at the big guy as we settled into our seats and the rickshaw driver set his feet to pavement. I could confide in him, couldn't I? And he ate a lot. Maybe he had more knowledge of dining etiquette and its correlation to relationships than I did.

"Can I ask you something, Quinto?" I said as the rickshaw wheels clattered over the cobblestones.

"Yeah, sure," he said.

"What do you think my partner meant by that comment of hers?"

"What comment?"

"The bit about the sandwich," I said. "How she didn't want one."

"I assumed it meant she wasn't hungry," said Quinto.

"Oh." I hadn't considered that possibility. In retrospect, it seemed the most likely option.

Quinto lifted an eyebrow at me. "Now do you mind if I ask *you* a question?"

I glanced at the big guy. "Sure."

"What's up with you and Steele?"

I responded in my typical witty fashion. "Huh?"

Quinto rubbed his chin. "Hmm. Let me see if I can rephrase that... Nope. I can't. Seriously, what the heck's up with you two? You've been spending more time around one another. You've been going out to eat more often—"

"Not going out," I said. "Eating together, yes. But *not* going out."

"What's the difference?" said Quinto.

"Oh, trust me," I said. "There's a difference."

Quinto peered at me quizzically.

"Ok, I admit," I said. "Steele's grown on me over the past few months. She's an excellent homicide detective. Smart, quick-witted. And she's far easier on the eyes than Griggs ever was, even in his pre-mummified years."

"That's not exactly what I was getting at," said Quinto. "You like her, right?"

"Whoa," I said. "I didn't say that. You did. But, yes, I guess, you could say that, in a way, I like her. Why wouldn't I? But I'm not *in like* with her, if that's what you mean."

"That's not even a phrase, Daggers."

"Sure it is," I said. "You're just not down with the street lingo like I am."

Quinto rolled his eyes and shifted in his seat so he could better see the scenery. We were approaching the East Bay Bridge, a part suspension, part bascule system which everyone in the city merely called the Bridge for reasons of simplicity. The drawbridge portion in the middle of the Bridge, controlled by a team of strong but lethargic oxen, was down, so traffic progressed along it at an even canter.

Thinking of the oxen drew my mind to the Bock Industries reciprocating engine I'd seen the other morning with Steele. Surely such a machine could do the work of two dozen oxen, and do it far faster, which was a good bit of news for every rickshaw driver, pedestrian, and frigate captain that made use of the Bridge's services, but not necessarily good news for the oxen.

The street arched slightly as we approached the Bridge, and our rickshaw driver huffed and puffed under our heavy load and the incline. A breeze curled off the sea, up the cool waters of the Earl, and buffeted me in the face as it passed me by. It smelled of salt and sand and wide open spaces, of turning seasons and ocean swells. I filled my lungs with it.

As we passed over the drawbridge, I tried to strike conversation back up with Quinto. "So how's your clandestine relationship progressing?"

Quinto shifted his eyes from the wide expanse of the Earl to me. "You mean with Cairny?"

"Unless you're seeing someone else on the side, yes," I said.

Quinto's face lit up. "It's going well. Really well. Man, she's a blast to be around. And funny, too!"

"You're kidding," I said. "We're talking about the same Cairny, right?"

"I know you wouldn't guess it from the way she acts at work," said Quinto, "but it's true. She's quick on her mental feet. I think that's a common trait of funny people."

I'm not sure if Quinto meant that as a compliment, but I took it as one given my own humorous inclinations. "And the two of you haven't had any...how should I put this? Difficulties? Arguments?"

"Not really," said Quinto. "Though we haven't been dating that long. We're still feeling each other out."

"Figuratively, I hope," I said.

Quinto frowned. "I'm not going to delve into that. You're a friend, Daggers, but not *that* good of a friend."

The breeze died down as we came off the Bridge and rolled our way into the dock district, the whistle of the wind and the cries of seagulls replaced by the banging of crates and the yells of longshoremen.

"You know, there's one thing I still don't understand about you two," I said.

"That being?" said Quinto.

"How did you and Cairny become a couple?" I asked. "How did you convince her to go out with you?"

"Oh, that's simple," said Quinto with a smile. "I just asked."

What a novel concept. I'd never have thought of the same thing myself.

22

I thought our rickshaw driver might lose a lung before we arrived at the Our Lady of Hope and Salvation halfway house, but despite a sudden coughing fit that nearly brought the poor guy to his knees near the end of our trip, we made it. Quinto gave the driver a hefty tip, which was only fair given the months we'd shaved off his life through the taxing endeavor.

We unloaded from the solid wooden rickshaw right in front of the halfway house, a lime-green two-story pile of bricks and timber that looked like it might fail a fire code inspection but nonetheless outshined pretty much any tenement you'd find in the Erming proper. The shutters in the front had been thrown open, welcoming in whatever traces of cool sea breezes might straggle in from over by the river, and a sign over the front door, black paint on wood, read 'Welcome Children of the Birth Mother.' I wasn't sure which particular Lady the supervisors of the halfway house bowed their knees in prayer to, but I gathered they believed in one of New Welwic's many pagan religions.

Next to the building, a number of teens and pre-teens loitered in a fenced in lot that, besides copious amounts of dirt, held a rudimentary playscape, including a seesaw, a slide, and my own mongrel's favorite—monkey bars. The kids on the playground all looked a little too old for the equipment, so I assumed the half-way house catered to troublemakers of all ages.

One thing the kids in the dirt lot weren't too old for was that favorite of young adult pastimes—mockery of others. A trio of pimple-faced gnomes who barely scraped their noses against the top of the fence surrounding the playground catcalled us as we walked up to the Hope and Salvation house.

"Hey, guys. Look what the cat dragged in," said the one in front, a kid with a red striped shirt and a pair of hand-me-down corduroy pants. "A couple of donut eaters."

Although I knew what the kid was getting at, I didn't think the dig was particularly apt. One of the reasons I'd shed a good ten or fifteen of my excess pounds over the past few weeks was that I'd limited my stops at Tolek's mobile kolache cart from once a day to once or twice a week—and then I limited myself to one per visit, as opposed to however many I could fit into one of his paper bags.

Regardless, I didn't let the kid's wisecrack get to me. If I couldn't outwit a testosterone-riddled gnome youth, I didn't deserve my crown as the precinct's king of quips.

"Hey, squirt," I said. "What's got you down? Or is that due to genetics?"

One of the kid's gnome friends joined him at the fence, a youth with a green-striped shirt to match the other's red one. He sniffed the air. "Do I smell bacon?"

"Nope," I said. "That's the grease on your face. Don't worry, it'll clear up when you hit puberty. You know, in a decade or so."

The second gnome kid's face reddened.

"You kids seen Zander?" asked Quinto.

"What's it to you?" said the first.

"We're trying to piece some things together," I said. "Like who we can implicate alongside him in our current case. Any of you interested in some obstruction of justice charges? Or maybe a perversion of justice charge instead?"

That shut the kids up. One of them pointed to the halfway house. "Talk to Miss Eckles. She can tell you about Zander."

I smiled my most reassuring smile, tossed the kids a lazy thanks, and wandered inside. A hall of lime green stretched out before us, and hints of the color peeked out from rooms to my left and right. The contractors must've gotten a deal on the bold paint. Only the stairs had avoided the touch of the painter's brush.

"Was that really necessary?" said Quinto.

"You mean with the kids? You can't show weakness with brats. Otherwise they'll run all over you." I wondered if I should try in back or up the stairs first.

"All I'm saying," said Quinto, "is you catch more flies with honey than you do with vinegar."

"Have you ever tried it?" The back made more sense, but sometimes these old homes had the offices upstairs.

"Tried what?"

"Honey and vinegar," I said. "Flies love vinegar. Seriously."

Quinto frowned at me.

I decided to try the lazy man's method of finding the halfway house's administrator. "Miss Eckles!?"

"In the back," came a feminine voice.

I led the way and motioned for Quinto to follow. Crammed into a cubby under the back of the stairs was a tiny office, and in the office was a tiny woman—maybe five feet tall and a hundred and five pounds after a solid breakfast. She wore a modest black and white dress that covered her from neck to toe, and a few strands of gray wove in and out of her otherwise black mane of hair.

"Miss Eckles?" I said.

She took one look at us and said, "Uh oh. Who's in trouble now?"

I glanced at Quinto before turning my peepers back onto the headmistress.

"Oh, don't give each other that look," she said. "I've spent my life around hellions, bless their hearts. I know you're cops. So who did what this time?"

"We're looking for a teen by the name of Zander," I said. "Ring a bell?"

"Of course it does," she said. "Toby."

"Toby?" I said.

"Tobias Zander," she said. "He likes his last name better."

"Do you know where we can find him?" I asked. "We need to ask him a few questions."

Miss Eckles waved her hand dismissively. "I don't know. You'd have a better idea of that than I would, wouldn't you?"

I scratched my head. "I don't understand. Doesn't he live here?"

The headmistress snorted. "He did. Until he got arrested again for robbing a greengrocer. He's been in your custody for the past four days."

"You're kidding," I said.

Quinto clapped me on the shoulder. "Well, so much for that angle."

"Yeah," I said. "Do you know which precinct he's being held at? We need to double check his whereabouts for the past day or two."

Miss Eckles pointed us toward the nearest police house, the one on the southwest corner of the Erming. I thanked her and excused myself, feeling like something of an idiot after my exchange with Shay where I'd floated the possibility of the kid's involvement. I was sure she'd give me a hard time over it, so I tried to console myself with the knowledge that lunch was imminent and for once my partner wouldn't be able to steer me clear of a nice, simple sub shop.

23

Quinto and I popped by the precinct where Zander was supposedly being held, the one situated on the southwest corner of the Erming. Police stations stood at each of the Erming's four corners—silent, stoic sentinels dedicated not so much to keeping the peace inside the wretched slum but to make sure the chaos, poverty, and depravity within didn't spill out into the surrounding neighborhoods. Given their limited resources, the gumshoes and bluecoats assigned there did an admirable job, though from friends and colleagues I knew who'd spent time at the slum stations, the turnover was high. Not necessarily because of the danger involved—it had more to do with the mental strain associated with dealing with slum dwellers on a day in, day out basis. My job was mentally taxing, too, but at least for the victims I worked with, their lives couldn't get any worse, something that wasn't true for most slum rats.

The Erming Southwest location's stone exterior was run-down and dingy, and it still stood out like a beacon of brilliance compared to the dilapidated red brick back-drop of the slum that stretched out behind it. Quinto and I sauntered in and found the precinct's jailor, a stereotypical barrel-chested man with red cheeks and a handlebar moustache. He escorted us to the holding cells, where we found Zander loitering among a group of likeminded hooligans and where I suffered my first real surprise of the trip—Zander, like his compatriots at the Our Lady of Hope and Salvation halfway house, was a *gnome*.

The jailor, who went by the handle of Carbonaceous Carbuncle—a name I can only assume was his honest-to-goodness given name because why else would any-one go by such a daft moniker—confirmed Zander had been imprisoned since robbing a local produce vendor at knife point, making it quite impossible for him to have committed our homicides. As much as I believed him, I didn't really need the confirmation anymore. Looking at Zander's slight, teenaged gnome frame, I doubted there was any way he could've hogtied, tor-tured, and murdered a fully-grown man like Darryl Gill even *if* he'd been on the loose.

Much like his smart-mouthed buddies back at the halfway house, Zander had a few choice words for Quinto and I, which made his newfound cellmates chuckle. I laughed alongside with him and told him his sense of humor would serve him well. Guys his size and complexion always did great in prison, I assured him.

Leaving the appropriately cowed Zander in our wake, Quinto and I caught a rickshaw back over the Bridge to the west side of town, where, before arriving at the precinct, we stopped by a new sandwich shop by the name of Grinders. I'd heard from some of the other flatfoots around the precinct that the place could slap toppings between slices of bread with the best of them, and while I was a fan of a different shop by the name of Loaders, I was willing to give Grinders a try, despite the ludicrous name.

I snagged a ham and cheese with mustard and pickles to go, and Quinto, possibly still on his cod and potato high from yesterday, opted for a smoked pepper mackerel sandwich that reeked of mesquite smoke and the aftermath of a summer algal bloom. The thing could only have looked more dubious if the heads had still been attached to the filets. We grabbed a more normal hoagie for Rodgers, and, in a fit of enthusiasm and lunacy, I picked up a turkey, bacon, and tomato half-sandwich for Shay, consequences be damned.

Quinto's and my sandwiches disappeared within a few minutes of us leaving the shop, so it was with only a slim paper bag in hand that the big guy and I walked back into the 5th Street Precinct. As we passed through the wide front doors, I spotted the back of Shay's head at her desk, her dark brown hair hanging lazily past her shoulder blades. Past her, in *my* chair, at *my* desk of all places, sat Rodgers. The pair giggled over some clandestine joke, probably one with me as the punch line if I knew them as well as I thought I did.

I walked up and deposited the paper bag on my desk. "You're in my seat."

"Oh, hey Daggers," said Rodgers, getting up. "Just keeping it warm for you."

"I hope you didn't ruin my butt groove," I said.

Shay snorted and shook her head.

"Very funny," said Rodgers.

Cushions were something reserved for those public servants with real pull, people like the mayor and the DA and the Captain. Honestly, I'm not sure how the bulldog had added his name to that list. He must've blackmailed someone somewhere along the line.

"So what did you get me?" asked Rodgers, eyeing the bag.

"Smoked pepper mackerel," said Quinto. "I had one and it was *delicious*." He licked his fingers as proof.

Rodgers' face fell. "You're kidding."

"Sort of," said Quinto. "I had one. We got you roast beef."

Rodgers clutched his heart. "Oh, man. You had me there. Especially because I could smell a strange fish funk coming off you."

I eyed Quinto. "That scent does have a way of lingering."

Rodgers opened the bag and pulled out both sandwiches. "What's this one?"

I nodded to the half-sandwich. "That's for Steele."

"What?" Shay raised an eyebrow. "I told you not to get me anything."

"Yeah, but I don't want you wasting away," I said. "What if we get into a scrape and I need you to back me up? You're not going to be much use if even an arthritic grandmother could push you around. After you finish that sandwich we're going to do some pushups and wind sprints out on the sidewalk."

Shay accepted the sandwich with a begrudging smile. Maybe she was right. Maybe I couldn't read facial expressions. I certainly couldn't tell if her current attempt at a grin indicated subdued annoyance or heartfelt affection.

Shay unwrapped her turkey, tomato, and bacon and took a bite.

"Good?" I asked.

She nodded. "So...tell us about your adventures with the reformed teenage gang member."

"Well, Zander's not our murderer," I said, sitting down in my still warm chair. "And I know that because he's far from reformed. He's been incarcerated for the past few days on charges of aggravated robbery. Plus he's a gnome, so murdering humans with a claw hammer is probably a little out of his wheelhouse."

Rodgers shook his head as he unwrapped his own sandwich. "That's a shame, Daggers. Well, not the part where he didn't murder anyone. More that you went to all that hassle. Fortunately—" He brandished a finger in the air. "—you have a partner with a few licks more sense than you do."

I propped my arms up on my desk and rested my chin on a palmed fist. "I take it you two discovered something during your secret trip to...oh, I don't know. I'm going to guess the Municipal Department of Boredom and Tears?"

"Close," said Rodgers as he took a bite. "The bank."

Quinto looked confused. "But I already went over Gill's finances."

Shay swallowed a mouthful of bread and turkey. "Not Darryl. Mel and Anya. Daggers, remember how Mel said he was a guidance counselor?"

"Of course I remember," I said. "I just went chasing after one of his snot faced appointees wrongly thinking he might be involved."

"Then you'll also remember how he mentioned Anya was unemployed until she recently started her own events planning business."

I nodded. "So? What are you getting at?"

"Well," said Steele. "If Mel was telling the truth—and as far as we know he was—how is it he and Anya were able to afford to buy their very own, nicely furnished brownstone row house?"

I almost slapped my forehead, but I held back on the self-mutilation. "Holy crap. How didn't I see that? There's no way they could afford a place like that on a single counseling salary. What did you find at the bank?"

Rodgers answered as Shay took another run at her sandwich. "Turns out Mel deposited a large sum of money—*very* large—into his bank account a little over a year ago, and they used that as the down payment on the home."

"And what did Mel have to say about that large chunk of change?" I asked.

"Not sure. We haven't asked him yet. But he's still here." Rodgers pointed across the pit to the waiting room, where I spotted Mel curled up on the couch, perhaps asleep. "Steele thought it would be better to wait for you. She's better at the soft and fuzzy approach, but your tactics are better when you need to catch someone in a lie."

"So you admit I'm the bigger hard ass," I said to Steele.

She nodded as she swallowed another bite of sandwich. "I won't argue that point."

"Well alright then," I said, rubbing my hands together in glee. "Let's go see what Mel has to say."

24

had to rein my horses for a few minutes until Shay finished her sandwich, but as soon as she'd swallowed the last bite, I led the way over to the waiting room where Mel lay sprawled out, snoring on the tan leather couch.

I knocked on the open door none too gently, startling sleeping beauty awake.

"Howdy, Mel," I said.

Mel sat up and blinked, his hair a disheveled mess. "Oh, um...hello." He rubbed his eyes. "What time is it?"

"Just after lunch," I said. "Twelve thirty-ish."

"Oh. Wow." He blinked again and seemed to realize Shay and I were both at the door. "Did you already find the killer?"

"No. Sorry," I said. "We're here to ask a few more questions. Mind if we sit?"

He nodded.

I introduced my posterior to the face of the club chairs. "So, if you don't mind, Mel, can you refresh me on what it is your wife Anya did?"

Mel looked around as if he'd misplaced something. Perhaps his coffee. "Yeah. She was an events planner. Like for parties."

"But she'd stared that business recently," I said. "She'd been unemployed before that, right?"

"That's right," said Mel.

"How was business?" I asked.

"It was ok," said Mel. "She had some clients lined up, but nothing to write home about. Why are you asking?"

"We combed through your bank records, Mel," I said. "Turns out you deposited a *substantial* quantity of cash into your account about a year ago. Money you used to buy your house. You mind telling us where that money came from?"

"Oh, uh, right. That money." Mel rubbed his neck. "It was...from an inheritance."

I could smell the lie on him. "Whose, exactly?"

"My, uh, uncle," he said. "Daniel Crestwick."

I glanced at Steele. She said nothing.

"So...you wouldn't mind if we check on that, then," I said. "Just to make sure we have the story straight."

"I, uh... I mean..." Mel glanced at the door, and he rubbed his hands together. "Ok, look. That money? It wasn't from an inheritance. It was from...something else."

"Go on," I said.

Mel sighed. "This is going to sound bad, but...someone paid me to find out more about Anya's father. But there's no way this has anything to do with Anya's murder!"

I performed a quick double blink. "Huh?"

"Look, I know what you're thinking," said Mel. "But I loved Anya. By the gods, I loved her... I'd never do anything to hurt her! It's just that, well...we've been married for about four years now. And we've never had much, between my meager salary and her nonexistent one. So when someone approached me to seek out Anya's father, offering to pay me several years worth of my salary for the information, I figured, what harm could it do? Anya didn't know anything about her father anyway. He's long gone. A recluse. So I took the money and told Anya it was an inheritance from my uncle. And we used it to buy our house."

"Whoa, whoa. Slow down," I said. "You're going to have to back things up. Someone wanted you to track down Anya's father? Why?"

"I don't know," said Mel. "They wanted to meet him, or get his help on something, I suppose. I didn't ask questions. Like I said, I knew Anya didn't know where the man lived. But I was happy to take that much money to try and find out more."

"Hold on," said Shay. "Who, exactly, *is* Anya's father?"

"Buford Gill," said Mel. "He's a scientist specializing in astronomy and, uh...theoretical physics, I think. As I said, he's a total recluse. Anya hasn't seen or talked to the man in over a decade. He used to be a professor at one of New Welwic's universities, but as far as I know, he angered some of the brass there and was fired. Nobody's seen him in years. The only reason anyone knows he's still alive is because he occasionally publishes papers in scientific journals."

I scratched the back of my head. "And who paid you a boatload of cash to locate him?"

"Uh..." Mel chewed his lip.

"Look at me, Mel," I said. "You're not implicated in any wrongdoing...*yet*. But I have plenty of time to change my mind about that."

Mel continued to chew his lip, but he relented. "Ok. He told me to keep it quiet, but these are sort of extenuating circumstances, so I'm sure he'll understand. It was Linwood Bock."

I tried to rouse the hamster in my mind and get him on his wheel. "Wait...the wealthy business magnate?" I recalled the man as I'd seen him at yesterday's fair, aging, wearing a pinstripe suit and with a white doorknocker beard over his lip and chin.

"Why did Linwood Bock hire you to find Anya's father?" asked Steele.

"I already told you, I don't know," said Mel. "I assume he wanted his help with something, a research project of some sort. Buford Gill's a curmudgeon, and he's a little off his rocker—or so I understand, I've never met him—but by all accounts, he's a genius. He'd surely be an asset to Bock Industries."

"And you have no idea where to find the man?" asked Steele.

"None," said Mel. "Honest."

I looked at the guidance counselor: his posture, his demeanor, and, most importantly, his eyes. An experienced detective could tell a lot about a person from the contents of their eyes, and I had enough seasons on me to discern the motives of an entire sack of potatoes. Mel was an idealist, a romantic, and possibly a bit of an idiot, but he wasn't a murderer, and I didn't think he was hiding anything from us in regards to his relationship with Anya's father and Linwood Bock.

I tapped my chair's armrest. "Alright, Mel. Those are all the questions we have for the time being. You're free to leave if you want, but if someone killed your wife to get to her father, well...they might come to you for information next. Why not hang out and enjoy the coffee?"

Mel's eyes widened and he gulped, and I realized perhaps there might've been a better way to break the news to Anya's husband. I glanced at Steele and reminded myself to let her take care of the warm and fuzzies. Unwittingly, I might've ensured Mel's catnap was the last he indulged in for days.

25

Upon returning to our workspaces, I found an even greater act of sacrilege had been committed than the one preceding my interview with Mel. Rodgers had reinvaded my desk, and he'd convinced Quinto to conquer Shay's. Their elbows and leftover lunch wrappers littered our desks like so many soldiers enjoying a post-battle snooze.

"Don't you guys have anything better to do?" I asked as Shay and I approached.

Quinto shot his partner a glance. "Doesn't he know?"

"Know what?" I asked.

"We're officially on the case," said Rodgers.

"Really?" I said.

Quinto nodded. "The Captain assigned us this morning. Yesterday we were lurking because we didn't have anything of our own to investigate, but now we're lurking in an *official* capacity—again, because we don't have anything of our own to investigate."

I grunted. "Hmm. I'll let it slide, but only because nobody else being murdered over the past day puts me in a good mood."

"This is you in a good mood?" said Steele.

I glared at her. She smiled back at me brazenly, which melted my frown like a pair of wax lips under the hot rays of the sun. Try as I might to invoke my inner sourpuss, I found it harder and harder the longer I spent around my partner.

"So," said Rodgers. "What did you learn from Mel?"

"That this case possibly goes far deeper than we'd initially imagined," I said.

I glanced at the side of my desk. Something was missing. Something I'd noticed earlier but hadn't brought up as a point of discussion. I pointed to the gaping hole beside my desk that allowed light to drift in from the Captain's office windows. "Say...where's the corkboard? I swear I left it here yesterday."

Quinto looked around, his furry eyebrows pressed together. "Huh?"

"It's the janitor," said Shay. "He rolls it into its cubby at night so he can sweep the floors."

I raised an eyebrow. "How late are you staying at work, exactly?"

Shay shook her head. "It's not that. I've noticed it before, and I asked him about it. That's what he told me."

"Oh, good gods," I said. "I'll bet you know the guy's name and everything. Well, don't get any ideas. I've already befriended Boatreng. That's enough social fluttering to hold me over for another few months, at least."

"I'll keep that in mind," said Steele. "Now quit bitching and go get the board."

I did as I was told, without slinging a single quip or zinger in my defense before I left. And they say an old dog can't learn new tricks.

When I returned, Shay had reclaimed her chair, and one of the Rodgers and Quinto pair had brought over seats enough for the rest of us. I repinned the sketches of Scar Face and Cheeks, now better known as Harland Wyle, up onto the corkboard while Shay put her creative skills to use fabricating sketches of Darryl Gill, Anya, and Mel Crestwick. The sketches of the victims, or of Mel, weren't particularly necessary, but ever since revealing her artistic abilities a month or so ago, Shay had insisted on sketching anyone she deemed important to the case and adding them to the board. I think her motivations were twofold. For one, she enjoyed stretching her artistic muscle, and what better time to do it than on company time? But I also think Shay was more of a visual learner, and having the faces on the board helped her make connections she otherwise wouldn't.

My deductive system was far simpler. I just swilled coffee and listened to my gut.

Once Shay had finished her drawings, she added them to the cork and stepped back. "Alright," she said. "Let's try and make sense of what we know. Rodgers and Quinto, this applies to you, too, since you're on the case. Daggers, you like to hear yourself talk—" She followed that jab with a sly smile. "—so bring us up to speed."

"My pleasure," I said. "Why don't we go over what we absolutely know, and then we can bring in all the things we *think* we know."

I got a few nods in response, so I stepped over to the board and pointed at Shay's sketch of Darryl Gill. "We know Gill was murdered early yesterday morning via a heavy blow to the skull. The techs found a set of prints from someone other than Gill on various surfaces in his apartment. The night prior, Gill visited an elven gigolo by the name of Passion Faust at a club called the 9's, and the bouncer at the club reported seeing a man following him. Later that day, eyewitness accounts have a different man, who we now know as Harland Wyle—" I pointed to Boatreng's sketch. "—breaking into Gill's apartment. CSU found his prints, which we've since confirmed, on letters and curios.

"Then today, we found Darryl Gill's sister, Anya Crestwick, murdered in her home, also by a blow to the skull. We found Wyle on the scene going through Anya's personal effects." I turned to Steele. "Do we have the CSU report from Anya's place yet?"

"I haven't seen it," she said. "I can go bug the techs later."

"Alright," I said. "So for the time being, that's all we *know*. Now, here's what we *think* we know. We think the man the bouncer spotted outside the club followed Gill and murdered him. We don't think Wyle's the killer because his prints weren't on the scene prior to his break-in at Gill's apartment yesterday afternoon. Given that Anya's murder was performed in the exact same manner as Darryl's, chances are Wyle didn't murder her either, although we won't have any evidence to support that until we get the CSU report."

I stuck a finger in the air. "Now, here's where the story gets weird. Wyle claims he's a time mage sent from the future to prevent the murder suspect, who we're calling Scar Face for obvious reasons—" I pointed to Boatreng's first sketch. "—from ending the future as he knows it. Wyle doesn't claim to know why or how, but he's adamant about his mission. Clearly, he's a nutball. But what's his connection to the murders?

"And, the more important question is, why were Darryl and Anya murdered? Previously, we'd operated on the assumption that perhaps Darryl was slain by an angry client of his repossessions business or by a jilted ex-lover, but the evidence doesn't support that. Similarly, Gill's finances were in order, and his apartment wasn't robbed. Money may not be involved. So why kill him?

"I'd suspected for a while now that the killer, and Wyle for that matter, were after information, but what? Well, thanks to Steele's intuition—" My partner flourished her hand in recognition. "—we now have a clue. A year ago, Mel, Anya's husband, was approached by none other than Linwood Bock, the wealthy industrialist, to try and locate Anya's father, Buford Gill, who we'll call Gill Sr. to avoid confusion with Darryl. Gill Sr. is, by Mel's account, a brilliant scientist who could be of use to Bock's empire, but he's a recluse and hasn't been seen in years. Now, let's keep in mind Mel was approached over a year ago by Mr. Bock. With that said, however, I'd say it's probable, if not certain, that our mystery killer didn't murder Darryl and Anya for any reason other than to locate Gill Sr.. The question, of course, is why?"

I went back to my chair and took a seat. Steele, Rodgers, and Quinto all sat, quietly, staring at the cork board.

"Any ideas?" I said.

Quinto cleared his throat. "Have you had this Wyle guy undergo a psychiatric evaluation?"

"Not yet," said Steele. "But we could. He's in holding. Why?"

"Well," said Quinto. "It seems to me he's not crazy."

Steele raised an eyebrow. "Don't tell me you're going to pull a Daggers-esque theory out from between your toes."

Quinto smiled. "That's a nice way of putting it. Daggers usually picks a different orifice. But no, it's more simple than that. If this guy's crazy, how is it he made his way to Gill and Anya's places in the immediate aftermath of their deaths? I guess he could be a stalker, but the timing's off. As Daggers said, he's looking for something, which means he's not crazy and henceforth he's lying. I'm not sure what his involvement in these murders is, but he must know something that can help us solve them."

Steele nodded. "Good point. We could always interrogate the guy again. Change our tactics. See if he modifies his story."

I stared at the board, my chin cupped in my hand, using my fingers to squish my lips together.

"Uh oh," said Rodgers, noticing. "Daggers is doing that fish face thing again. I think he's dangerously close to coming up with an idea."

I glanced at him without moving my hand. "Maybe. And I doubt you or anyone else will like it."

"That's never stopped you from sharing before," said Steele. "Go on. Out with it."

I shrugged, leaned back in my chair, and clasped my hands. "Alright. What if Wyle's telling the truth?"

Steele rolled her eyes and Quinto snorted.

"Not the whole truth, by any means," I said. "But there might be a kernel of truth to his story. Think about it. He said Scar Face is a member of a radical anti-technology group bent on preventing the spread of science into the future. Buford Gill is a brilliant scientist, one who's still working on his research from some unknown, secluded location. He could be on the verge of an important scientific discovery, and if he ends up collaborating with Linwood Bock, whose resources are nearly limitless, couldn't that change the future of our world? And we still don't know how he found Anya."

"Look, Daggers," said Steele. "I'm willing to agree with Quinto that Wyle probably isn't crazy. But he's lying, about *everything*, including all that stuff about time ripples and how he used them to locate Anya. Clearly, he found her address on one of Gill's letters, or he tracked the murderer to her house."

"I'm not necessarily saying I believe it myself," I said. "I'm just putting it out there as an option. Either way, I think we're all in agreement that we need to have another chat with our dapperly dressed prisoner. Rodgers and Quinto, care to join us?"

26

The precinct's holding cells were located in the back of the building, each of them built about ninety percent underground except for the top foot. In that space, small, bar-reinforced lookout windows graciously allowed the prisoners access to a few hours of natural sunlight each day, in addition to the occasional sidelong view of the feet of anyone who happened to walk through the adjoining alleyway on the other side of the jail walls.

It was a slow day. Wyle had an entire cell to himself, though the compartment opposite him had a resident— a permanently drunk half-orc by the name of Goakey Joe who inevitably ended up in the pens every few days. Thankfully, the orc lush was still in the throes of unconsciousness. He could get pretty rowdy when awake and sober.

Harland stood and approached the cell's bars as we descended the stairs into the holding chamber, his deep violet robe flapping as he walked. "Oh, thank goodness. I was afraid you'd abandoned me here in this prison."

"This isn't a prison," I said, coming to rest outside the wrought iron. "It's a jail."

"There's a difference?" said Wyle.

"Of course," I said. "A prison is a place for people who've been convicted of a crime. Jails are for short term detention and people awaiting trial."

"Ok, well, whatever," said Wyle, shrugging. "Are you going to let me out or not?"

"That depends," I said.

Harland's brows furrowed and he blinked. "What? What do you mean, *that depends*? I thought you believed me."

"Let me introduce you to a few of my friends," I said. "This handsome fellow is Detective Rodgers. The walking mountain is Detective Quinto. And of course you remember Detective Steele. She's hard to forget."

Quinto tipped his head and Rodgers gave a mini salute. Shay just smiled, whether at me or Wyle I couldn't tell. Probably because I couldn't read her signals, gosh darn it!

"Um, nice to meet you," said Wyle. "Now what's it going to take to get me out of here? You know we have limited time, don't you?"

"Why don't we go through your story again," I said. "You know, to make sure we're clear on the specifics."

Wyle gripped the bars of the cell and rested his head on his hands before bringing it up again. "Oh, come on, Detective...what was it? Dagger?"

"Daggers," I said.

"Yes, that's right, Daggers," said Wyle. "Look, I already told you, we need to stop that psychopath from Citizens for Simplicity before he kills again. I'm guessing he hasn't because I haven't felt any pulses in the time streams since this morning, but as far as I'm concerned, we've gotten lucky. Yes, he's murdered a couple people, but I'm certain he hasn't found his target yet. If he had, the sensory flood from the time streams would've been seismic, to say the least."

"And you know this because..." I said.

"Good question," said Wyle. "To be fair, our knowledge of major historical changes due to temporal interference is purely theoretical. We've never tried to change history for the fun of it. But I assure you, the theory *is* sound. We've done tests with temporal distortionists. I'm certain we still have time. At least...I hope we do."

Quinto leaned over to Steele. "Sorry I didn't believe you earlier. You were right."

"Right? Right about what?" Wyle looked at Steele's face, then Quinto's, then mine and Rodgers'. "Oh...I see. You all just came back to laugh at the nutcase. Well, guess what? I'm not crazy! This is real! Maybe to you it isn't, because you don't have the knowledge I do, and it's not your future on the line, just mine. You're all free to live a new, non-premeditated future, but not me! I'm trying to save what I have, and what the rest of the sentient races put together."

"Let's cut through the lies, Harland," said Steele, tapping on one of the cell bars. "What do you know about Buford Gill?"

"What? Who?" said Wyle.

"Buford Gill," repeated Steele. "Darryl and Anya's father."

"I...don't know," said Wyle. "I'm not familiar with him."

"He's an important scientist," I said. "If you're from the future, surely you've heard the name."

Wyle stared at the floor for a second and blinked. "Um...no. I can't say I have."

"What about Linwood Bock?" said Steele.

"No," said Wyle. "I don't know who that is either."

"Your story's sounding flimsier by the minute," I told Wyle. "Bock's a wealthy industrialist, owner of Bock Industries. Surely *that* name rings a bell."

"Well, it doesn't, ok?" said Wyle. "None of the history texts from my age mention any Bock or Bock Industries. It's all Sherman Industries, so I don't know what this line of questioning is supposed to accomplish. Unless..." Wyle let go of the cell bars and stepped back. "Oh no. Oh CRAP."

"What's up?" I asked. "Did one of the time steams spring a leak?"

"No, no, don't you see?" said Wyle. "The theories? Maybe we were wrong. Maybe the killer's work is already done. I don't know how he did it—I was sure I'd sense the change in the time streams, but it's the butterfly effect. It has to be. He must've already changed history. Sherman Industries doesn't exist—or rather, it never *will*. It's all Bock now. Oh, gods..."

Wyle slumped onto the flimsy bench inside his cell and rested his head in his hands. I thought I heard a sob.

"The what effect?" whispered Rodgers.

"I don't know," said Steele. "But this was clearly a waste of time. Let's head back up."

My detective compatriots headed for the stairs, but I lingered for a moment, casting my gaze Wyle's way. The guy seemed pretty shook up. Would a nutcase get that emotional? Wouldn't they change their story to fit their delusion? Or would they believe as Wyle apparently did, that his world had ended?

I caught up with the rest of the gang at the top of the stairs, the image of Wyle on his jail bench still fresh in my mind.

"Thought I'd lost you," said Steele as we walked back into the pit.

I smirked. "Despite that old adage about men, most of us have very acute senses of direction. I can find my way back from the holding cells, and even if I couldn't, there's a fire escape map in the stairwell."

"So," said Rodgers as we neared the desks. "How's that theory of yours about Wyle telling the truth feel now, Daggers?"

"I never said I believed it," I reminded him as I plopped back into my chair. "I said it was a possibility. Now? I don't know. I can't tell if the guy's crazy or lying, and if he's lying, I don't know what his game is. There's something off about him."

"No kidding," said Quinto, stuffing his hands in his pockets. "Multiple things. *Way* off."

"Well, regardless of what's wrong with him," said Shay, "his role in these murders is still very much unclear. But he does have a role. I guarantee it. Quinto, Rodgers, why don't you work the Harland Wyle angle? Try to figure out who he is, his background, where he's from, who his friends are, all that stuff. If we can learn more about him, perhaps we'll stumble across a connection to Scar Face."

Rodgers glanced at his elephantine partner. "Well, it's not as if we have much to go on—other than maybe checking with New Welwic's specialty clothing stores and costume shops. But yeah, sure. We'll try to slap together a dossier on the guy."

Quinto chuckled. "As useful as that tactic might be, we might want to start with Public Records. If he's crazy, chances are he's been institutionalized. We'll be able to find a paper trail."

"Great," said Shay. "Daggers, you're with me."

I tried not to stand at attention, but I had to put some effort in. Steele was assuming a leadership role, and doing a fine job at it. Rodgers and Quinto hadn't even grumbled when told to dive into another mound of paperwork in the name of justice. If I wasn't careful, she'd take my place in the Captain's chair before I ever had a chance to ascend to the throne.

"You got it, partner," I said. "But, if you don't mind my asking...what are *we* going to do?"

Shay smiled. "We're going to find Buford Gill."

27

Our first stop was back at Taxation and Revenue where we managed to locate our young, bowtie-clad friend Teller and get him to track down yet another Gill name for us. Unfortunately, our luck held steady from earlier in the morning.

Teller produced the file they had for Gill Sr., but it was marked as severely delinquent. According to the records, Gill Sr. hadn't paid his taxes in close to a decade, and that meant he wasn't anywhere near the address they had on file for him, otherwise the city's ordained tax thugs would've collected on his debts long ago.

Luckily for me, the pretty head my partner carried around on her shoulders had more than cooking tips, chemical know-how, and gumption coursing through it, which is how we found ourselves elbow deep in the scientific periodicals section of the New Welwic Municipal Library.

I dug out a pile of research journals from a gloomy stack and lifted them into my arms, filling my lungs with the scent of their dusty, acid-eaten pages. Turning, I headed back along the deserted aisle, my footsteps sounding off the marble floor beneath me before echoing off the walls a good hundred paces away. Grunting under the weight of the manuscripts, I worked my way back to a long refectory table situated under a high arching window at the side of the periodicals wing. I dropped the journals onto the polished wooden surface with a thud.

Shay looked up from her article. Somehow, she'd finagled it so whenever it was time to grab more journals, I was the one who did the heavy lifting. Imagine that.

I sat down across from her and picked up a few items off the top of the recently-deposited pile. Two of them were from *Physica Modernica* and one was from the far more rationally titled *The Journal of Astrophysics*. Flipping open the first issue of *Physica Modernica*, I checked the table of contents and found Buford Gill's entry, a mouthful if I'd ever seen one. It was called: *A Treatise on the Physiomechanical Principles governing Tangential Motion in the Phase Field, Part 1: Theoretical Proofs Concerning the LaTrobe Vector in Inverse Space.*

My eyes glazed over as soon as they hit the page. Luckily, I wasn't particularly interested in anything Gill had to say on phase fields and inverse vectors. I only cared about the portion at the top of the article, under the title, that contained the man's contact information. I cracked a knuckle, closed the journal, and tossed it to the side.

"I don't know how you managed to come out so normal, considering your dad's a scientist," I said to

Shay. "I feel like anyone raised in one of those house-holds is practically exposed to a foreign language."

"Chemistry isn't quite so bad as physics in that regard," said Shay as she turned a page. "At least, I think so. But maybe I'm biased because I grew up with a chemist and I understand the lingo."

I grabbed another journal, the astrophysics one this time. A glance at the table of contents revealed a more normal-sounding article, albeit one whose title I still didn't understand: *A Prediction of Tidal Radii based on Orbital Eccentricities*. What did an orbit's quirks have to do with tides? Or was I missing something?

After glancing at the article's contact information, I tossed the journal in the pile with the rest of the rejects.

"This is useless," I said. "All these old journals list Buford Gill's work address at The University of New Welwic's Department of Physics and Chemistry, except for the newer ones that list a separate address at the Department of Physics and Astronomy. Either way, we know he hasn't worked at the university in years. And the few journals that show his home address list the same place we got from Taxation and Revenue. We're not going to find him this way."

Shay glanced at me and smiled. "Well, not with that attitude we're not. Try thinking outside the box."

"I thought I was pretty good at that," I said, "but sifting through these papers makes me feel like I didn't even know there *was* a box."

Shay lifted her head from her manuscript and looked at me. "Don't be so hard on yourself. Everyone's talents are different. I doubt Gill Sr. could do what you do."

I snorted.

"I'm serious," said Shay. "He's clearly a genius, but a lot of people like him struggle in all kinds of other areas, from their ability to interact socially to application of common sense. If you plopped the man into the middle of a crime scene, chances are he'd be as useful at solving a murder as a bricklayer or a window washer."

I glanced at my partner, at how the sun at her back glimmered off her dark brown hair, how it illuminated the tips of her pointy ears while sending the rest into shadow, and how, despite any and all physical explanations a man like Buford Gill might be able to provide to the contrary, her smile always seemed to shine despite the angle of the sun.

"Thanks," I said.

Shay smiled demurely and turned her head back to her reading material.

"So," I said, "have you come up with any bright ideas about how these articles might help us track down Professor Gill?"

"I have," said Shay. "Two, actually."

"Really?"

Shay looked up again and tapped the pages of the magazine she was reading. "Yes. These are some of the most recent journals in which Gill Sr. published."

"I know," I said. "You were all too eager to dive into them when presented with the option of doing that or digging out more from the stacks. I'm telling you, that sandwich you ate isn't going to do any good unless you put in some long hours of heavy lifting to go along with it. I'm thinking we should put you on a regimen."

My partner smiled and shook her head, ignoring my witty tangent. "My point was going to be that even though none of these recent articles list a contact address for Gill, they do provide clues. For one thing, Buford published two articles this past year in the same journal, *Philosophical Science Letters*—" She tapped the periodicals in question. "—which just so happens to have its offices right here in New Welwic. If Gill sent his articles to the journal headquarters via courier, it's possible he left them with a return address for correspondence. Or, perhaps he dropped by the offices himself. Maybe someone there knows where we might be able to find him.

"And there's more. Both of the articles published in *Philosophical Science Letters* list a coauthor, someone by the name of S. Tanner. Unfortunately, they don't list an address, personal or professional, but if we could find this person, chances are they could point us in the direction of Gill."

I scrubbed a hand across my mouth and chin as I grunted.

"What is it?" said Shay.

"I'm trying to figure out how I didn't see that earlier," I said, which wasn't a lie, but it wasn't the whole truth either. I had a fairly good idea of what had distracted me, and she had pointy ears, dark hair, and a smile that shone even outside of direct sunlight, apparently. Thankfully, my partner cracked as many head-scratchers as she prevented me from solving with her feminine wiles, so I suppose the overall situation was a zero-sum game, although it did make me look like a fool in front of the other detectives on occasion...

"So, if you've figured that out, what are we sitting around here for?" I asked.

Shay shrugged. "I don't know. I guess I got caught up reading this article on space tensors."

"You know, I was sort of kidding earlier about the whole separate language business," I said, "but now I'm changing my mind."

"Look, I don't understand *all* of it," said Shay. "But sometimes it's interesting to delve into the mind of a genius, just to see what's lurking there."

Was that a not-so-subtle dig at me?

"Well, your passing interest in geometrical tensors can wait," I said as I stood. "We've still got a murderer on the loose, in case you don't remember. So let's wrap this up. And while we're at it, let's bring some of these journals with us for evidence purposes. You'll have to put them on your library card, though."

Shay furrowed her brows. "Huh? Why?"

"Because the librarians here still haven't forgiven me for the last...*incident*. As it turns out, they frown upon people who overturn a centuries' worth of documents from a series of library stacks in one full-bodied blow. Now come on, let's hustle."

28

The address we gleaned from the pages of *Philosophical Science Letters* led us to a nondescript, four-story, multi-tenant office building on the north side of town, west of the Earl. I stood with Steele across from the second floor landing outside a door with a frosted glass pane set into it at roughly face height, assuming one was human or elven. Etched into the glass were the words "Philosophical Science Letters" and the address.

"I think we've found the right place," I said.

"What gave you that idea?" said Steele as she knocked, making the door rattle in its frame.

"Just a hunch," I said. "I'm clever like that."

A tired voice responded from the other side of the glass, one that quivered and creaked, possibly from disuse. "Come in."

I wrenched on the doorknob and opened the door—or at least tried to. It stuck on something after I'd pushed it to about a thirty degree angle.

"Oh, sorry about that," came the voice again. "Here, give me a moment."

I heard a rustling of paper and a soft scuffing of shoes on lumber. The door jerked in its hinges, and I heard a muffled curse.

"Oh forget it," said the voice. "Look, you'll just have to wriggle your way around. I'm sorry. I hope you're not one of the city's jumbo-sized inhabitants, otherwise you simply won't be able to fit."

I looked in through the door gap, but all I could see was a wall covered floor to ceiling with journal reprints held in place by round metal tacks affixed to the upper left-hand corners.

"After you," I said to Steele.

She shot me a fake smile. "You're such a gentle-man."

Steele slipped a foot into the opening and slid around the not even halfway open door, her slim frame making the curve with ease. As I readied myself to follow, I heard her voice from the other side of the door.

"You, uh...might have to suck it in, Daggers. It's a little tight in here."

"Yes, yes, I know," said the mystery voice. "I'm terribly sorry about the mess. It piles up over the years, you understand. And I can't get rid of it. Too attached to it, you see. Although I suppose I could put some into storage, but I don't know how I'd manage that in my condition. Regardless, there's a path there to the left. If you shuffle a little..."

I shoved myself sideways into the opening and squirmed around the edge of the door, barely squeezing my bulk through the gap, at which point I understood

Shay's comment. It didn't refer to the entryway, but rather the office as a whole.

Mountains of paper occupied almost every cubic inch of the room, in every way, shape, and form: books, magazines, journals, pamphlets, and circulars, some bound in hard or soft covers, others loosely collated with staples and binder clips and shiny brass brads. Some sat on their sides on bookshelves, which occupied two full walls of the room, but the majority stood in huge stacks on the floor or rose up in a massive, rectangular pile in the middle of the space. Only after I caught a glimmer of glossy wood from underneath the pages did I realize there was probably a desk underneath the mound.

Narrow corridors snaked around the room, allowing passage to the far corners and the various stacks of knowledge that resided there, assuming you were the sort of person who enjoyed jogging and had an aversion to food.

The latter at least seemed to apply to the source of the quavering voice: an old, rail-thin man, probably in his seventies, with thinning gray hair, knobby hands, wearing wire-rimmed spectacles and sporting a conspicuous liver spot on his forehead over his right brow. Either he or something in the room smelled like my grandfather's prized sweater collection. We locked eyes.

"Um...hi," I said.

"Oh, uh, yes. Hello." The old man blinked and shook his head. "Where are my manners? I'm Dr. Lester French, editor-in-chief of Philosophical Science Letters. How may I be of service?"

Shay spoke up. "I'm Detective Steele. This is Detective Daggers. Do you mind if we ask you a few questions?"

"*Detectives?*" Lester's eyebrows shot up. "Don't tell me there's an academic fraud scandal brewing?"

"No, Dr. French," said Steele. "That's not the sort of...*crime* we investigate."

Lester sighed. "Oh. Thank goodness. There's nothing worse than fraud. That sort of thing can affix a black stamp to a scholarly journal for years."

"Well, *you* may think there's nothing worse than fraud," I said, sidling past a particularly wobbly-looking stack of reprints. "But I assure you the victims in our department think there's at least one crime worse."

Based on the look the old guy gave me, I don't think he got my joke.

"Yes, uh, well, anyway," he said, "why don't we sit and discuss...whatever it is you wish to discuss."

"We'd be happy to," said Steele with a raised eyebrow, "but if you don't mind my asking...where are the chairs?"

"Oh, they're there," said Lester. "I'm sure of it. You might need to rearrange a few things to get to them, and move a few papers once you get there—"

"It's alright," I said. "We'll stand."

The old man looked pained. "You won't hold it against me if I sit, of course? My arthritis acts up more than it used to. It's a miracle I can still get up and down the stairs every day."

Steele and I both nodded. With a sigh, the old man shuffled back behind the massive pile of documents that covered his desk and collapsed into his chair, which I could actually see once I got close enough to peer over the mound of paper.

"So, if you're not investigating fraud," said Lester, "what exactly *are* you investigating?"

"Homicide," I said.

Lester sat up straight, something I wasn't sure he was capable of given the state of his joints. "*What?* Someone's been murdered?"

"No one you know, in all likelihood," said Steele. "But we have reason to believe someone you're familiar with may be in danger. Do you know a scientist by the name of Buford Gill?"

"Oh, yes, Buford. Of course I know him," said Lester. "Anyone who reads our publication would be familiar with his name. You're saying his life is at risk?"

"Possibly," I said as I glanced at a mound near Lester's desk that I suspected might be hiding a chair. "What can you tell us about the man?"

"Well, he's brilliant, for one thing," said Lester, leaning back in his seat. "I'd dare say he's one of the sharpest minds of our age. Makes me feel like a first-year undergraduate at times with the intricacy of his theories—" A bit of a bitter frown crept across his face as he said that last part. "—but, regardless, I'm glad he chooses to publish with us. The issues featuring his papers always sell better than those that don't."

"He's popular, then?" said Shay.

Lester French rolled his eyes. "Well...in a sense. Let's just say that, while Gill's papers inevitably get published, they always engender a healthy debate, both during the peer review process and afterwards. While many of our readership look forward to Gill's publications to read his insights, others look forward to them simply to try and find holes in them."

The old man chuckled and shook his head. "And Gill's never been one to shy away from debate. He's always been very combative toward others who try to disprove his theories. So invariably, Gill will publish a paper, and someone will publish a rebuttal to his points, and Gill will publish a fiery counter-rebuttal. Honestly, we usually see a spike in our circulation for several issues *after* Gill's initial publication for just such a reason."

"That's great," I said, not entirely truthfully, "but the real question that concerns us is, do you know where to find him?"

"Ah, no, unfortunately," said Lester. "He's quite the recluse, which I assume you probably already know if you're asking me about his whereabouts. I suppose you could ask around his old department at the University of New Welwic. Someone there might have some idea where he disappeared to. And by old department, I mean Physics and Astronomy, not Physics and Chemistry. That department was shuttered years ago at the same time the building housing it was condemned for chemical contamination. Damned shame, really. It was a nice building."

"You can't tell us you honestly have no clue where the man might be," said Steele, resting an elbow on a stack of textbooks. "He publishes in your journal. Surely you have some open method of communication with him? Otherwise how would he be able to submit his findings?"

"Well, that's the clever part," said Lester, waggling a finger. "I've seen Gill a couple times over the past few years—chance occasions, mind you—but after he lost his position at the University following that spat with the offices and the departmental changeover, he went into hiding and, for lack of a better term, became very...*wary* of people, including me. I mean, he'd always been antisocial, but he just got... Well, it doesn't matter. Long story short, we set up a system whereby he could submit papers remotely."

"Remotely?" said Steele.

"Yes," said Lester. "When he has a paper he wishes to submit to us, he sends it in via courier from—well, who knows where, honestly. Our reviewers read his work and supply their comments and suggestions, and we bundle those together with his original paper and any correspondence we get from readers and leave those in the communal mail slot in the lobby downstairs. Gill then comes by and picks up the bundle, though he must do so very early or very late because I've never bumped into him at the office since we instituted the program. Overall, it's rather inefficient—he only checks the mail slot once a month or so—but it works."

"That sounds like a lot of effort to go through to make sure one author gets published," I said.

Lester shrugged. "As I said, the man's brilliant. And more importantly, he sells journals. Figuratively speaking, of course. He's not on our payroll."

I glanced around the office one more time, wondering to myself if there was *anyone* other than Lester on the magazine's payroll.

"So you have no idea where we might be able to find him?" asked Steele.

Lester shook his head. "No. I'm sorry. As I said, try his old university. He might still have a few friends there."

Steele wasn't willing to let the matter go that easily. "We noticed a few of his recent publications had a collaborator. An S. Turner? Do you know where we might be able to find this person?"

Lester removed his spectacles and rubbed the bridge of his nose, gesturing with his glasses as he talked. "Unfortunately, no. I know even less about that person than I do about Gill. The first time I saw the name was on Gill's second most recent paper. Given they're a coauthor, I have no correspondence system set up with them. We only do that for lead authors."

"Come on," said Steele. "Think. You must know something that could lead us to Gill. Maybe a piece of information he dropped in passing. Anything!"

Shay's jaw was set tight, and she punctuated her remark with a slap of a stack of journals, which made Lester jump as he returned the glasses to his face. The performance was out of line with her normally even keel behavior—in fact, I'd only seen her like this during our good cop, bad cop interrogations. I wondered what might be agitating her, until I realized our current case might be hitting a little too close to home. Perhaps I shouldn't have drawn so many parallels between Buford Gill and Shay's father while at the library.

I approached my partner and put a hand on her shoulder. "Steele. We'll find him, but Dr. French doesn't know where he is. We'll have to try something else."

Steele turned to face me. In her eyes I saw fierce determination, but the fire within melted away after a second or two. "Sorry. You're right. Dr. French, thanks for your time, and apologies for—" She mimed slapping the books. "—well, you know."

"Don't worry, dear," said Lester. "No offense taken. I imagine your profession must be far more stressful than mine, at least in most senses. Which reminds me...before you go, could I ask *you* a question?"

"Sure," said Steele. "Why not?"

"Well," said Lester, adopting his best set of wide puppy eyes, "academic journals aren't exactly a high margin enterprise. Perhaps I could interest the two of you in a couple subscriptions? Or some for your friends?"

I glanced at Steele. Suddenly her determination and remorse had turned into apprehension. I could understand the feeling. I felt like a holiday party guest being cajoled into trying Aunt Millie's famous fruit cake that tasted of sawdust and fossilized raisins.

I considered it a minor miracle when both of us emerged from the office, minutes later, without having purchased a single copy.

29

We took Lester's advice and visited Gill's old colleagues in the Department of Physics and Astronomy at the University of New Welwic, but the few professors and staff who had anything nice to say about the man knew less about his whereabouts than they did about modern fashion conventions. By time we'd finished knocking on office doors and asking questions, I'd had it up to my eyeballs in four-buttoned vests and extra wide Balthus-knotted ties. Frustrated and disappointed, Shay and I indulged our moods in a bit of silence and quiet contemplation on our rickshaw ride back to the precinct.

Upon arrival, we found Rodgers and Quinto at their desks looking not much happier than we did. Rodgers nursed a mug of hot coffee, and Quinto had broken out the mug he reserved for his strongest brews of tea, which couldn't be a good sign.

"Tell me you've had better luck than we have," I said as Shay and I approached the pair.

Quinto looked up from his desk. "Hey Daggers. Steele. Your trip went that bad, huh?"

"Are you kidding?" I said. "Buford Gill's a ghost. Taxation and Revenue's file on him is a decade out of date. Nobody knows where to find him—colleagues, professional acquaintances, nobody. Not even the journal he publishes with regularly has any idea how to contact him. He has a special drop box system in place with them to allow for anonymous pick-ups and drop-offs. If not for the fact that he checks the box every month or two, I'd think the guy had evaporated off the face of the earth, or at least high-tailed it out of New Welwic for greener pastures."

"Well, it could be worse," said Rodgers as he set his coffee down on his desk. "If Gill Sr. is a ghost, then Harland Wyle is a will-o'-wisp."

I raised an eyebrow. "A what now?"

"A will-o'-wisp," said Shay. "It's a flickering light in swamps people talk about in folklore. But I have to admit I'm struggling with the metaphor, Rodgers."

"Alright. Let me try again." Rodgers flourished a finger in the air. "If Gill Sr. is a ghost, then Harland Wyle is a breeze on a gust of wind."

I frowned and glanced at Quinto.

"Don't look at me," the big guy said. "I have no idea what he's talking about."

Rodgers sighed and rolled his eyes. "I was *trying* to come up with a way to say that even though you've had a hard time locating Gill, Harland Wyle's been even harder to find. I mean, not in the literal sense. We know exactly where he is—in holding. But at least there's a paper trail indicating your guy exists. Not so for Wyle. He has no arrest record, and we stopped by Public Records to see if he'd ever been admitted to a psychiatric ward. No dice. We even stopped by Taxation and Revenue, but they didn't have a file for him either."

"All of which corroborates our theory that the guy's been lying to us about everything," said Quinto. "Including his name."

"So, basically, we're no closer to solving Darryl and Anya's murders than we were this morning," said Shay.

"Basically," said Rodgers. "Although, on the bright side, if Gill Sr. is *this* hard to find, chances are Scar Face hasn't found him either. At the very least, there haven't been any runners tearing through our halls with bad news."

I crossed my arms. "Forgive me if that doesn't make me break out in dance. Both of our murders have occurred early in the day. Who's to say Buford Gill's death would be any different? And, of course, it's always possible the man's already been murdered and nobody's found the body yet—which wouldn't surprise me if the man's as big a recluse as everyone says."

"Well, I don't know what to tell you," said Rodgers. "I'm not sure what our next move should be, unless you want to turn the screws on Wyle some more and see if he changes his story, but seeing as we already tried that..." He shrugged and took another sip from his mug.

I frowned. I still hadn't figured out what it was about Wyle that bothered me. There was his ludicrous time travel story, of course, but I could deal with craziness and lies. What I couldn't deal with was craziness and lies that fell just close enough to the truth to make me go 'Hmm.' The timing of his break-in at Darryl's apartment and his intrusion at Anya's house seemed more than coincidental, and I wasn't sure I believed Shay's simple address-based explanation of how he tracked down Anya.

I tapped my chin. "You know, maybe we should talk to Wyle once more."

"Again?" said Shay. "What's your angle going to be this time?"

"My angle," I said, "is that regardless of whether or not he's a whacko or he's manipulating us, he knows something about the murders we don't. If he's crazy, perhaps by playing into his delusions, we can get him to reveal a clue we haven't yet uncovered. And if he's not crazy, perhaps by making *him* believe *we* believe in him, we'll achieve the same effect."

"I'm not sure I totally follow," said Quinto.

"It's ok," I said. "Come with me and follow my lead."

Most of the time a command like that resulted in jeers or at the very least some mild resistance, but apparently everyone was really and truly stumped. As I turned toward the back stairs, everyone followed me without so much as a snort or a roll of the eyes.

I led my entourage down the back stairs to the holding pens. Drunken Goakey Joe had been set free, but Harland Wyle still sat in the same cage he had earlier in the day. He stared at the rough stone floor of the cell, neglecting to look up at the sound of our octuplet of pattering feet.

"Hi, Harland," I said as I stopped in front of the wrought iron bars.

Wyle kept his gaze trained on the floor. "What do you want this time?"

"I want to go over one part of your story, again," I said.

"Not this again." Wyle sighed and turned his face up to meet mine. "Why should I? So you guys can have another laugh at my expense? This may be funny to you, but I'm still agonizing over the possibility that everything I've ever known and loved is gone—or rather never existed. Dealing with your mockery in addition to that is more than I can deal with."

"*Possibility?*" said Steele. "So you're no longer convinced your future has changed?"

Wyle shrugged. "I may have overreacted. Trust me, it's easy to get emotional when you think your world just winked out of existence, but I thought it over. The theories we developed regarding time reconstruction are solid. If my reality was extinguished, I should've felt a substantial wave in the time streams, even accounting for the spatial gap between me and the psychopath from Citizens for Simplicity. Either that, or I shouldn't exist anymore. Either way, I'm pretty sure my future still exists, which means there's time to right the ship. I think..."

I regarded Wyle and his crop of wavy black hair. The guy's wacky robe and implausible story were overt sign of lunacy, but even though I didn't have any formal training in psychology, I'd met enough drunks, whack jobs, and nutcases to get a feel for the group. Wyle didn't fit. That meant he was lying—but boy, he was a pretty good actor.

There was, of course, a third option besides madness and pathological insincerity that explained his story, one I'd joked about earlier in the morning but hadn't given any real credence to. It was an option I weighed in a dark corner of my mind. As much as I disliked it, if it turned out to be true, it was my responsibility as a detective to prove it.

"Alright, Wyle," I said. "Let me be frank. We think Buford Gill, the father of the two people you found murdered, may be in serious danger, but we can't find him. This morning, you mentioned how you tracked down Anya. You said you followed disturbances in the time stream, or something along those lines, to find her. Is that right?"

"That's an imprecise way of describing it," said Wyle. "But yes. Close enough."

"Ok," I said. "So my question for you is, can you use that method to find Buford Gill?"

I heard a feminine groan and a derisive snort that may have originated from a half-troll. Rodgers, however, apparently managed to keep whatever scorn he felt to himself.

I turned to face my detective buddies and gave them a stern flick of my eyebrows which I hope conveyed that I wanted to them to hush and play along.

When I turned back to the cell, I found Wyle had stood.

He gazed at me intently. "Are you serious?"

"I can't vouch for the officers of the law behind me," I said. "But yes, I am. Dead serious—no pun intended. If you can help us find Buford Gill—or even better, Darryl and Anya's murderer—that's all I care about."

"Well, that's the thing," said Wyle, approaching the cell's bars. "I can't track down this Buford Gill guy. As I said, I've never heard of him. But I might be able to track down Scar Face. He's the one who altered the time streams. But if you're serious about collaborating, we need to move now. We call them ripples for a reason. They disappear quickly. As it stands right now, I'll be lucky if I can still feel them."

I turned to Quinto. "Can you find the jailor?"

"You're serious, then?" he asked.

"Absolutely," I said. "Get the keys. We've got work to do."

30

We followed Wyle through the streets of New Welwic on foot, heading south. Given how much walking I'd already endured throughout the day, I would've preferred to take rickshaws, but several forces conspired against their usage. For one, five was an awkward number to transport via the biwheeled contraptions, as they normally fitted two people abreast. Although my gut told me Wyle wouldn't make a break for it, he obviously needed to be kept under close supervision, but the most important reason we fueled our travel via the power of our own legs had to do with Wyle's powers, such as they were.

The astronomically-garbed young man walked through the city's maze of avenues and boulevards in spurts, pausing every now and then at street corners or at the mouths of alleys. He claimed his ability to sense the fluctuations in the time streams—which he described as rivers flowing through the fourth dimension, whatever the heck that meant—was akin to the sense of touch, but from watching Wyle perform his tracking maneuvers, he appeared to be *listening* for signals rather than *feeling* anything.

Because of the way he described it, I thought Harland might need a tool to help him in his search, whether a wand or a divining rod or some futuristic doohickey I couldn't envision, but he progressed with his hands empty and his arms hanging loosely at his sides. He'd pause and squint, then turn his head to and fro as if he'd heard a rustle or a rush or the flop of a time fish. After thinking silently on the invisible, inaudible cues he received, he'd set off again at a brisk pace until the next break in the action.

I found Wyle's act fascinating, if for no other reason than because I found myself comparing it to Shay's fingers in the air, eyes rolled back in the head, psychic trance. I couldn't help but wonder how much the two shared in terms of both actual ability and showmanship. For the sake of all of us, and of Buford Gill, I hoped there was a glimmer of a method behind Wyle's madness, but I'd be willing to accept a routine packed with hogwash and malarkey so long as there was a vein of knowledge and useful intent seated behind it.

Rodgers and Quinto trailed behind Shay, Wyle, and me, seemingly resigned to accept the jerky stop-and-go venture for what it was, but my partner couldn't leave Wyle in peace. She kept pestering him for information regarding his methodology and time magic in general, which I found hilarious. Nonetheless, I kept my chuckles constrained to the interior of my chest cavity. I doubted my mirth would help advance our nebulous relationship in a positive direction.

"So, explain again to me," said Steele, "how exactly you perceive the time stream."

"I already told you," said Wyle as he stopped and glanced into an alley populated by dented steel trash cans and yellow-eyed cats. "It's exactly like it sounds. A stream of actions, liquid and indistinct, rushing by all around me. I can't pick out discrete events because they bleed into one another."

"So...like ink?" asked Steele.

"Exactly," said Wyle. "Imagine taking a pipette of ink and squeezing a drop of black into a stream. As soon as the droplet hits the water, it disintegrates, incorporated into the rushing waters, but the ink's still there. It's just hard to discern because it diffuses so quickly. If you poured an entire jar of ink into the stream, you'd see it, and the color would spread for a while, but eventually it, too, would disappear."

"And yet you keep describing the disturbances in the time stream as ripples," said Steele, crossing her arms. "So your analogy seems a little...*contrived.*"

Wyle stopped and turned. "Why are you giving me such a hard time about this? Out of this group of detectives, aren't you the one with magical knowledge? I'd think if anyone would understand, it would be you. You can't describe magical powers in terms of the traditional senses. Wading through the time stream *isn't* like seeing or hearing or feeling. It's a totally different sensation, one I have a hard time describing because it's so different to any of the other, traditional senses. But it's *most* similar to the sense of touch, which is why I describe it that way."

Steele stood her ground. "I'm just trying to learn about your abilities. If time magic *is* real and it *does* exist, it's a massive breakthrough that'll change the face of magical theory."

"Um, yeah," said Wyle. "It does, actually. And it's not supposed to happen for another hundred and twenty years. So quit asking me about it."

Shay grit her teeth, and she looked as if she might tear into Wyle, but I managed to distract her with a wave. She walked over to me, her lower lip jutting out comically over her chin. It made her look cute, in a way, but I kept that tidbit to myself.

"What are you doing?" I said in a low voice. "We're supposed to be playing into his delusion to see what he knows. If you keep attacking him, chances are he'll clam up and we'll lose any progress we've made with him."

"I *am* playing into his delusion," said Steele. "That's why I'm asking so many questions. If I wasn't, I'd be breaking into a rousing rendition of 'Liar, Liar, Pants on Fire.'"

"You sing?" I smiled. "I'd pay to see that."

"I'm sure you would." Shay's pout diminished somewhat. "But be honest with me, Daggers. You don't believe a word this guy's saying, right? He's so full of crap, I'm surprised he hasn't burst yet."

"I don't know what to believe," I said. "But I meant what I said at the precinct. If he can lead us to Gill Sr. or to Scar Face, I won't care how he did it. Well, I will, but I'll figure it out later. Right now I'm interested in results."

"Yeah, well, we're not getting much of those, either," said Steele with a glance at Wyle. He was still peering into the trash can-filled alley.

"Give it a bit longer," I said. "Perhaps he'll surprise us. Besides, it's not as if we have many other leads to follow."

As the words escaped my lips, Wyle straightened and his eyes widened. "There! There it is! I felt something. A ripple, a recent one. Come on, this way!"

Steele glanced at me. I shrugged in reply and hurried after Wyle.

31

We jogged a few blocks farther south before ultimately stopping at a flophouse located on the outskirts of New Welwic's dwarven quarter, derogatorily referred to by many of the city's residents as Little Welwic. The interior of the dwarven sector was dwarf only—not in the sense that intruders were tarred and feathered, but in terms of design and function. All the buildings featured six foot stories, and the furniture in the shops and restaurants, though robust enough to support a wide dwarven frame, wasn't particularly suited to guys my or Quinto's height. I'd only had to venture inside one of the dwarven apartment buildings once in search of a suspect, and I hoped never to have to repeat the experience. My back didn't forgive me for a week.

Luckily, the flophouse Wyle led us to catered to species of all heights, though if external appearances were any indication, it didn't offer many amenities. Faded bricks containing elements of dull browns and even duller tans climbed the side of the building, and a huge crack arching through the bricks ended in a hole near eye level where a few dozen of the clay blocks had fallen out, revealing rotting wooden interior paneling.

I thought about cracking a joke about structural issues and insurance scams, but I feared it would fall flat. Wyle presence had unbalanced our detective quartet's humorous center of mass, and besides, I think we were all anxious to see where, exactly, the self-professed time mage's powers had led us.

"So this is the place?" said Quinto, staring at the faded building exterior.

"This is it," said Wyle.

"And by it," I said, "you mean Scar Face's whereabouts?"

"By *it*," said Wyle, "I mean the epicenter of the most recent time ripple. Unless someone else I'm unaware of travelled backwards in time to this era, I'm assuming Scar Face had something to do with it. But I don't know if this is where he currently is, a place he recently visited, or a place he will visit."

"*Will* visit?" said Rodgers.

"Do you remember what I told Detective Steele earlier about the ink droplets?" said Wyle.

Steele rolled her eyes.

"Right, right," I said. "Diffusion. Streams. Rushing water. We get it. It's complicated. Quinto, join me up front. Rodgers and Steele, bring up the rear. Wyle, you're in the middle. Everyone keep your eyes peeled."

Hinges squealed in protest as I pushed open the flophouse's front door. I paused for a moment in the building's meager lobby, letting my eyes adjust to the gloom as the rest of the troupe filled in behind me.

"Can I help you?" said a gruff voice to my left.

I blinked a couple times before I discerned a short, bearded figure behind a low desk darkened by pipe ash and old elbow grease. A dwarf. Figures. They loved gloom. The dude's hair fell around his face in an untamed mane, scraping the top of the grungy clerk's desk, and I thought I smelled the lingering funk of burnt high-mountain pipe weed.

"Hey, dude," I said. "You own this place?"

"I run it," said the dwarf. "And the name's Sheila."

Whoops. Dwarf gender was a tripping point for me due to the whole bearded women thing.

"Sorry. It's the whole..." I mimicked stroking my chin. "Well...you know."

Sheila chewed on something and spat, her spittle impacting the floor with a wet slap. "I'm guessing based on your magisterial appearances you're not looking for a room to party in for a few hours, but if I'm wrong..." She glanced at Steele and jingled some keys. "Sorry, honey."

I don't think I'd ever seen Shay blush, but she did so now. Or maybe it was just the gloom. I'm sure she'd use that as cover if I asked her about it later.

I flashed my badge. "We're looking for someone. Human. Grizzled guy. Old scar under his left eye. Did anyone bring the sketch?"

Shay shook her head while Quinto checked his pockets.

"Don't need one," said the dwarven manager. "I know who you're looking for. Third floor. Unit six."

I blinked and shook my head. "Wait...what? *Seriously?*"

I don't think I hid my surprise particularly well. I know Shay didn't. She openly stared at Wyle, who grinned in response.

"Yeah," continued Sheila. "Been here a few days. Paid for the whole week ahead of time with real silver. Shaved some right off a solid block with a knife. Whacko..."

"Is he here right now?" I asked.

"Not sure," said the dwarf. "I think he left about a half hour ago. I could be wrong though. I don't pay much attention to people leaving. It's the people entering who need to pay. Feel free to check. But for the love of the gods, use a key." She chucked one my way and I caught it. "You and the big brute look a little too eager, and I don't want to replace any locks, you hear?"

"Thanks." I waved for everyone to follow me and headed up the rickety, worm-eaten stairs. I reached into my jacket and snagged Daisy as I propelled myself up the steps, two thoughts prominent in the front of my mind: one, how the dwarf lady had known about my proclivity toward kicking in doors, and two, how Wyle had known Scar Face had taken up residence in this rathole—if, of course, he'd discovered the knowledge through rational means.

I didn't have long to contemplate the matters. Within seconds, Quinto and I stood in front of the door to unit six, the rest of the crew standing behind us. With my foot twitching in false anticipation, I slipped the key into the lock, twisted, and threw open the door.

Quinto burst into the room first, but I was right behind him, Daisy clenched in my fist like a gleaming, foot-and-a-half long bringer of headaches and bad news.

Quinto headed right, as did I, given it was the only direction in which motion was possible. The room was barely bigger than a closet and held only a bare, wire-framed bed, a battered dresser, and an enameled washbasin that had lost the majority of its enamel over the years. Together, we confirmed what the front desk clerk had already suggested.

"He's gone," I said.

Quinto nodded, and the Rodgers/Steele/Wyle triumvirate poured into the tiny room like so much meat into a sausage casing. Luckily, the shutters on the room's sole window had been thrown open, otherwise we might've soon run out of air.

Wyle didn't seem to notice the cramped conditions. He pushed forward past me, muttering to himself. "Yes. Yes. He was here. I can feel it. It's like the ripple just started, like it's still spreading. *Wow*, it's strong. Much stronger than I'd thought it would be. I wonder what that means? Nothing good, I bet. Perhaps some big event happened here? But there's no dead body, so perhaps the event has yet to transpire..."

I started barking orders. "Quinto, see if you can find anything in that dresser. Shay, check the bed. Rodgers...oh, just stay by the door. This place is too small for us all to move at once. And Harland, buddy. Focus." I snapped my fingers at the guy. "Don't get me wrong. I'm impressed you led us here. But in case you didn't notice, we have a problem. Scar Face isn't here. So where is he?"

Wyle shrugged. "I don't know. I told you, I can't track people, only fluctuations in the temporal vibrations."

"So you have no idea where Scar Face is?" I asked. "Surely if he's not here, there must be some other vibrations or whatnot going on elsewhere. Stuff you *can* track?"

"I, uh...don't know," said Wyle. "This stuff is indistinct, sometimes. The time streams ebb and flow, kind of like the tides. Maybe the ripples are ebbing right now."

Steele had knelt next to the bed and patted it down. She'd stuck her head under the mattress to check for hidden loot—it was amazing how many times we found clues under beds—but at Wyle's latest remark she pulled her head back and stood.

"Oh, come on," she said. "Vibrations? Ebbing and flowing like tides? What can't these time streams do? Except lead us where we need to go, of course. That would be too convenient. And there's nothing under the bed, by the way."

"Not much in the dresser either," said Quinto, his big bass voice rumbling and his arms stuck elbow deep in the drawers. "No food. No extra clothes. And no claw hammer. That would've been nice to find. But there does appear to be one thing the guy left behind."

Quinto pulled his arms out, and in his hands he held a small notebook. From my vantage point next to him, I could see a clear spot pattern on the front cover comprised of small red dots. A blood spatter.

"Holy crap," I said. "Quinto, set it on the dresser. Let's have a look."

"Here, let me see," said Steele. She shoved Wyle down on the bed none too gently as she squeezed past to get beside me and Quinto.

"Don't worry about me, guys," said Rodgers. "I'll just, uh, stay here by the door. You know I don't care much for solving convoluted, brain-bending mysteries, any-way."

I would've felt bad for Rodgers if I wasn't so desperate to find out what secrets the notebook's pages held. With a reverential hand—or as close as Quinto could get, his paws were like oven mitts—he flipped the blood-stained journal open to the first page. Among the stains were a few short notes, scrawled in a sloppy script:

> <u>D. Gill:</u>
> B. Gill? No dice. Crazy. Dementia? Not buying it. Last seen ~6 years ago. Met for lunch. Destello's, uptown. Worth checking. Sentimental. Old haunts?
>   - Try old department. U of NW. Physics & Astronomy? Stakeout.
>   - Last known address: 4044 Wayland Ave., Apt. 212 – Check. No go.
> D. Gill <u>USELESS</u>. Too bad, so sad. smash smash time Gill
> A. Gill (Crestwick?): 516A Bartleby Ln.- Try next
>   - No B. Gill address damnit

"They're Scar Face's notes," I said. "From when he murdered Darryl Gill. He's looking for Buford."

"He took everything else, but left the notebook?" said Quinto. "That can only mean..."

We all knew what it meant.

"Next page," I said. "Quick."

Quinto flipped to another blood-spattered page.

A. Gill/Crestwick:

Last correspondence with B. Gill: 4 years ago. Better.

    - B. Gill not in right mind? Drugs? Doesn't make sense. Science papers clear.

    - Recluse. Set in ways. Resistant to change. Back to childhood home, perhaps?

    - Try Folsom Park. Mornings. Sentimental. *OLD HAUNTS*

    - Brookside Cemetery. Wife's grave. GOOD.

    - Physics and Astronomy Dept? No go, sweetie. Tried & failed.

Four fingers down. No address. A. Gill a <u>WASTE</u>.

The page ended in a bloody trail of what I could only assume was Anya's spent life force.

"That can't be it," I said. "Try the next page."

Quinto obligingly flipped again, this time to a page populated by doodles and scrawls interspersed with the occasional loose word or phrase. A few words had stars next to them, or clusters of dots nearby, as if someone had tapped a pencil against the word in thought over and over again.

Drugs. Dementia. Mental Ward?...   ...   ...Physics is the key?
    OLD HAUNTS...   ...   Dead wife's grave is cold. No flowers...

Come out come out, wherever you are Gillsey...   ...   Uptown? Sentimental..?   ...   Astronomy. Good view for telescopes. Where?

In addition to the doodles and scrawls, the words 'OLD HAUNTS' had been circled several times.

"Anything else?" I asked.

Quinto flipped, but the rest of the notebook appeared to be empty of everything but stains that had bled through from the other pages.

"Mind if I have a look now?" said Rodgers.

"Sure, sure," I said. I passed the journal to Shay and she handed it to Rodgers.

"So, Scar Face is out there looking for Gill Sr.," I said. "But he doesn't know where he is. Unless he finally figured it out. An old haunt of his, if his doodling is any indication. But where? The graveyard? An observatory?"

"Look, Harland," said Shay to Wyle, "if you were holding anything back earlier, *anything* that might help us find Gill and save his life, this would be the time to come forth."

Wyle stammered. "I... I told you. I don't know. I swear. The time streams led here. I don't know why. Maybe Gill's not important. Maybe it doesn't matter if he dies after all."

"Excuse me?" said Shay. "That's not exactly how we operate around here. And unless you want to be implicated—"

I racked my brain as Shay silenced Wyle with a stern talking to. What could Scar Face have discovered? Darryl and Anya had both apparently thought Gill Sr. was a little out of his right mind. Why? He was sentimental, and he was attached to old haunts. That was the key. But what were his haunts?

If only we knew more about the man: the places he frequented when he was younger, his favorite eateries, his likes and dislikes, the methods behind his apparent madness. But all we knew about him were his professional exploits, the details of his career as a scientist, a physicist, and an astronomer...

I felt a prick in my mind, the bite of a sudden thought. It wasn't a common occurrence, by any means, but I knew it when I sensed it.

"Steele," I said.

She paused midway through her impromptu interrogation of Wyle. "Yeah?"

"Your dad's a chemist, right?"

Steele narrowed one eye. "I can't even recall how many times I've told you the answer to that question."

"Does he or did he by any chance work at the University of New Welwic?" I asked.

My partner shook her head. "No, he's a working professional, not a professor."

I clicked my tongue. "Damn."

"Where are you going with this, Daggers?" said Steele.

"It's something the guy at that research journal headquarters, Dr. French, mentioned," I said. "He said Buford Gill was fired after a dustup following the Department's restructuring into Physics and Astronomy from Physics and Chemistry. He mentioned the old building was condemned, but he didn't say anything about it having been demolished."

"So?" said Quinto. "Some of those university buildings are pretty old. It's possible the university wanted to tear it down but the city designated it as a historical landmark."

I held up a hand and ticked off fingers. "Physics. Astronomy. Sentimental. Old haunt."

"Wait," said Steele, her eyes widening. "Are you suggesting...?"

"I am," I said. "Let's go."

32

Despite the difficulties involved in transporting five people, one of them a prisoner, via rickshaw, we did it anyway because time was of the utmost priority. Steele and I stuffed Wyle between us and told our driver to hoof it to the university stomping grounds.

As the wheels clattered and our driver huffed and puffed, Shay suffered a sudden recollection. She *did* know why the old Physics and Chemistry building had been condemned. Her father had related the news in passing once. An experiment conducted by one of the chemistry professor's graduate students had gone horribly wrong, leading to a large release of mercury vapor throughout the building. That had been the impetus for the separation of the fields and the establishment of the new Physics and Astronomy department.

As soon as the word 'mercury' escaped Shay's lips, I recalled Scar Face's scrawl about dementia, and I knew my suspicions were correct. I told our struggling rickshaw driver to hurry, promising yet another silver eagle from the precinct coffers as motivation.

After what seemed to me an eternity but was probably only about twenty minutes, we unloaded in front of the old U of NW Physics and Chemistry building, which according to the somewhat vine-covered plaque next to the boarded-shut front doors was actually the Professor James T. Oroblatt Memorial Physics and Chemistry building.

I'd expected to find a boarded up husk of a building with bricks crumbling to dust and mortar falling out in chunks, opening yawning chasms into an inky, black, ruinous interior, but other than the boarded up part, I couldn't have been more wrong—or at least, I think I was. I couldn't see enough of the bricks to know what sort of condition they were in. Green tendrils coursed over the building's two-story exterior, thick, leafy vines that twisted and turned and dug their prickly feelers into the tiny crevices between the bricks to gain a foothold. They swarmed over the façade and onto the roof, turning the structure into a living, breathing green rectangular box.

"Tell me what you're feeling, Wyle," I said as I scanned the front of the building for gaps in the boards which a human might be able to fit through.

"I'm not feeling anything," he said.

"Really? Nothing?" I said. "No ripples, no tides, no underwater temporal farts?"

Wyle rolled his eyes at my last comment. "No. None."

I frowned. I was losing confidence in the guy. Either he'd used information he'd chosen not to share with us to lead us to Scar Face's flophouse, or his tracking powers, whatever they might be, were so anemic as to be essentially useless. Without asking, I already knew which of the two options my partner suspected was true, which was about as close to psychic ability as I could muster.

Quinto and Rodgers dismounted from their rickshaw behind us, less than a minute off our pace. I didn't bother bringing them up to speed on Wyle's lack of helpfulness.

"Alright," I said. "We need to find a way into this place. Let's spread out and—"

"No need," said Shay, pointing down and to the right. "Missing basement window. We should be able to squeeze in through there. Might be a tight fit for Quinto, though."

I had to squint to see it, but sure enough, half-hidden behind an overzealous dog rose bush, was an open basement lookout window, and Steele hadn't been kidding. I'd have to hold my breath to get through. Quinto might have to jog a few miles and rearrange his ribs to accomplish the same.

"Ok, follow me, everyone," I said. "And watch out for those prickles. They're a pain if you get them under your skin."

"Wait," said Wyle. "Even me?"

"Especially you," I said. "I don't want you out of our sight until we have Scar Face under lock and key at the precinct."

Harland had the gall to look indignant, but he swallowed the look away after Quinto jabbed him in the back toward the open window.

True to my word, I led the way. I pushed the bush to the side, slipped my feet through the opening, pinched my shoulders, and slid down. My feet hit the floor with a crunch, turning the window's broken glass fragments into slivers. In the dim light, I could make out a few lonely metal tables, some with built in cabinets underneath, but not much else. The space appeared to be a lab, but everything of value had long since been removed.

The broken glass crunched in agony as the rest of the crew descended into the basement, including, to my surprise, Quinto, who came last.

I eyed the big guy. "Nicely done. You lose any skin?" I rubbed my ribs in emphasis.

"Not even sand paper has much of an effect on me, Daggers," said Quinto. "In a fight between me and a window sill, I think the entire frame would give way before I'd be affected."

"Good to know," I said. "I'll save my money instead of getting you that pumice stone for your birthday, then."

Quinto chuckled.

"Are you done?" said Shay. "We have a murderer to catch, if you recall."

"Sorry. Just trying to lighten the mood in case Buford Gill is already dead." I reached into my jacket pocket and retrieved Daisy. "Rodgers. Quinto. Why don't you start with the basement? Keep Wyle with you. Steele and I will head up to the top floor. You work your way up and we'll work our way down. If we meet in the middle without either of us having found anything, we'll reevaluate. Keep your eyes peeled and watch out for murdering psychopaths. And stay quiet."

I nodded to my partner. She gulped and nodded back, a familiar look plastered across her face, one I'd come to associate with a combination of nerves, fear, and excitement. I experienced the same cocktail of emotions anytime I anticipated action, but I don't think it showed on my mug as clearly as it did on Shay's, possibly because my cheek and jaw muscles had lost some of their flexibility after a decade of taking punches and truncheon blows to the face.

I stepped into the hallway, carefully working my way toward the stairs as my eyes continued to adjust to the thick, murky gloom. Despite the bright, late afternoon sun shining outside, the interior of the Physics and Chemistry building was as dark as a tomb thanks to the heavy planks nailed over the windows. My feet stirred dust motes up from the floor, sending them drifting lazily through thin rays of light that squirmed through the gaps between the boards.

I picked up speed as I reached the stairs, pausing only to make sure Shay stayed close behind. Two flights up, I pushed through a swinging door, my nightstick held before me, and stepped into a deserted hallway.

I moved efficiently and, despite my size, quietly, checking rooms to my right and left with nothing more than a couple glances, a pair of pricked ears, and the occasional sniff. Most were empty, and all smelled of must and cold metal. Shay stayed two paces behind me the entire time, making no more noise than a mouse wearing moccasins.

After peering into a half-dozen rooms on either side of me, I noticed an aura of brightness ahead emanating from an open doorway at my right, what would be the back side of the building. An unshuttered window, I reasoned. I crept forward, pausing at the lip of the door. I glanced at Steele and brought a finger to my lips. She nodded.

I sprung forward into the light—caused by a single loose window board, I soon realized—into what essentially amounted to a squatter's den, but not just any squatter. I spotted two bookshelves packed with textbooks and scientific journals up against the left wall, a mobile chalkboard covered with complex equations, and a shiny, brass telescope propped up underneath the window, its objective lens placed in the gap liberated from the fallen board.

Given my keen deductive sense, I surmised we'd found Buford's Gill's private quarters, and I would've realized that even if I hadn't seen the old man's body, lifeless and bloody, prone on a mattress in the middle of the floor.

I approached the body and kneeled. "Shit. We're too late."

I tried to tell myself the old guy could've been any random physics- and astronomy-obsessed squatter retiree, but the lines in his face and along the side of his jaw shared too much with those of Darryl and Anya for that to be possible. It was definitely Buford Gill lying on the ground before me, the left side of his skull a bloody wreckage of bone fragments and gray matter. I glanced at his hands. He wasn't bound, and his fingers hadn't been smashed. Apparently, unlike his progeny, he hadn't been tortured, but that didn't make him any less dead.

Shay stepped into the room and to my right, over by the guy's feet. "How recent is it?"

"Recent," I said. "I don't have Cairny's expertise, but I'd say—"

I paused, thinking I'd heard footsteps, when a blood-curdling scream rent the air.

33

A hooded figure, bearded, scarred, and crazy, burst out of the shadows behind Shay with a roar, a bloody claw hammer grasped in his right hand. He lunged at my partner, swinging the hammer in a wide arc.

Shay screamed and danced to her right, avoiding the killing blow by a hairsbreadth, but she couldn't avoid the psycho's following punch with his left. Scar Face clocked Shay in the mouth, knocking her to the ground, and funneled his momentum back into his hammer hand.

Time slowed around me, not due to anything Wyle or Scar Face might've done but due to the gravity of the situation. I saw Scar Face, his teeth bared in a brutal sneer, lift the bloody hammer over his head, his eyes wild and unfocused. Light gleamed off the hammer's head as it began its descent. Complete and utter emptiness filled my mind—an inability to comprehend the events unfolding before me. Not that it mattered. No thought—mine or hers—could save her now. It was too late for that.

Thankfully, I'd never relied much on my brain in life and death situations. I didn't even realize I'd risen and lunged until my shoulder collided with Scar Face's midsection, driving him at full force into one of the packed bookshelves. I heard a crack—whether of shelving material or ribs, I didn't know—and felt my own tackling blow reverberate through Scar Face, off the wall, back though him, and into me.

Scar Face's hammer rebounded off the floor with a clang, and we both toppled to the hardwood under a rain of leather-bound books and periodicals. I fell flat on my back. Scar Face landed on top of me, driving the wind out of my sails.

Suddenly, time had shifted. No longer were Scar Face's movements progressing at the pace of a snail, but rather they came fast and furious, faster than time should've allowed. I felt a whistle of wind and twisted my head to the side, narrowly avoiding a heavy punch. Scar Face's knuckles dusted the floor, and he grunted in pain.

I grabbed his shoulder with my right hand—where had Daisy gone? I couldn't remember—and threw my left elbow at his face, but Scar Face pulled his head back, causing me to miss. With his center of mass off from the dodge, I tried to push him off me, but Scar Face twisted and pushed and dug a knee into my kidneys. Based on his size, I was sure I outweighed him by a good twenty pounds, but like a trained wrestler, the crazed killer used his position to its full advantage.

I dished out a few half-strength punches to Scar Face's clavicle and midsection, taking an elbow to the chin and a karate chop to the neck in return. Sensing his advantage, Scar Face worked in closer, pressing his torso against me and wrapping his hands around my neck in a chokehold. His beard scraped the side of my face, and the scent of his rotting teeth and stale sweat filled my nostrils.

I tried to punch him in the back of the head, but I couldn't generate any power from my position on the floor, and try as I might, I couldn't shake him.

His thumbs dug into my neck. Air rasped through my throat as I tried to breathe, and I started to see spots. I needed to change tactics, and fast. Scar Face knew proximity was his best friend, so I decided to use it to my advantage as well.

I grabbed the back of Scar Face's skull and pulled it toward me while at the same time straining forward, ignoring the pressure of his thumbs into my windpipe. I bit down, as hard as I could, into the side of Scar Face's jaw. I tasted blood as flesh tore.

Scar Face recoiled with a howl, but rather than pressing his hands to the wound as I'd hoped, he whipped his arms forward and drove a haymaker into my temple.

The room swam. I flailed. I think I might've punched Scar Face in the jaw. I heard another howl and grunting. And pounding—footsteps, heavy ones.

The walls coalesced back into focus, and I caught sight of Scar Face's shoes, which seemed to me a blur as he sped into the hallway.

I stumbled to my knees and shook my head, the punch-induced grogginess fading fast. I could discern the footsteps now. They came from the direction of the stairs—Quinto and company if the weight of the sound was any indication.

I knelt there.

Scar Face had caught me off guard, but we had him trapped in a boarded up building with a single known exit. I could get up, take off after him, and coordinate with Rodgers and Quinto. We'd catch him in our web.

And still I knelt there.

Every ounce of my gut screamed at me to rise, to run, to chase down the murdering psychopath. Every bit of my sense of justice and right and wrong urged me to ignore the pain in my skull and RUN. CHASE. CAPTURE. But for perhaps the first time in my life, my gut got shouted down, and not by my brain or my loins, but by my heart.

I rose. I turned, and knelt by Shay.

My chest clenched as I laid eyes on her. My lungs froze, my throat narrowed, and the pressure of ten feet of water pressed down on my brain, but the sensation was fleeting. No blood. I'd remembered correctly. The hammer *had* missed.

Her eyes were closed, but her chest rose and fell evenly, and when I pressed a finger to the side of her neck, her pulse pushed back, strong and steady. Her hair, normally styled into a pompadour and pinned back or held in a loose pony tail at the back of her head, now lay partially across her face, loosened by Scar Face's blow.

I reached out a finger and brushed it across Shay's brow, gathering the loose strands and tucking them behind a delicate, pointed ear. A scent of lilacs filled my nostrils, but there were other hints there, too, scents entirely unique to Shay. Soap and freshly-washed hair and clean skin, all combining to form an aroma I'd come to know well and yet had never fully deciphered until now.

Shay's eyes fluttered and opened. Rather than drawing my hand back, I let it linger, gently cupping her ear and the back of her head. My partner's eyes darted to the right, then the left, before coming to rest on me, kneeling before her.

"Hi there," I said.

Shay drew air into her lungs slowly, blinked, and rested her warm, full eyes on me. When she spoke, her voice came heavy and breathy. "Hi."

In that instant, there were no walls between us. There was no guarded Detective Steele, no jaded and hesitant Detective Daggers. Only a hurt but not wounded, beautiful, intelligent, compassionate Shay, and kneeling next to her, a concerned but relieved, genuine, caring Jake full of heartfelt emotions and fading worry. Shay's lips were full and red and inviting. Our eyes locked, and her exhaled breath became my inhaled one. Yearnings and desires filled the cavity in my chest that had once been empty but now threatened to explode. I wanted to lean down and...and...

Quinto and Rodgers tore into the room, Wyle in tow. They surveyed the room in a few rapid glances.

"What happened?" said Rodgers.

With a herculean effort, I tore my eyes away from Shay. "Scar Face. He took off for the far stairwell. Quinto, see if you can cut him off. Rodgers, stay here with me. Watch Wyle."

Quinto nodded and disappeared. Rodgers looked displeased, but apparently he understood Shay and I were in no condition to watch over Wyle on our own. Or at least, that's what I supposed. At the moment, I didn't care. I turned my gaze back to Shay.

"You ok?" I said.

Shay brought a hand up to her face and worked her jaw muscles gingerly. "I think so. I don't...remember everything."

"Scar Face hit you with a hook," I said. "Knocked you out, though only for a minute or two. I'm not entirely sure how long it was, to be honest. Time wasn't functioning the way it normally does for me."

I heard a confused grunt from Wyle, but I ignored him.

"Scar Face got away?" asked Shay.

"For now," I said. "Maybe Quinto can catch him."

"Why didn't you go after him?" she said.

I didn't answer. I didn't have to. She stared into my eyes, and she knew.

I felt the heat of Rodgers and Wyle's eyes on us, and I felt crowded.

"Can you stand?" I asked Steele.

"Yeah, I think so," she said.

She gave me her hands, but paused before I could help her up. "Daggers?"

"Yes?" I said.

She looked deep into my eyes. "Thank you."

The look she gave was more of a response than the words. I nodded and helped her to her feet. As I did so, I noticed Wyle staring at the bloody corpse of Buford Gill.

"You finally hear any bells ringing?" I asked him.

Wyle looked up at me, confused. "Huh?"

I nodded toward the body. "You said you didn't know anything about Buford Gill. That the name didn't ring a bell. Well, here he is, and in case you hadn't noticed, he's dead. So...care to modify your story?"

Wyle shook his head. "No. In fact..."

"In fact, what?" I asked. Not that I cared much about his answer, but talking to Wyle gave me something to do other than stare at Shay and wonder how much she suspected regarding my feelings toward her or if anything had changed between us.

"Well, it's that...I didn't feel it." Wyle lifted his eyes from the body and looked at me. "The fluctuations in the time stream, I mean. I didn't sense his death at all. Now that I'm here, I can feel some of the expanding ripples, but they're faint. Indistinct. If Scar Face killed this man, there should've been a greater disturbance— certainly if he was important enough to merit being murdered."

"So, what?" said Rodgers, nodding at Gill. "Are you saying this guy is a nobody? That he's not Scar Face's ultimate target?"

"I don't know," said Wyle. "Honestly, I really don't know..."

Quinto's heavy footfalls gave him away before we spotted his big round mug back in the door frame. I guessed his news before he opened his mouth based solely on the dejected look on his face.

"Sorry, Daggers," he said. "I raced down to the basement as fast as I could, but either he already got away, or there's another exit out of this place we don't know about."

I frowned and sighed.

Shay stepped up beside me and placed a gentle hand on my shoulder—an *especially* gentle hand. Intentional, or not?

"It's ok, Daggers," she said. "We'll find him."

"I know," I said. "I know. The question is if we'll find him before anyone else dies."

No one had any witty remarks to add to that statement. In fact, everyone had developed a sudden interest in the tips of their shoes.

"Come on," I said. "It's time we enrolled some backup. This case is getting out of hand."

34

I gave the Captain a rundown of the day's events upon returning to the precinct, everything from progress with Wyle to the trail that led us to Buford Gill to me and Shay's encounter with Scar Face. I didn't pull any punches. I told the whole truth, and nothing but the truth, as I remembered it. I'd expected a reproach for not going after Scar Face when the chance had presented itself, but I'd received none. Maybe the Captain knew more than he pretended to about the chemistry developing between me and my partner, or perhaps not. He'd always been a proponent of the old code, one of the most fundamental mantras of which was to never leave a partner behind, no matter the circumstances.

I'd also expected some resistance upon asking for help, purely due to the added financial strain of giant manhunts upon the department's coffers, but the Captain surprised me yet again. He pulled out all the stops. He ordered for an all points bulletin to be issued for Scar Face and sent beat cops to stake out the old Physics and Chemistry building, the flophouse outside Little

Welwic, and both Darryl's apartment and Anya's brownstone. He sent teams of technicians to the flophouse and the condemned science building to sweep every last nook and cranny for evidence that might help lead us to Scar Face's next location. Cairny was instructed to double time it on her coroner's reports. And, in a return to his sensitive, caring form, he growled at Rodgers and Quinto to pour through Scar Face's journal while yelling at Shay and I to keep leaning on Wyle until he cracked.

So it was that I found myself standing over Harland Wyle, who sat in my desk chair with his head hanging low, while Shay perched on the corner of my massive desk, overseeing the action. Shadows stretched out from each of us as the sun dipped low in the sky, sending rays glancing at acute angles through the Captain's office windows and into the pit.

"Keep talking to me, Wyle," I said. "We need to work through this together."

"I don't know what else to tell you, man," he said. "We've gone through what I know a dozen times already. My story isn't going to change."

Says you, I thought. "Then let's go through it once more. Some say thirteen's a lucky number."

Wyle groaned.

"Tell me again what you know about Buford Gill," I said. "Surely there's something important about the man. Some reason he was murdered."

With Wyle, I'd kept operating under the pretense that his story held water instead of insisting it was a total crock. It made conversation easier, as I didn't have to preface each statement with 'Let's assume you're right and...' or 'If what you say is true, then...', but the fact was I didn't know what to believe anymore. Part of me, the open-minded part, wanted to believe Wyle's time travel hypothesis—it would explain a lot—but the man made that so hard, with his constant waffling and imprecise descriptions of his own magic. The whole case would be much simpler to understand if I could catch Wyle in a lie, but I'd yet to do so. What was his angle, and how did he know where Scar Face had been hiding?

"Look," said Wyle, "I've told you. To the best of my knowledge, Buford Gill isn't an important historical figure. His death, which barely altered the time streams, supports that."

"But then why did Scar Face kill him?" I asked. "Why torture Darryl and Anya to find him if he's not important? Is it possible this isn't about changing the fate of technology? Could there be a deeper connection between Scar Face and the Gill family?"

Wyle wiped a hand across his face. "Look, I don't know, ok? It doesn't make sense to me, either."

I tapped my fingers impatiently against the desk. "Give me something, Wyle."

Wyle spread his hands and looked bewildered. "Look, maybe...things are more complicated than they appear. Maybe Scar Face isn't who we think he is. Maybe he knows more than I gave him credit for. Citizens for Simplicity is a pretty radical sect. Maybe they're operating on a fringe theory of temporal reconstruction."

Shay rolled her eyes. "I'm going to brew some tea. You want any?"

I shook my head. "Grab me a coffee, though, will you?"

Shay nodded, hopped off my desk, and walked off toward the break room. My mind threatened to wander as I watched her sway, but I wrestled it back to the case at hand.

"What fringe theory?" I asked.

"There are a couple unpopular hypotheses," said Wyle. "One's known as period accurate temporal reconstruction. Which essentially means you can change the past, but only if you do so in a manner that doesn't *directly* contradict it."

My brow scrunched up in thought. "I'm not sure I understand. How's that even possible?"

"Let me give you an example," said Wyle. "Let's say someone came back in time and tried to kill, oh...I don't know, the mayor of New Welwic. Well, he couldn't just pop back and blast the guy with a heater in front of a huge crowd of people."

"A what now?" I said.

"A, uh...never mind," said Wyle. "The point is, he'd have to make the death seem possible, even likely. Maybe poison the man, or fake a cancer or, I don't know...hit him with a hammer, I guess."

I frowned. "And the other theory?"

"The other one's called anti-event temporal reconstruction," said Wyle.

"Say what now?"

"It's the idea that you can't change the past through *direct* action," said Wyle, "and that only by preventing established events from unfolding can you impact the future. Look, they're both convoluted theories, but they both operate under the assumption that to effect real change, you can't just *do* things, you have to...*nudge* the past in the direction you want it to go. I don't know how Scar Face would know what to tweak, but maybe that's what these murders are. Nudges."

I tried to see how many creases I could fit in my forehead when I noticed the Captain gesturing to me from the doorway to his office, a mug of coffee grasped between his thick, blacksmith-like hands. I sauntered over.

"Get anything?" asked the bulldog.

"Not really," I said. "But I'll keep trying. I just need more time, and maybe a fresh strategy."

"Well, don't take too long," said the Captain.

"Trust me," I said, "I know all too well with every passing second, the chances increase that the murdering SOB who took out the entire Gill family line will strike again."

"Yes, but that's not what I meant," said the Captain, taking a gulp from his mug. "We can't keep Wyle in custody forever."

"What?" I said. "Why not?"

"You know damned well why not," said the Captain. "Despite his lunacy and his apparent involvement with the Gill murders, you can't implicate him in any of the slayings, can you?"

I shook my head.

"Exactly," said the Captain. "And while we can charge him with a couple counts of trespassing, we have nobody left to pursue those charges. And as far as we know, he didn't even steal anything, so burglary is off the table."

"Just give me a little more time, Captain," I said. "We can hold him for twenty-four hours without anyone batting an eye. Then we can figure out what to do with him."

The Captain drew the mug of coffee back to his lips, but before he said anything, I heard the front doors to the precinct bang open. A panting bluecoat entered, spotted us, and jogged over.

"Captain...news," he said.

I stuck my fat mouth into the fray before the Captain could get involved. "Did we get a sighting on the APB?"

The beat cop shook his head. "No. Sorry. This is from the World's Wonders Fair. You know that wealthy businessman? Bock? He's gone missing."

"Linwood Bock?" My conversation with Mel Crestwick popped into the forefront of my mind. "This can't be a coincidence. Stay here. I'm going to get Detective Steele."

35

The sun had just set when Steele and I arrived at the home of Linwood Bock, a palatial estate smack dab in the center of the ultra-swanky Brentford neighborhood. Centenarian oaks and pines lined the property, set inside an eight-foot perimeter wall constructed of pale gray granite slabs that each must've weighted as much as one of Mr. Bock's patented reciprocating engines. The towering wrought iron gates at the front of the property stood open, admitting us to a curved cobblestone path leading to the house proper—a mansion in every sense of the word. Four stories of polished stone and beaten copper roofing, with rooms enough to house, feed, and pamper a small army, surrounded by grounds so meticulously manicured they'd make the curator at the municipal botanical gardens blush with envy—or suffer a more orgasmic response.

A throng of officers milled outside the mansion's front doors, including a handful standing at a table set between a pair of tall braziers that burned fiercely in the cool evening air. A mobile command center, if looks were any indication. A man, tall and lean, with a straight back and precisely trimmed black hair, leaned over the middle of the table staring at a map and giving orders. I headed for him and waved for Shay to follow.

"Excuse me," I said, pushing through the crowd to reach Tall and Slim. I flashed my badge. "You in charge?"

"Sort of," said the man. "Chief Investigator Reynolds is inside, talking to Bock's wife, Sophia. I'm Lieutenant Drake. Who are you?"

"I'm Daggers," I said. "She's Steele. Homicide." Shay nodded in acknowledgement.

Drake stood, straight as a rod, and his face lengthened. "Don't tell me..."

"No," I said. "Bock's not dead. Not that we know of, anyway."

"Oh." Drake sighed. "Thank the gods. Then why are you here?"

"It's complicated," I said. "But suffice it to say we have an active investigation that may tie into Bock's disappearance. You mind filling us in on what you know?"

"Sure," said Drake, "but forgive me if I'm brief. We're scrambling to stay ahead of this before the news spreads. Essentially, Bock was last seen at the World's Wonders Fair, behind the main stage an hour, hour and a half ago. They were prepping for the evening exhibition of his...*apparatuses*, or whatever you want to call them. Apparently, Bock visited the facilities and never returned. One of his protégés went to the bathroom to look for him and found signs of a struggle. A busted window, scuff marks on the tiles, and Bock's pocket watch, broken and discarded on the floor. We're treating it as a kidnapping, but that's all we know right now. No one's contacted the family. Yet, anyway."

"Thanks," I said. "And you mentioned the CI—what was his name, Reynolds?—is inside?"

Drake nodded. "Yeah. You going to tell me how this ties into your investigation?"

"I will," I said. "But I need to talk to Reynolds first. Time may be tight."

I pushed into the house proper and paused inside the broad front doors, momentarily awed by the foyer's opulence. I don't think I'd ever seen so much marble, which covered not only the floors but the ceilings—the ceilings!—although it was the sheer quantity of gilt that made me feel inadequate. It graced the walls in ornate filigrees, enrobed the banisters of the dual, sweeping staircases that curved around the sides of the three-story chamber, and glinted off the fierce light of a crystal chandelier, one with so many candles the Bocks probably employed a manservant whose entire job it was to light, extinguish, and replace the waxy cylinders.

A burly bluecoat standing guard in the center of the room gave us a fish-eyed look, but I flashed my badge again and told him I needed to see Reynolds. He grunted and pointed to his left.

Shay and I entered the hallway his finger had indicated and soon heard voices, one male and one female.

"But I don't understand how this could've happened," said the woman. "Weren't there guards or watchmen at the fair? At the very least there were crowds. How is it no one noticed my husband's disappearance? What sorts of lawless rabble do they allow into these damned things?"

"Look, Mrs. Bock, you have my sincerest condolences," said the man, "but know we're doing everything in our power to find your husband. We're throwing the full weight of our department behind this effort. Every man we have has been called in, and all of them have been placed on this case. We have dozens of officers canvassing the festival grounds and interviewing fairgoers. Someone will have seen something. We'll find your husband."

I turned the corner into a sitting room furnished with a quartet of old world provincial-style sofas, except no couch in the old world would've likely been built out of such fine leather or fur trim. Seated on one sofa was a woman wearing a violet gown and a cream-colored pashmina over her shoulders. An excessive amount of makeup caked her faced, partially obscuring the lines in her forehead and at the corners of her mouth, and her hair, held in a bun at the base of her neck, looked a little *too* dark given her age. She'd be Sophia Bock.

Across from her sat a square-shouldered man with a crew cut and a thick, graying moustache. He wore a police-issue jacket that looked as if it had been pulled right off the steaming rack. He'd be Investigator Reynolds, if I was anywhere close to being worth my salt as a detective.

I knocked on the door frame. "Excuse me. Detective Reynolds?"

The man turned. "Yes? Who the hell are you?"

"Detective Daggers," I said. "Homicide. This is my partner Steele. We heard about Bock and got here as quickly as we could. As it turns out, we're working a case that may be related to his kidnapping."

Reynolds and Sophia Bock glanced at each other, the former with a look of confusion and the latter with a look of concern, before turning their gazes onto Steele and me.

Reynolds scowled and stroked his moustache. "Homicide, eh? Brief me."

"We're after a man—someone we've been calling Scar Face due to his appearance—who we believe has committed three murders over the past two days," I said. "We tried to apprehend him a few hours ago at an abandoned building, but he escaped our capture. Based on knowledge we've gathered in our case and the timing of his evasion of us, we believe he may be involved in Bock's disappearance."

I dug into my jacket pocket and produced a sketch of Scar Face—an alternate Boatreng had drawn for us on request. I handed it to Reynolds. "This is the man. You can distribute that sketch to your men at the fair grounds if you'd like. We have a spare. Mrs. Bock, does this man by any chance look familiar?"

Sophia Bock took one look and the sketch and shook her head. "No. Certainly not. I wouldn't associate with anyone like that, and I doubt my husband would either."

Reynolds pocketed the sketch. "I'll get this to my men immediately, but you're going to have to explain the situation further. How does this man connect to Mr. Bock?"

Steele piped up from my side. "The three murder victims are all related. They include Darryl Gill, his sister Anya Crestwick, and their father, Buford Gill, a physicist. We understand he was a professional colleague of your husband, Mrs. Bock."

Sophia Bock snorted. "You must be joking. Buford Gill was murdered?"

"Yes," I said.

Sophia laughed a bitter laugh. "Hah. Well good riddance."

I glanced at Steele. She peered back at me, eyes narrowed and mouth slightly open.

"Excuse me?" I said.

Sophia Bock stared at me coldly. "I don't know where you get your information, detectives, but my husband and Mr. Gill are not and were never *professional colleagues*. They despised one another. I'm not entirely sure what that blowhard Gill had against Linwood—likely he couldn't accept his immeasurable success—but it's no secret why my husband hated the man."

I raised an eyebrow. "That being...?"

"Well, Gill constantly derided him," said Sophia, "at every opportunity, public and private, in speeches and in publications, constantly ripping his work to shreds because his interests were more commercial than scientific. It all came to a head years ago after that man Gill all but assaulted my husband at a charity function. Apparently he'd just been fired and was half drunk, and my husband's never been the sort of man to stand for that. He threatened Gill with his life, and thankfully that put an end to it. Gill went and hid under some rock, though he still lambasted my husband on occasion in publications. I thought his firing was karmic justice enough, but I certainly won't shed any tears over his murder."

Silence filled the room in Sophia's wake. Reynolds stared at her, as did Steele and I. I recalled Dr. French's words earlier about how Gill had been combative in defense of his theories, but I hadn't quite envisioned this.

Sophia Bock flushed. "What? Why are you all looking at me like that? We're the victims here. *My* husband's the one who's been kidnapped."

"Yes, yes, of course, Mrs. Bock," said Reynolds, assuring her. "It's just that it's an interesting...*coincidence*, that's all."

"*Very* interesting." I turned to Steele, rubbing my chin. "Interesting enough that I'm wondering if there are any *other* coincidences we haven't uncovered yet."

My partner tilted her head and raised an eyebrow. "You're getting that look again. The one where you're forming a theory."

"Starting to," I said. "But it's not fully cooked yet. It needs time to simmer. In the meantime, let's get back to the precinct. There's someone I want to talk to."

36

The 5th Street Precinct buzzed with activity despite the late hour. Lanterns blazed above the wide front doors, illuminating the faces of a dozen beat cops chatting and shuffling their feet in the soft evening breeze. Runners shuttled memos back and forth between mobile street teams and the head brass, their bare feet slapping the concrete as they flew up and down the precinct steps two at a time. An air of tension hung over the street corner like a dense fog.

Despite the cool weather outside, the interior of the station steamed like a sauna. Bluecoats massed together, clutching mugs of coffee that trailed hot vapors as they carried them to and fro, clenched in fists alongside witness affidavits and report forms. The break room overflowed with guys I'd never even seen, much less whose names I remembered.

Amid the bustle, the Captain sat alone in his office, chewing his cud and looking as if he might set his teeth into anyone dumb enough to enter his bubble of thought. I spotted him looking my way and gave him a determined nod, trying to convey my commitment to the case without risking the bulldog's physical presence. I didn't want to get any spittle on my coat.

Like everyone else on the police payroll, Rodgers and Quinto were still at work, but instead of hovering around, buzzing and stinging people and being huge annoyances, the pair sat at their desks, manuscripts grasped tightly between their fingers.

"You guys find some interesting new reading materials?" I asked.

Each half of the mismatched detective pair startled. Perhaps amidst the elevated activity in the pit, they hadn't heard us approach.

"Oh, hey Steele. Daggers," said Rodgers.

I glanced at Shay and raised an eyebrow. "Look at that. He mentioned you first. Have you been slipping these guys bribes while I'm not looking?"

Shay smiled seductively. "Oh, I have more effective ways of changing minds than bribes."

I gulped. I knew she did, but I hoped she wasn't wasting those skills on Rodgers and Quinto when I was so readily available.

"I was just trying it out," said Rodgers. "You know, for kicks. Although, I have to admit, I think I like Daggers followed by Steele better. Sorry, Steele." He shrugged.

"It's ok," said Shay. "I'm the rookie. I understand. But enjoy it while you can. Some day you'll be referring to me as *Captain* Steele."

Rodgers smiled. "I'll look forward to it, if for no other reason than to see what new, horrid partner you stuff Daggers with."

"Hah," I said. "Not likely. I'll be long retired at that point, living it up in a tiny shack surrounded by empty whisky bottles, weather-beaten paperbacks, and my own faded memories of the past."

Quinto chuckled and shook his head.

"So," I said, "did you guys learn anything while Steele and I made our excursion to the Bock estate?"

Before leaving, I'd tasked Rodgers and Quinto with digging up whatever back story they could on Gill and Bock to see if any shiny bits stuck out.

"Interesting you should ask," said Quinto. "You know how you'd mentioned during your interview with Mel, Mel said Bock had paid him to track down Buford Gill? And Mel thought Bock wanted to hire the man to work for his company?"

"Let me guess," I said. "Not so much?"

"Probably not," said Rodgers. "Let me read you a passage from one of Gill's manuscripts, a review paper entitled *An Analysis of Disparate Theories regarding Phase Changes in Closed Systems*. Let's see, where was it..." Rodgers flipped through one of the many journals we'd brought back from the library, drawing his finger down a page. "Ah, here we are. *Bock's suggestions on the nature of gaseous processes in closed systems are so laughably inadequate as to border on scientific slander. While he and his teams have produced impressive results under controlled conditions, Bock's explanations regarding the phase changes in his prototypical 'engines' are completely unsubstantiated by traditional theories, showing conclusively that his many exploits are due to the coercion of other's minds for profit and not to any production of his own intellect.*"

"His papers are littered with these sorts of insults," said Quinto. "But...based on the looks on your faces, you already knew that."

I shrugged. "Bock's wife spilled the beans."

"Apparently, the animosity between the pair goes beyond verbal insults," said Steele. "Sophia Bock told us Gill accosted Bock at a party some years back, and, tired of his insults, Bock threatened Gill with physical force. We didn't get many details into precisely how it occurred, but the really curious part? That was right before Gill went into hiding."

Quinto tapped his chin. "Are you implying that incident was the impetus for Gill's disappearance?"

"It's a possibility," I said.

"Daggers is working on a theory," said Steele.

"Ooh, a theory." Rodgers rubbed his hands together. "Well, don't be shy. Let's hear it."

"Not yet," I said. "I haven't figured out all the details. There's still an important piece of the puzzle I can't fit into place yet."

"Which is?" said Quinto.

I shook a finger at the big guy. "Not so fast, Quickdraw. I'll share when I'm ready."

Quinto rolled his eyes. "Ok. Well, regardless of your theory, we still have a major problem. None of the teams the Captain sent out have seen hide nor hair of Scar Face, and as interesting as these papers of Gill's are—" Rodgers snorted at that part. "—we're no closer to finding our bearded murderer than we were when we left the abandoned Physics and Chemistry building. So I hope you learned something other than Gill and Bock's ten year history while out and about."

Shay grimaced.

Quinto leaned forward in his chair and his eyes widened. "You didn't?"

"Daggers said he has a plan," said Steele.

"And are you willing to share *that*?" asked Quinto.

"Sure," I said. "I'm going to ask the final piece of the puzzle to take us to Scar Face."

37

My instructions to Wyle, who'd been placed back into one of the overnight holding cells, were simple: take me somewhere. He'd asked what I'd meant and I'd reiterated my statement: take me anywhere you think we should go.

I hadn't pushed the whole Gill/Bock angle. I hadn't even mentioned it. But I had played along with Wyle's worldview, emphasizing his own statements from earlier in the day about the time streams ebbing and flowing like tides. Surely, I told him, the ebbing had abated. Surely, I told him, someone with his abilities could detect disturbances in the flow of time, no matter how minor. Surely, I told him, you can feel *something*. So close your eyes, find your inner quiet spot, do whatever it is you need to do—but take us wherever it is your magics draw you.

I'd expected resistance from my compatriots, and I got some in the form of snorts and rolled eyes from Quinto and Rodgers, but surprisingly enough, I didn't get any pushback from Steele. Not a word. That caught me off guard. She merely stood at my shoulder and smiled, and when I'd asked what she thought of my strategy, she'd said she thought it was worth a shot. I couldn't tell if she was yanking my chain, letting me hang myself in my own noose, but I doubted she'd do that, not at this point in the investigation with a serial killer on the loose and lives at stake. She wouldn't risk the wellbeing of others to teach me a lesson, which could only mean...*she trusted me.* She might not agree with my methods or my strategies, which perhaps explained her silence when I'd asked her for her opinion, but she trusted me enough to follow along with whatever wild plan I concocted, because even if she didn't believe in my methodology, she believed in *me* as a detective.

It was a sobering thought. Shay trusted me. In a sense, I think she always had—or least she had after our first painful couple days together—but she'd done so as a natural course of action. I was her partner. I'd have her back, and she knew that. But now she trusted me *implicitly.* So what changed? Was it our encounter with Scar Face, where rather than chase after the lunatic, I'd stayed to make sure she was safe? Could that have affected her so strongly?

Luckily for me, I didn't have to focus on the case at hand while following Wyle through the streets of New Welwic, because once the realization about Shay hit me, my deductive powers turned to jelly. So I walked and thought and stayed close to Wyle's heels, a lantern confiscated from the precinct's supply room clenched in my right hand to help banish the night's encroaching demons. I paused when he paused, I turned when he turned, and I fought back my rising tide of unrest as our journey stretched well past the hour mark.

Together, Shay, Wyle, Rodgers, Quinto, and I walked across the Bridge, over to the east side of town and into the industrial district where foundries spewed smoke and ash and where the ringing of metal on metal and the grunting of men lifting crates and weighted sacks formed an ever-present sonic backdrop.

Wyle led us along a wide thoroughfare deep into the heart of the industrial district. A cart drawn by two burly fellows in shirtsleeves, piled high with rolled metal bars that clanged together, clattered past, and workers chatted as they walked along the side streets, swinging supper pails as they headed into factories to start their night shifts.

Wyle paused in mid stride. Our detective troupe stopped behind him, me on the far right and Quinto, who also carried a lantern, on the far left. I gave Wyle a minute, thinking he needed to reassess and continue as he'd done dozens of times already, but he just stood there, his jaw set.

Eventually, I spoke. "Is there a problem, Wyle?"

"I...think this is it," he said.

I looked around at the looming factories with their jutting chimneys and high walls, all eerily lit from within, whether by lanterns or burning fires or by the radiating pools of molten metal that were the source of the business owners' livelihoods.

"What do you mean, this is it?" I asked.

"I mean, this is where the ripples led," said Wyle, "but they're gone now. I could feel them a moment ago—faint, to be sure, but they were there. Now? Nothing. Either they've faded completely, or we've reached the center of the drop."

I inferred what Wyle meant by his metaphor, but I wasn't happy about the result. "Seriously? Your time magic led us to the middle of a street?"

"Yes," said Wyle.

"And...what?" I said. "Where's Scar Face? Where's Bock? There's nothing here. Literally. Nothing."

"I...I know." Wyle hung his head. "I'm sorry."

I pressed a hand to the bridge of my nose, pressure building in my sinuses and in the back of my brain. This couldn't be how it ended. I'd been sure Wyle was involved with Scar Face, somehow, in some way. I was sure he knew more than he'd let on, sure he'd lead us to another clue or a lair or something. But this? The middle of a street? Was that really the best the man would, or could, offer?

"You've *got* to be kidding me," I said slowly.

Wyle shrugged while keeping his eyes on the ground, the actions of a beaten man.

"Damn it!" I exploded. "Come on, Wyle. Give me something. Anything! I know you know more than you're letting on. Tell me what you know. TELL ME!"

No one said a word, though I felt a few heads turn my way from the direction of the factory workers, their eyes working in tandem with my own embarrassment to heat my cheeks and neck.

Quinto broke the silence. "Maybe we should pack it in, Daggers. Head back to the precinct. We'll try again tomorrow."

"Yeah, Daggers," said Rodgers. "Let's go."

"No," said Steele.

I turned to face her, but she wasn't looking at me or Wyle or anyone else. She gazed, brows furrowed, down the street.

"No?" I asked.

"No." She turned to me and smiled. "What do you notice about this area of the city, Daggers? What sticks out to you?"

"Nothing," I said. "That's the problem."

"Sometimes I wonder how you ever solved any cases without me, Daggers. You're great at putting the puzzle pieces together, but sometimes you can't see the pieces at all. At least, not without *my* help." Her eyes twinkled. "We're smack dab in the middle of a metalworking district. Even though it's evening, there's foot traffic. Workers are heading to night shifts. The fires of industry burn bright all around us, lighting the skies. Behind us. Across the street from us. To our left, the way we came. And..."

Shay held her hand out to her right, in the direction she'd been staring, toward another large, industrial facility, one that stood dark and cold and silent in the early evening. Shay turned to one of the passing factory workers. "Excuse me...sir?"

The guy, a squashed-faced dude that could've passed for Quinto's younger, leaner cousin, looked around, confused, and pointed at himself. Perhaps he wasn't used to unsolicited advances from pretty, professionally-dressed elves standing around in thoroughfares.

"Yes, you," said Steele. "Can you tell us what that building over there is?" She pointed.

"Durr, dat's uh, a Bock Industries place," said the guy, scratching his bulbous nose. "Da plant where dey make dose big mechanical doohickeys."

"Does it normally shut down at night?" asked Steele.

Schnozz Derpsalot had to think about that one. "Duh, nope, nope dey don't. I dink dey shut da place down for dat fair. You know, da one downtown."

Someone grabbed the rope that descended from my mind and gave it a mighty tug, giving the bell inside a furious ring. I wanted to slap Wyle on the back and plant a big, wet kiss on Shay's cheeks—or lips—but I did neither. Instead, I patted my jacket to check on Daisy and hefted my lantern into the night.

38

I stumbled through the near darkness, the now-shuttered lantern grasped in my right hand. I held my left hand out before me, feeling for exposed metal rods and heavy pieces of industrial equipment that secretly thought nothing funnier than seeing me bang my head against them.

"Dear gods," I said in hushed tones. "It's darker than a..."

"A what?" whispered Shay, her voice coming from my right.

"Um, nothing," I said. "I was going to say something rude and possibly offensive. I thought better of it."

"You're kidding," said Shay.

"Huh?" I said. "What do you mean?"

"You thought before you spoke?" she said. "This is a big day. We should celebrate."

"With drinks?" I said. "Sure. You buying?"

Wyle's voice came from between us. "Are you guys always like this?"

"Pretty much," I said. "Unless I've said something to piss Steele off, or I'm moody because she's one-upped me."

"Yeah, that sounds about right," said Steele.

I couldn't see her smile in the darkness, but I felt it.

We stood in the cavernous interior of the temporarily closed Bock Industries factory, surrounded by silent sentinels: mechanical behemoths with wide metal chests and thick iron flywheels as legs, connected together with ligaments of belts and chain and with spent coals lingering in their bellies. Heavy lifting hooks hung from cables which disappeared into the gloom like the cords of giant marionettes, waiting to be attached to the machines to bring them to life in herking, jerking spurts. A chill crept into my bones, more from the ominous environs than the temperature, and I smelt cold steel and long dead fires and industrial lubricant.

Upon reaching the factory, I'd sent Rodgers and Quinto to swing around the back while I went in the front with Shay and Wyle. For once, I'd decided to keep the time mage with me, despite the fact that I knew it would be dark inside and that he could probably overpower Shay if given the opportunity. Perhaps I took on the task as a favor to Rodgers and Quinto—neither of them put any faith into Wyle's rambling predictions and I didn't want to burden them with him, *again*—but it was more than that. I honestly didn't think Wyle would make a break for it. He'd had plenty of opportunities since we'd snagged him early in the morning, yet he'd intentionally stuck with us, for reasons that, despite my best efforts to pry them out of him, were still his and his alone.

The shuttered lantern released only the barest dribble of light, and so I snaked forward through the factory slowly, watching for low-hanging lifting hooks and piles of cans I might clumsily knock over, creating a ruckus that would awaken the dead, as well as Scar Face should he be hiding nearby. At the same time, I kept my eyes peeled for signs of life or of a recent struggle: discarded bottles or takeout food containers, drag marks on the floor, or, most tellingly, the light of another lantern. Of course, I let Shay do most of the heavy ocular lifting. Being half-elven, her eyes were quite a bit better than mine.

"See anything?" I asked, again keeping my voice low so as to not alert anyone.

"Other than heavy machinery and darkness, you mean?" said Shay.

"Yes," I said.

"Not so much," she replied.

"What about you, Wyle?" I asked. "Did the ripples or whatnot pick back up? Can you give us any direction?"

"Um, no," he said. "The trail ended in the street outside. But since you asked, I do feel *something* here. Not a ripple in the time stream, or even a fluctuation, but a sensation of sorts. Kind of like being underwater, perfectly still. A temporal pressure, if you will."

"How convenient," said Shay. I think she rolled her eyes, but I couldn't tell in the gloom.

We kept moving, and suddenly I experienced an incredible sensation of déjà vu. Around a corner—and by corner, I mean the edge of an enormous cast iron cauldron—I noticed an increase in brightness, just as I'd spotted while stalking the abandoned halls of the Physics and Chemistry building in search of Buford Gill. I hissed at Shay and Wyle to slow as I peered around the edge of the cauldron.

A few dozen paces away, next to an empty foreman's shack, two chairs faced one another, made visible by the light of a lantern set to the side on a table most likely designed to hold engineering diagrams.

In the first chair, the one that faced us, sat a portly individual in a rich wool coat, pinstriped slacks, and glossy black shoes—a man, based on his body shape. A tan gunny sack obscured his head, and from the way his arms wrapped around the back of the chair and his feet splayed out next to the chair's legs, I assumed he was tied to the thing. Though he didn't move, I didn't spot any blood or other evidence of a struggle.

Across from him, with his back to us, sat another individual, slouched low and with his feet stretched out and crossed before him. His head was also obscured by a hood, but not a makeshift one fashioned out of a potato sack, rather that of his hooded jacket—a ratty, worn thing I remembered quite well from my brush with death earlier in the afternoon. Scar Face's hood. Like the man across from him, he lay motionless, and unless my ears deceived me, I heard something coming from the direction of his chair.

Snoring.

Ever so carefully, I laid my lantern down at my feet and slipped Daisy out of my jacket. I held a finger to my lips for Steele and Wyle, pointed at them and the floor, then pointed at myself and the chairs. Apparently, my pantomime classes had paid off, as both Steele and Wyle nodded, catching my drift.

Like a two hundred and ten pound shrew, I scuttled across the expanse between me and my quarry. First one step, then two, then three.

The hooded one didn't move.

I kept closing, more swiftly now, a couple steps at a time. The man in the gunny sack struggled intermittently against his bonds, weakly, as if without hope. The snoring became more clear, more distinct. I was sure it came from the figure nearest me.

The hooded one didn't move.

My feet became a silent blur. My heart raced with anticipation. I held my breath to keep from uttering a single warning sign.

And still the hooded one didn't move.

I swung Daisy in a rapid arc and clocked the man in the hoodie upside the head. A yelp like that of a kicked dog escaped his lips, and he crumpled to the floor.

"Daggers!"

Steele's voice pierced the silence behind me, and the man in the potato sack startled and shook and started emitting muted moaning sounds. The hooded figure lay motionless and silent at my feet.

"What?" I asked.

Steele rushed up to join me, the hem of her jacket fluttering as she ran. "You can't go around indiscriminately bashing people in the head."

"You do recall this man nearly killed you, right?" I asked. "And that he tried to kill me as well?"

"Scar Face did," said Steele. "But we don't know who this is. This could be a setup. It could be anyone behind this hood. Why, it—"

I bent over and used Daisy's tip to push back the floor-snoozer's hood. Scar Face's bearded, scarred face appeared from within, complete with bite marks on his jaw. He didn't look quite as wild and crazy as before, most likely because the dude's eyes were closed.

"Oh." Shay's face fell. "Sorry. As we approached, I got this weird feeling like it wouldn't be him. Like it would be someone else pretending to be him, here to lure us out."

I snorted. "I don't think Bearded and Ugly here is smart enough to pull off something like that. I'd accuse you of reading too many hackneyed mystery novels, but that description applies to me not you."

With Scar Face momentarily incapacitated, I peered back toward the cauldron. Luckily, Wyle still stood there. Apparently my gut instincts regarding the guy had been well-founded. I motioned him over.

"Is it him?" asked Wyle. "Did you get him?"

"Sure did," I said. "Scar Face, in the flesh. Did you feel anything pulse through the magisphere when I smacked him?"

Wyle shook his head. "Nothing. But maybe that's a good thing, right?"

A few indistinct mumbles from the direction of the still-occupied chair drew my attention, but Shay beat me to the punch. She walked over to the figure and pulled off the hood, revealing a man with tousled, graying hair, a white circle beard, and a pair of chins. He blinked in the sudden light and tried to speak, but thanks to the rag in his mouth held in place by a length of hemp cord, all that came out was a grunt.

Shay untied the rope and, with more grace than I could've mustered under the same circumstances, plucked the spit-soaked rag from the man's mouth. "Linwood Bock?"

Bock spat, rubbing his tongue against his teeth, and nodded. "Yes. Yes, that's me. Who are you?"

"Detective Steele," she said. "This is my partner Daggers and our...*consultant*, Mr. Wyle. You're safe now. Detective Daggers apprehended your assailant. In a sense..."

Bock glanced at Scar Face's motionless form and at Daisy, who I still clutched in my fist. "Yes, I can see that."

"Are you hurt? Did this man torture you?" I pointed at Scar Face with my baton.

Bock shook his head. "No. Physically, I'm unharmed. Though I'm parched. And these restraints are digging into my wrists, so...if you'd please?" He tilted his head toward the back of the chair.

I got to work on the knots. "Steele, let's find Rodgers and Quinto and tell them the good news. I'll free our captive and secure Scar Face. And Mr. Bock? I hope you're not too tired, because we have a lot to talk about."

39

Steele and I emerged from the precinct's sitting room and headed toward our desks, avoiding the civilian crowd that milled in the hallway. The insect-like buzz infesting the station's interior had subsided once we'd returned with Bock and Scar Face in custody, replaced instead with an exhaled cloud of relief as beat cops and detectives alike were given the all clear signal and allowed to return to their wives and families.

However, as soon as the horde of flatfoots and officers abated, their warm bodies had been replaced with those of Linwood's hangers-on: friends and family relieved to hear of his rescue, bodyguards—probably newly hired in the wake of his disappearance, cronies, journalists, and, of course, lawyers. *Lots* of lawyers. More than Bock could possibly need—unless he had something to hide. And given how tight-lipped Bock had been until their arrival, despite me and my partner's affable and encouraging approach, I guessed he might have a secret or two up his designer coat sleeves. I even thought I knew what said secrets might be. Proving my suspicions, however, was a different story, and so it was that Bock walked toward the exit, free as a bird, surrounded by his posse.

Quinto and Rodgers intercepted us on route to our desks. While Steele and I had interviewed Bock, they'd taken a run at Scar Face in one of the interrogation rooms. Apparently, they'd already finished their round of questioning, which didn't surprise me. Bock's lawyers had taken their sweet time arriving at the station.

Quinto crossed his arms and eyed the retreating crowd. "Quite the welcoming party, eh, Daggers?"

I glanced at Bock's entourage and shrugged. "When you're as rich as that guy is, I'd expect it. Hell, if I had his kind of money, I'd probably pay people to hang out with me. Make me look cooler than I really am."

"Who's to say *he* isn't?" said Rodgers.

"Well, he is, in a sense," said Shay. "But I don't think lawyers ever helped anyone look cool."

I chuckled. "Good point."

"So what did you guys learn from the magnanimous Mr. Bock?" asked Quinto.

"Not a whole heck of a lot." I skirted around Quinto's broad shoulders and slumped into my chair. "He basically confirmed everything we already suspected. The killer, Scar Face—"

"Cedric Mitchell," said Rodgers.

"Excuse me?" I said.

"His name's Cedric Gene Mitchell," said Rodgers. "That's one of the few things we got out of him. But I'm interrupting. You finish. We'll fill you in on our side in a minute." He waved for me to go on.

"Right," I said. "So anyway, Bock said Scar Face...err, I mean, Cedric, accosted him in one of the World's Wonders Fair bathrooms. Punched him and beat him. He'd brandished a knife and told him if he screamed he'd kill him. Then he gagged him and slapped the sack on him, and according to Bock, his next breath of fresh air—heck, the first time he even knew where he'd been taken—was when we de-hooded him in the middle of his own factory."

"Wait a second," said Quinto. "So according to Bock, Mitchell managed to transport him from the middle of the fairgrounds all the way to the industrial district without anyone wondering why he had a gunny sack over his head?"

Shay hopped onto the corner of my desk, the fabric of her pants stretching as it pressed against her skin. "Well, that's one of the many interesting things about Bock's version of the events. He also claims he *thinks* he and Mitchell took a rickshaw out to his factory, but he doesn't fully remember. He was too *terrified.*"

Quinto and Rodgers shared a look.

"Exactly," I said. "Anyway, Bock claims he's never met Mitchell before, and he has no idea why the man kidnapped him. He said he assumed he'd make a monetary demand sooner or later, but Mitchell didn't say anything of the sort to him. According to him, Mitchell didn't say much of anything, but Linwood wasn't particularly forthcoming with answers when we questioned him. He refused to go into any detail without his lawyers present, and once they showed up, his answers became even skimpier."

Quinto stroked his chin. "Well...I guess the part about Mitchell's silence at least sounds believable."

"It does?" I said.

Scar Face had remained unconscious for the vast majority of our return trip to the precinct, but when he'd finally awoken, he'd flipped out. We'd tightly bound his arms and wrists, and with Quinto holding him in a vice-like grip, he couldn't inflict any physical damage, but that hadn't stopped him from spewing as much vitriol as humanly possible.

At first he'd stuck to the usual prisoner fare—insults, including plenty of choice bits about our mothers and what we could cram into our various orifices, but that didn't last long. He'd quickly ascended into shouts of a different nature: threats, mostly, peppered with cries for help from passersby. Then he'd gone silent. When he spoke again, he'd tried to appeal to our sense of civic duty, or something along those lines. 'It's fine, take me,' he'd said, 'so long as you hold Bock in custody as well. At least for a few days. Please.' As if us holding Bock would've made him feel better about his own failed plans. Eventually his varied appeals died off and turned into raving mumblings of the 'I was so close...' variety.

"Yeah," said Rodgers. "Apparently Mitchell's chattiness was a one time occurrence brought on by the loving caress of your truncheon. By the time we'd let him simmer in the interrogation room and gone to question him, he'd reconsidered his legal strategy. I'll give you one guess as to the only question he answered for us."

"His name?" I said.

Rodgers snapped his fingers. "And that's why they pay you the big bucks."

"Right." I rolled my eyes. "I'm raking it in compared to the rest of you. That's why I'll be able to afford a new jacket in a year or three."

"Like you'd ever willingly replace that old piece of leather," said Shay.

I smiled and shrugged.

"So," said Quinto. "Speaking of your deductive prowess, I seem to remember you had a theory that explained all of this."

"More or less," I said. "But it's all pretty obvious at this point, isn't it?"

"Oh, um, of course." Quinto crossed his arms and shrugged them a little as he averted his eyes. "But, uh, why don't you tell us your version so we're all on the same page."

Shay snickered, causing Quinto's cheeks to turn a delightfully rosy shade.

"Sure," I said. "Keep in mind the evidence to support this is only circumstantial, but I think it's pretty clear Linwood Bock hired Cedric Mitchell to murder Buford Gill. And not just kill him, but murder his entire family and use that knowledge to inflict even more pain upon Gill before his eventual death.

"I mean, think about it. It was Bock's intimidation of Gill that sent him into hiding in the first place. Clearly Gill took Bock's threats seriously—and why wouldn't he? The man mocked Bock mercilessly at every opportunity, and Bock's an incredibly powerful man. And let's not forget Bock paid Mel a near fortune to locate Gill. I don't think he did that for kicks and giggles."

"But if you're right," said Rodgers, "why did Mitchell kidnap Bock?"

"Because Mitchell isn't as crazy as he'd like us to think he is," I said. "Vicious? Yes. Bloodthirsty? Yes. But crazy? No. He probably realized a man with Bock's wealth and pull wouldn't leave a loose end like him lying around. That after completing the hits on Gill's family, he'd be expendable. Maybe Bock wouldn't kill him, but he'd at least find a way for him to end up in our clutches with Gill's blood still fresh on his hands. So he preempted Bock's double-cross and kidnapped him in an extortion attempt to get his snuff money."

Quinto frowned, and Rodgers sucked on his lips.

"It would explain why Bock's version of the kidnapping doesn't add up," said Quinto. "Because he knew his assailant. He probably went along with Mitchell willingly, to start."

"And only later realized he was being kidnapped," said Rodgers.

Shay rapped her fingers on my desk as she peered at me. "You know, Daggers, the scenario you've laid out is definitely plausible, but there's one glaring, outstanding issue with it."

I gritted my teeth and took a deep breath, letting the air out through my nose slowly. "I know. The evidence, or lack thereof. We won't get a confession out of Bock. He's too smart, and even if he wasn't, his lawyers are. And I doubt the man left a paper trail tying him to Mitchell. Which leaves leveraging Mitchell as our best shot, but he's a serial murderer. He's not exactly a credible witness. And on top of that, if his silence during your interrogation is any indication, he's already realized he's screwed. He knows he's going to jail no matter what, and he might've come to grips with the fact that opposing Bock will just cause him more trouble in the long run. I doubt he'll admit the truth of the matter to us, either."

"Well, yes, there is that," said Steele. "But I was referring to Wyle. We still don't know how he fits into any of this, or how he knew where to find Mitchell and Bock." She raised an eyebrow. "Unless you have some ideas you've yet to share..."

I sighed. "I wish. I know, I'm usually an endless font of crazy, unfounded theories and wild possibilities, but I honestly can't explain Wyle. Maybe if we talk to him, just once more. Now that we've apprehended Mitchell, maybe he'll change his tune."

I glanced at the break room. I didn't have the heart to stuff him back in the holding cells, but the sitting room had been occupied by Bock, so I'd told Wyle to enjoy our fabulous coffee and asked a beat cop to stand guard at the door to make sure he didn't make a break for it. But as I glanced at the room, I didn't spot anyone there—neither Wyle nor the guard I'd assigned.

My heart sank, and I suffered a horrible sensation of fear. Could I have been wrong about him? Had he played me like a fiddle? Had he somehow masterminded the entire ordeal and now that I'd finally learned to trust him, at least to a degree, he'd bailed on me?

As my mind struggled with the possibility, the Captain's voice erupted behind me.

40

I turned, and, luckily for me, the bulldog's company precluded my oncoming heart attack. At his left stood a middle-aged man with unkempt finger-length blond hair and a stubble beard. He wore a heavy gabardine trench coat over his shoulders and a practiced scowl-and-frown combination on his face. Between him and the Captain stood none other than Harland Wyle, alternating his glances between the bulldog and the guy in the trench coat, a bewildered look in his eyes. The new guy wrapped a meaty hand around Wyle's upper arm, grasping him in a way I sensed had more to do with function than friendliness.

The Captain eyed the four of us gumshoes. "Gentlemen, Steele, and Daggers—" He said that last part with a gleam in his eye. "—let me introduce Detective Marcellus Ledbetter. He's with white collar crime downtown. I think he'll be able to shine some light on one of the...*sticking points* of your current case."

Ledbetter gave a curt nod. "Detectives, first let me commend you on your handling of the Bock case. Losing someone of his stature could've left a black eye on all of us for months, but instead you've helped instill a little faith into the populace. Faith that we can and *will* stop nefarious plots in their tracks, and that we'll pull out all the stops in the protection of our citizens—so long as said citizens are uber-wealthy business tycoons."

A smile escaped Ledbetter's scowl following that last part. "But beyond that, detectives, you also have my thanks. If not for the publicity of the Bock case, I never would've found out you had this man, who's been presenting himself to you as Harland Wyle, in custody."

Wyle glanced at Ledbetter and the iron grip he held on his arm. "Um, my name *is* Harland Wyle."

"Sure it is," said Ledbetter. "Just as it's also Tank Richards, or on occasion Harold Drambuie. But none of those monikers have much of a lasting appeal. Isn't that right, Mr. Turtledove?"

Wyle raised an eyebrow. "Excuse me?"

Ledbetter shifted his gaze back onto us. "This man, whose given name is François Turtledove, isn't who he pretends to be. Let me guess, detectives—he presented himself as a mystic? Or a seer? Or perhaps something more lavish? A scientist on the verge of a portentous discovery with as yet undiscovered technology at his disposal?"

"He said he was a time mage, actually," said Steele.

"That's because I *am* a time mage," said Wyle.

"Stuff it, François," said Ledbetter with a jostle of Wyle's arm. "As it turns out, Mr. Turtledove here isn't any of those things. He's something much more mundane. A corporate spy. Isn't that right?"

"I honestly have no idea what you're talking about," said Wyle. "And could you please let go of my arm?"

"You want to keep playing this game?" Ledbetter's scowl deepened. "Alright. I guess I'll have to do the talking then. You see, me and my partner have been after Turtledove for years. He's what I like to call a roving spook. Goes wherever the money takes him. And for the recent past, the money's taken him in the direction of one of Mr. Bock's largest overseas competitors, a corporation by the name of the Fleetwood Conglomerate. They're a decent company—they have a solid manufacturing arm—but they don't have the same technological innovations and expertise Bock Industries does. Isn't that right?"

Wyle stared at Ledbetter, then turned his eyes to the floor and blinked twice. Then he looked at the Captain. "Can I get a lawyer, now?"

Ledbetter ignored him and kept talking. "You see, Mr. Turtledove's been trying to steal trade secrets from Bock Industries for well over a year—anything that could be used to give the Fleetwood Conglomerate a fighting chance in the upcoming industrialization arms race. But Turtledove couldn't get his mitts on anything valuable. At least, not until he caught wind of the lingering feud between Buford Gill and Linwood Bock.

"As it turns out, the folks over at Fleetwood are pragmatic. They don't so much care about being better than Bock Industries, they just don't want any competition. So they figured, as good as it might be to produce better products than Bock, it would be even better to have Bock exit the picture entirely. So they instructed Mr. Turtledove to fan the flames between Gill and Bock, hoping the resulting quarrel between the two would incriminate Bock and shutter his business. At the very least, it would irreparably stain his reputation. But as you wove your tangled web of lies and deception, you didn't know it would lead to murder, did you Mr. Turtledove?"

"Ok, seriously," said Wyle. "I have no idea what this man is talking about. Daggers, come on. Help me out. I've been nothing but honest with you. I helped you find Buford Gill. And Bock—"

"And how exactly did you do that?" asked Ledbetter.

"Um, by...following the time streams," said Wyle sheepishly.

"Sure you did," said Ledbetter. "And I'm sure a jury will believe that."

"What?" said Wyle. "You can't be seri—"

Ledbetter cut him off again, yanking on his arm as he did so. "Detectives, thanks again for your help. I don't entirely understand Turtledove's connection to Mr. Bock's kidnapper—what was his name? Mitchell?—but I plan on finding out. In the meantime, I'm transferring him downtown to the Grant St. Precinct for questioning. Captain? I owe you one."

"Not a problem, Detective," said the Captain. "Grab one of our officers at the door to help you with the transfer. I'll take care of the paperwork."

Ledbetter dragged Wyle toward to the door, who couldn't quite believe what was happening. He turned his head toward us to plead for assistance. "Detectives, please! I don't know who this man is! He could be a serial killer, or a nutcase. You can't leave me with him!"

Quinto grunted. "Nutcase? Doesn't he see the irony in that?"

As Ledbetter wrestled Wyle out the precinct's front doors, the Captain's harsh bark brought me back to attention.

"Detectives," he said. "Good work today on the Gill case. You didn't catch Mitchell before he notched a couple more victims, but you got him before he brought harm to Bock, and trust me, the commissioner won't forget that come time to hand out commendations."

"Or raises, I hope," I mumbled.

The Captain snorted. "Don't get your hopes up, Daggers. Now go on. Get out of here. You can finish the paperwork in the morning."

With that, he turned tail and headed toward his office. It wasn't much of a thanks, but given the Captain's heart had been surgically replaced with a sack of rocks, it was about as good as we were likely to get.

"Well, he doesn't have to tell me twice," said Rodgers. "I'd better get home before Allison kills me. See you guys tomorrow."

Quinto nodded and gave a two finger salute. "Likewise."

As my two detective buddies wandered off, I lingered in my chair. I don't think I did a very good job of hiding the scowl that was slowly spreading across my face. Shay, with her butt still pressed against the hardwood of my desk, eyed me with a raised brow.

"Now, now, Daggers," she said. "Just because there ended up being a perfectly logical explanation for Wyle's abilities doesn't mean you have to go looking like someone drowned a cat."

"Are you kidding?" I said. "I'd be smiling if that happened. This is my 'not enough cats were drowned face.'"

"You know what I mean," Shay said.

"Yes, I do," I said. "But that's not what I'm glum over. I'm upset about this whole Bock fiasco. The Captain may be happy but only because I haven't shared with him my theory about Mitchell, Bock, and Gill."

"It's just a theory," said Shay. "You could be wrong. Either way, we'll sort through it. If Bock's guilty of conspiracy to commit murder, we'll get him."

I snorted. "You're far less jaded than I am. With his wealth and connections? I don't know... And in the meantime, we have to accept everyone's accolades and pats on the back for saving the guy. If we can't implicate him... This could be one of those things that bothers me for the rest of my career."

I chewed on my lip, and my stomach growled.

Shay tilted her head. "You, uh...want to get a bite to eat?"

I glanced at my partner. She sat there, a smile splayed across her lips and her feet dangling above the floor as her legs hung over the side of my desk. She seemed upbeat and eager, as if she really *did* want to share in a bit of dinner and conversation. But there was that same terminology again. *Get a bite.*

I wasn't much of a linguist, but her word choice bothered me. Had I really expected her to suddenly shift her attitude toward me? And because of what? Because I'd saved her life? Because we'd shared a moment on the floor of an abandoned physics building while the corpse of an old scientist oozed blood and viscera a bare arm's length away?

Was that what bothered me so? Or was it precisely what I'd told Shay—that I couldn't stand the idea of some rich, bloated liar skating away from the triple murder of his greatest rival and his children while I was lifted up as the man who'd saved him.

I grunted and stood. "Maybe another time, Steele. I've got a lot on my mind. See you tomorrow."

41

Dawn's initial foray arrived far too early, so I counterattacked in the only way I knew how—by ignoring it entirely. I slept until around nine, then dragged my sorry hide out of bed and headed to work.

Clouds had rolled in overnight, cloaking the city in a hazy gloom, which seemed appropriate given my lingering foul mood. No one else at the precinct believed me, but I was certain the gods paid far more attention to my own personal highs and lows when determining the weather than they did anyone else's. Given the state of my psyche—and my stomach, which I'd barely pacified the previous night with a hummus and chicken-filled pita purchased off a street vendor—I had no choice but to make a pit stop on my way to work.

Afterwards, I walked into the station, a white paper bag held in my right hand, and headed toward my desk. As expected given the hour, Shay was already in, and based on the stack of papers on her desk and the pencil grasped in her delicate hand, I could only assume she was hard at work on the paperwork the Captain had so graciously told us we could postpone until today. And Shay wondered why I came in to work late so often...

"Hey there," I said.

Shay lifted her head and glanced at the white bag. "Kolaches?"

"I got you one." I opened the bag.

"Let me guess," she said, peering in. "The apricot one's yours?"

"And the honey one's yours," I said. "Come on, I know you as well as you know me."

"Well, that's debatable, but what isn't?" Shay plucked the honey kolache from the bag and took a bite. "Mmm. These *are* good, don't get me wrong, but weren't you down to two a week?"

I shrugged and sat down at my desk. "Yeah, but there were extenuating circumstances this morning."

Shay lifted her eyebrows and tilted her head. "Don't tell me you forgot to eat last night? See, this is part of the reason I asked you to come with me."

"No," I said pointedly. "These are more for emotional support purposes."

"Ah, I see," said Shay. "You're still upset about how things unfolded last night following the interrogations, aren't you? With Mitchell and Bock?"

I shrugged. "Yeah, that's a big part of it."

"So I take it you haven't heard the news, then?"

I raised a brow. "What news?"

Shay took another bite of her kolache. The honey glistened on her fingertips. "Linwood Bock fell down a flight of stairs in his mansion this morning. Broke his neck. Died on the spot."

I blinked. "What? You're kidding."

Shay shook her head and tore off another chunk of the glazed donut.

"And there wasn't any evidence of foul play?" I asked.

"Nope," said Shay.

"I find that hard to believe."

"Well, as crazy as it may be, the evidence supports it," she said. "His wife Sophia, the Bock's butler, and one of their gardeners saw it happen, and they all tell the exact same story. The guy tripped and landed on his head. Didn't move after that. There's a team at the estate grounds now, surveying the place to make sure there's no evidence of...well, anything. But the body should be here soon. Cairny's going to take a look. If he died from a fall and a broken neck, it should be pretty easy for her to tell."

I sat there and stared at Shay, my apricot kolache sitting in the paper bag, untouched.

My partner finished the last of her pastry and licked her fingers. "You don't seem terribly pleased. I take it you don't believe in karmic justice?"

"It's a hell of a coincidence, is all," I said.

Shay shrugged. "People slip and fall all the time. It's not that rare with guys approaching Bock's age. And from what I understand, even though we didn't find him with one last night, he normally walks with a cane. Maybe his balance wasn't that great. Or maybe his legs were tired after walking all the way back here from his factory last night."

"Yeah. Maybe," I said.

I must not have looked convinced. Shay jerked her thumb towards the far set of stairs. "His body should be here any minute. I was going to go check with Cairny while she did her analysis. Want to come?"

"You're going down there while she's cutting into people?" I asked. "And after having eaten? Who are you, and what did you do with my partner?"

Shay chuckled. "I've been working on my intestinal fortitude. For example, you don't disgust me the way you used to."

"Fair enough," I said.

Shay jerked her thumb again. "So...you coming?"

I tapped my fingers on my desk. "Not right now. I'm just going to sit here and enjoy the aroma of my apricot pastry."

Shay rolled her eyes. "Alright. Don't hurt yourself up there while I'm gone." She tapped the side of her head. Clearly, she didn't buy my explanation of why I wanted to sit back and cool my heels.

"I'll try," I said.

Shay stood and headed toward the stairs. As much as my partner thought herself my intellectual equal, she didn't understand there were actually *three* reasons I wanted to stay back instead of joining her in the morgue. Yes, I did want to think, but I also needed time to eat my kolache, and—a very underrated reason—by hanging back I got to enjoy the sight of her swaying backside.

Unfortunately, the sight lasted only a few seconds, and soon enough, I was left with the unsightly void of the pit's interior. I opened the paper bag and removed my kolache. I set my teeth into the gooey, sugary dough, seeing if the activation of the flavor receptors in my tongue might help awaken whatever part of my brain I needed to help me make sense of Bock's death.

They didn't have long to work their magic. Before I'd finished my second bite, a young man approached me from the direction of the front door.

42

The fellow who walked toward me sported a crop of tousled, medium-length brown hair to go along with a thin mustache that needed a few years and several ounces more hair before it would look respectable. A blazer with patched elbows hung over his narrow shoulders, one that looked like it had been snatched up from a retired professor's rummage sale. He walked slowly, glancing to his sides. I couldn't tell if he was nervous or merely uncertain, but unless he planned on making a sudden detour, he seemed to be headed my way.

I rested the uneaten portion of my kolache on the paper bag. "Can I help you?"

"Um, yes," he said, stopping at my desk. "At least, I think so. Are you the detective in charge of the Bock case?"

"One of them," I said. "But I guess it depends. Are you referring to the kidnapping, the murder investigation, or the falling down the stairs episode?"

"Um, the latter, I suppose."

I wasn't sure who'd been assigned to that particular event—I wasn't sure if it was even a detective from our precinct—so my first instinct was to tell the kid to get lost. But he looked perplexed, and gosh darn it if Shay's compassionate influence hadn't shaped me for the better. Besides, something about the kid seemed familiar.

"Why don't you tell me what you need and I'll see if I can help?" I asked.

"Well, I'm here to deliver some notarized testimonials from the Bock residence, specifically the written statements of the witnesses regarding Mr. Bock's fall." He reached into his blazer pocket and produced a sealed envelope. "I'm one of Mr. Bock's assistants—or at least, I was. I quit this morning. Anyway, the point is, Mrs. Bock asked me if I could bring these over here as one last favor."

The kid's statement jogged my memory. "Ah! That's it. That's why you look so familiar. I saw you at the World's Wonders Fair a couple days ago. You were working the levers on that lightning hickamabob."

"The electrical generator?" he asked.

I snapped my fingers. "Yeah, that's it."

The kid nodded. "Yes. I'm very proud of that exhibit. It's exciting for people to actually *see* electricity. But it's the implications of the generator that are far more interesting. Of course..."

"What is it?" I asked.

"Oh, nothing," he said. "It's just that, with Mr. Bock's death, I don't know how that's going to affect the pace of the projects, including the ones involving electrical experimentation. Without Mr. Bock's leadership, I have no idea what'll become of the company. His children certainly aren't up to the task of running it, nor is his now-widow. Not that it matters to me much. Even if I hadn't quit, I wasn't going to last long at Bock Industries, at least not after...well, it doesn't matter. I'm rambling. None of this is your concern. Here." He held out the envelope.

"Thanks," I said, taking it. "I'm not sure I'm the detective these need to go to, but I'll make sure they end up in the proper place. Before you leave, though—can you give me a name? So I can pass it along to whoever ends up getting these?"

"Oh, yes," said the kid. "I'm Sherman. Tanner Sherman, technically, but everyone calls me by my last name."

Both of those names tickled my brain, and in different ways. The first was due to something Wyle had said, something about how in his futuristic society, all the history texts referenced a 'Sherman Industries'— but that had to be nothing more than an odd coincidence...*right*? The second way in which the name tickled my brain couldn't be a coincidence, however.

"Wait...Tanner Sherman?" I narrowed my eyes. "You knew Buford Gill, didn't you? The scientist?"

The kid started inspecting the floor. "Uh..."

I leaned forward in my chair. "Look, Sherman. I'm not the detective in charge of investigating Mr. Bock's untimely death. I'm the detective who was investigating Buford Gill's murder, and I know Gill collaborated on his scientific endeavors with someone by the name of S. Tanner. That's you, isn't it?"

Sherman held up his hands and shrugged. "Um, yes...*which* is why I mentioned I probably wouldn't have been working at Bock Industries for long, even if Mr. Bock hadn't passed. Mr. Bock didn't pay any attention to what Buford Gill had to say other than the insults he threw his way, but sooner or later he would've put the pieces together and realized it was me in those papers."

"So, hold on a second," I said. "You risked your job to collaborate with Linwood Bock's sworn enemy? Why?"

"Look, Detective...what was your name?"

"Daggers," I said.

"Detective Daggers," said Sherman. "Buford Gill, despite his personal failings, was a brilliant mind. I couldn't pass up the opportunity to work with him, even if it did cost me my job. And honestly, given how the past couple days have played out, I'm glad I was able to find him when I did. I learned so much from him. His murder is...tragic. But given what he taught me, at least I'll be able to continue his work."

Continue his work? My fingers felt numb.

"So, uh...what are you going to do now?" I asked, hoping my voice didn't betray any of my creeping concern. "Seeing as you're unemployed and all?"

"I don't know," said Sherman. "Continue my studies on electricity, one way or another. Maybe try to get a position at one of the universities. Or if Bock Industries doesn't pursue the opportunities, maybe I'll start my own company."

I swallowed. *Hard.*

"Anyway, I should get going." Sherman jerked his thumb toward the doors.

"Oh, yeah. Sure. Of course," I said. "Thanks for the depositions."

Sherman turned toward the door, and I sat there at my desk, my mind swirling with possibilities. Before I knew what I was doing, I'd stuffed the last of my kolache in my mouth, wolfed it down, and headed to the Captain's office.

The door was open. I knocked on the frame. "Captain?"

The old bulldog looked up from his desk. "Yes?"

"There haven't been any new murders today, have there?"

The Captain shook his jowls in the negative.

"Ok. Great," I said. "I have a few things to check out. I'll be back in an hour or two."

43

I wandered back into the precinct just shy of midday. Luckily for me, Rodgers and Quinto were nowhere to be seen, nor was my partner—which was good, because I needed a few uninterrupted moments to think. I plopped into my chair, leaned back, and rested my feet on the edge of my desk.

During my impromptu morning jaunt, I'd hit the Grant Street Precinct, Public Records, and Taxation and Revenue. At the Grant Street station, I'd muscled my way into the office of the local captain, a surprisingly polite elven fellow by the name of Dean Flyleaf. I'd asked him about Detective Ledbetter, and much to my surprise, the captain told me he'd never arrived at the precinct last night, meaning Wyle hadn't arrived either. Even more to my surprise, the captain told me Ledbetter wasn't a detective. In fact, no one by that name or his description worked at the precinct.

After that discovery, I wasn't particularly shocked when neither Public Records nor Taxation and Revenue had any records of a Marcellus Ledbetter. Nor did they have any records of a François Turtledove, Harold Drambuie, or any other alias of Wyle's Ledbetter had mentioned. According to the city's pencil pushers, neither Ledbetter nor Wyle, in any of their forms, existed, which of course meant one of two things: either they'd *both* lied to us, repeatedly, about their motives and identities, or the more chilling of the two possibilities—Ledbetter and Wyle simply...didn't...exist.

In my mind, I kept revisiting the conversation I'd had with the young scientist, Sherman. How he planned on continuing Buford Gill's research. How he might start his own business following his exit from the now doomed Bock Industries. And what Wyle had mentioned in passing. Sherman Industries. *Sherman Industries* dominated the future history texts.

Of course, there were plenty of logical scenarios that explained everything without my stooping to the sorts of wild, unfounded journeys on which my subconscious liked to take me. Ledbetter and Wyle were clearly conmen, and beyond that, partners. They'd worked together to steer our investigation in the direction they'd intended. To what purpose, I could only guess at, but my suspicions were the explanation Ledbetter had given was probably fairly close to the truth. Someone undoubtedly wanted Bock out of the picture, whether dead or because he'd been implicated in the sordid murder of his archnemesis, to help gain market share for their own industry. It all seemed convoluted, but plausible. I could convince myself of it—if not for one lingering bit of information.

I recalled Mitchell's ramblings as we'd dragged him to the precinct late last night. 'I was so close. *So* close,' he'd said. And the other part. 'It's fine, take me—so long as you hold Bock in custody as well. At least for a few days.' Mitchell had kidnapped Bock and held him at the warehouse, but he hadn't tortured him or hurt him in any way. When we'd captured him, he'd pleaded with us to keep Bock in custody. What would've happened to Bock if he'd stayed at the station overnight instead of heading home?

It seemed impossible, but...*could Mitchell have known Bock was going to fall down the stairs?* What was it Wyle had said? About anti-event temporal reconstruction theory? That established events couldn't be changed through direct action but instead had to be *prevented* from unfolding?

"Daggers! There you are."

I practically jumped out of my seat at the sound of my partner's voice. "Gods, Steele! You nearly gave me a heart attack."

Shay hopped up onto the corner of my desk, a spot which apparently was becoming a second home for her posterior. "Where'd you head off to? I leave for twenty minutes to go chat with Cairny and you disappear for the whole morning—or at least what was left of it following your inherent tardiness."

"I, uh...needed to run some errands, that's all," I said.

"On company time?" Shay tsk-tsked. "I can't imagine the Captain'll be happy about that."

"He gave me the go ahead," I said. "Or at least, he didn't say I *couldn't* go."

"Well, anyway," Shay continued, "you'll be happy to know Cairny's exam revealed Bock suffered two fractured cervical vertebrae resulting in a partial severing of his spinal cord. The guy slipped and broke his neck, just as all the witnesses claimed."

"Oh." I nodded and blinked a couple times. "Good. Great."

Shay narrowed her eyes. "Are you ok, Daggers? You seem out of it. More so than usual, I mean."

"Um..." My mind raced as I tried to sum up the implications of everything I'd gleaned over the course of the morning. How could I possibly substantiate the evidence in a way that would satisfy both Shay's scientific sensibilities and my own deductive gut sense? What was the logical synopsis that explained all the facts? And then it hit me.

There wasn't one.

"You know what," I said. "It's nothing. I'm just a bit off after yesterday, that's all. Talk about a whirlwind case."

"No kidding." Shay glanced at the windows on the far side of the Captain's office. "So...it's almost lunch time. You want to go out together to get something to eat?"

All thoughts of the Gill and Bock case were swept out of my mind with a few choice words. "Wait...*what did you say?*"

"I said, do you want to go out together to get some lunch?" One of Shay's eyebrows rose. "Are you sure you're ok?"

I hadn't imagined it. *Go out. Together.* Her exact words. With a swift verbal slice, our weeks of lunch and dinner non-date posturing had been stripped like so much chaff.

I pulled my feet off the desk and planted them firmly on the floor. "Yeah, I'm fine. More than fine. And lunch sounds good."

"Great," said Shay. "I was talking to Cairny earlier, and I thought you and me and her and Quinto might all go out together."

"You mean..." The obvious metaphor popped into my mind. At any other point I would've been afraid to use it because of its awkward connotations, connotations I'd convinced myself weren't founded in reality, but now? I figured what the heck. "...you mean like a double date?"

Shay smiled. "Yeah. Why not? I'll even let you pay."

"Wait. Hold the horses," I said. "I saved you from having your skull beaten in by a murdering psychopath less than twenty-four hours ago, and as a reward, you're going to allow me to pay for your meal?"

Shay's smile didn't dissipate. "What? I thought you might be amenable to that."

It wasn't an outright admission of her romantic interests, but it was probably the closest I'd get at the moment. I'd take it.

"Alright," I said. "I guess I can do that. *Today*. But next time we'll swap, and I'll let you treat *me* to a meal."

"Fair enough." My sprightly half-elven partner hopped off my desk. "I'll go snag Cairny from downstairs, and hopefully find Quinto—I haven't seen him in a while. Meet you outside the front doors?"

"Sure," I said.

Shay walked off, and call me crazy, but I think she had a little more pep in her step than usual. As I rose out of my chair and walked toward the exit, I realized—so did I.

I pushed open the precinct's heavy double doors, and the streets of New Welwic welcomed me with open arms. As I stood on the station's steps enjoying the breeze and the cool air, I couldn't help but feel that to me, it felt a lot more like spring than fall, and even though the morning's clouds hadn't abated in the least, the day suddenly seemed a whole lot brighter than it had a minute earlier.

ABOUT THE AUTHOR

Alex P. Berg is a mystery, fantasy, and science fiction author, a scientist, and a heavy metal aficionado. Connect with him at www.alexpberg.com. If you'd like to be notified when new books are released, please sign up for his mailing list on his website. You will only be contacted when new books come out, your address will never be shared, and you can unsubscribe at any time.

Word of mouth is critical to author success. If you enjoyed this novel, please consider leaving a positive review on Amazon. Even if it's only a line or two, it would be a *huge* help. Thanks!